Mystery Dym
Dymmoch, Michael Allen.

White tiger

WHITE TIGER

ALSO BY MICHAEL ALLEN DYMMOCH

The Fall
The Feline Friendship
Incendiary Designs
The Death of Blue Mountain Cat
The Man Who Understood Cats

WHITE TIGER

Michael Allen Dymmoch

Thomas Dunne Books
St. Martin's Minotaur ⧁ New York

THOMAS DUNNE BOOKS.
An imprint of St. Martin's Press.

WHITE TIGER. Copyright © 2005 by Michael Allen Dymmoch. All rights reserved. Printed in the United States of America. No part of this book may be
used or reproduced in any manner whatsoever without written permission
except in the case of brief quotations embodied in critical articles or reviews.
For information, address St. Martin's Press, 175 Fifth Avenue, New York,
N.Y. 10010.

www.minotaurbooks.com

Description of the road to hell, page 185, from *The Screwtape Letters* by
C. S. Lewis, copyright © C. S. Lewis Pte Ltd. Used by permission.

Excerpt from "Spring and Fall: To a Young Child," *Poems of Gerard Manley
Hopkins,* 3rd Edition by Robert Bridges, 1956. By permission of Oxford
University Press on behalf of the British Province of the Society of Jesus.

Line from *The Wizard of Oz* copyright © 1939 Turner Entertainment Co., A
Time Warner Company. All rights reserved.

ISBN 0-312-32302-6
EAN 978-0312-32302-8

First Edition: December 2005

10 9 8 7 6 5 4 3 2 1

For

THOMAS AAGAARD
MICHAEL BLACK
LARRY BURROWS
LARRY HEINEMANN
TERRY G. HILLARD
TONY HILLERMAN
HUGH HOLTON
DANIEL ODIS HYER
DR. MAURICE LEBOWITZ
RAND R. MERKER
TIM O'BRIEN
JOHN POPCO
RANDY RAWLS
CHUCK RUSSELL
AL SANTOLI
BUDDY SCHAEFER
DICK SCHAEFER
WALTER STANLEY
OLIVER STONE
MICHAEL TAFT
WALLACE TERRY
GINNY MORSE TIMMONS
WILLIAM TRACY
DALE WATTERSON
SHARON GRANT WILDWIND
BOB ZEMEROFF

ACKNOWLEDGMENTS

I want to thank Sergeant Dave Case of the Chicago Police Department, Sergeant Michael Black of the Matteson Police Department, and Stephanie Patterson, LCSW, for answers to various technical questions. I've taken liberties with the information given me. Any errors are my own.

Thanks also to my editor, Ruth Cavin, and her staff at St. Martin's Press; literary agents Jane Jordan Browne and Danielle Egan Miller; the reference librarians at the Northbrook Public Library, Northbrook, Illinois; Judy Duhl and her staff at Scotland Yard Books, Winnetka, Illinois; Janis Irvine and her staff at the Book Bin, Northbrook, Illinois; readers Mike Black, Libby Fischer Hellmann, Jesse Kartus, Chuck Russell, Ginny Timmons, Jeanne Timmons, David J. Walker; and the Red Herrings. You've all helped me bring Caleb and Thinnes to life.

Two of the veterans gracious enough to comment on this story were troubled by the portrayal of violence by U.S. soldiers in country, and the craziness of many veterans back in the world. The majority of those who served in the Vietnam War came back to resume productive lives, and I've tried to portray them as people who remained human under inhumane conditions. I hope *White Tiger* serves as a tribute.

My purpose in writing the book was to show how Vietnam helped shape the characters of my protagonists. In researching, I discovered that the war was like the blind men's collective description of an elephant—each person's picture depended on where he stood. I leave it to my readers to decide whether I've reflected their experiences. The only thing I know for sure is that if the war didn't make you a little crazy, you were already *beaucoup dinky dau.*

ONE

The body lay facedown, off the center of the clearing in a pool of bright early-afternoon sunlight. The usual jungle sounds were absent—pigs and monkeys, nameless birds. Only the buzz of flies disturbed the silence.

From the protection of the forest, Caleb fought the impulse and training that urged him to dash out and drag the man to safety. Caleb had been watching him die for twenty minutes, unable to move because the sniper who'd put three bullets in the victim was waiting for someone to do just that. Though there was no evidence the shooter was still around, Caleb could feel him, the way he could feel the stifling humidity, as certain as the smell of blood.

Soon it would be a moot point. A great part of the soldier's lifeblood had seeped away. The pitiless sun had pressed most of his remaining fluids into the hot, still air. In shock, nearly exsanguinated, he was no doubt beyond help already. And, patient as death, the sniper was counting on their inability to let him die alone.

The victim was as silent as his surroundings; his screams had bled out. Only his occasional blink, and the disturbance of the flies, told Caleb he was still alive.

Caleb felt suddenly that his own skin was too small to contain the rage within him, the blood and viscera. A pricking of the skin over his scalp and shoulders became a burning, as if from a mist of napalm. Adrenaline!

One of the others broke from cover and zigzagged into the clearing to a chorus of, "No! Buddy, don't!" His flight was punctuated by the nearly simultaneous *crack!* of rifle fire. Buddy's throat exploded in a spray of red.

A firecracker staccato of gunfire answered, then the soft thwack and swish of branches falling and leaves tearing, the rustle of vegetation as they scrambled for new cover. No one spoke. After months of living in each other's pockets they could almost read one another's minds.

Until one of them went crazy.

Red washed over Caleb's perception. Another wave of rage hit him like an amphetamine rush. His cry was an animal's scream. He was on his feet and moving. An M16 materialized in his hand. Whose? From where?

He didn't see the sniper's gun flash, but its smell spurred him as he burst through the clearing's far side.

Fragments imprinted: A green blur of foliage. The deep brown odor of humus. Crimson starbursts as his rounds tore into flesh. The pale oval of the dying sniper's face. Then silence.

"Jesus Christ!" Coming up behind him, the sarge put a hand on Caleb's arm. "Doc, you okay? Doc?"

Caleb heard himself screaming, felt something liquid trickling down his neck. Not blood. Tears? Sweat? He started trembling. His skin blazed but inside he was freezing. The sergeant took the gun. Caleb shook like a man in a seizure. He squeezed his eyes shut . . .

When he opened them, the only green was the monstera plant in the corner, the only wood his furniture, the only red the ruby splashes of the pattern in the Harati underfoot. His shirt was soaked with sweat, but it was silk, not cotton, and he was wearing Levi's, not fatigues.

He willed his body to stop shaking and tried to reconstruct what happened. His television flashed silently, news he'd inadvertently muted when the story broke that had triggered his recollection. The report had been of a death in Uptown, a Vietnamese woman found shot in her apartment. It left him feeling queasy, and he aimed the remote to turn off the offending images.

His arms ached. He noticed he'd dug his fingers into the up-holstery of the couch until they left impressions. He reached for the phone, dialed. When he heard, "Hello," he said, "Arthur, I've just had a flashback."

TWO

Uptown. Little Saigon. Thinnes had started thinking of it that way when the Vietnamese signs went up on Broadway and Argyle. It never failed to bring back memories—some more vivid than others. Today they were almost flashbacks.

The body was sprawled face up in the center of the room. A middle-aged Asian woman, thin and small, dressed in a long-sleeved cotton shirt, black pants, white socks, Reeboks. Her clothes were typical of Vietnamese women of a certain age; they told him nothing.

He could see one half-closed eye clouding over as it dried in spite of the humidity. There were three gunshot wounds—to the chest and abdomen. Major overkill. Judging by the placement of the shots, any one would have killed her. There was no other sign of trauma—no obvious bruises, no defense wounds. The woman's face seemed serene. There wasn't much blood, but the little that had seeped from the wounds was obscenely bright against the white cotton.

Franchi, his partner, stared at the body without comment. She was a head shorter and almost young enough to be his daughter, but she was tougher than any man he'd partnered with. They watched as the evidence technician recorded the remains with a Nikon. The man was one of the major crime scene specialists, an Asian, and a pro in the business of dealing with violent death. If he felt anything for the dead woman, he didn't let it show. When he noticed Thinnes's attention, he said, "We're nearly done."

"Okay to touch her?"

"Yeah, have at it."

Judging by the residue pattern, the shooter had been a good three feet away. Thinnes put on a pair of gloves and felt the hole in the woman's breastbone with the tip of his little finger. Nine-millimeter on a bet. Powerful enough to punch through bone and innards. Powerful enough.

As he reached for one of the small hands, he felt a flash of déjà vu, but he ignored it. This wasn't Saigon. *This* woman was the victim of a robber or a murderous neighbor or relative. The system *here* would do what it could to find her killer.

The hand was cool and limp, the arm still rigid. Rigor had come and was passing away. Have to remember to ask what the room temperature was like. There was a gold band on her left ring finger. Where was her husband?

He studied her face. He had the feeling he knew her. Not possible, of course. He knew only a handful of Asians in Chicago, all of them cops, none Vietnamese.

The room was clean, the furniture good quality, if sparse. Except for the mail she'd been holding when she fell, nothing seemed out of place. The little Catholic shrine behind the door gave him another hit of déjà vu. He must've started, because Franchi said, "What is it?"

His answer was interrupted by raised voices.

"You can't go in there!"

"Of course I can! I live here!"

The man who plunged through the doorway, with the beat cop on his heels, was Asian, too. At least part Asian. He had black slanted eyes and high cheekbones, but he was six feet tall and light-skinned. Mid-twenties. Clean-cut.

Franchi stopped him with a hand flat against his chest. "This is a police investigation." He was nearly a foot taller; her hand was small against his white shirt.

He seemed to give her his whole attention. "Of what?"

"A murder."

"Who?" He looked from her to Thinnes.

Thinnes stepped aside so he could see the dead woman.

The man's face became perfectly still, not registering any emotion.

Thinnes said, "Do you know her?"

"My mother."

THREE

They found the super on the third floor, vacuuming the hall carpet with an old Hoover upright. Light from a window at the far end of the hall surrounded him like a halo. He must have sensed them; he shut the machine off and turned around. In the dim light, the lines in his face looked like cracks in old wood. He was thin, in his fifties, Asian, wearing a blue cotton coverall, snow-white socks, sandals.

"Mr. Hung?" The sergeant had called him Hung Duc Minh.

Thinnes was introduced to Vietnamese nomenclature long ago, in Saigon, by his FTO: *The Vietnamese put their surnames first, like the Chinese do. I know that seems bass-ackwards to you-all, but they been doin' it that way for five thousand years, so maybe it's us got it wrong.*

Thinnes showed Hung his star. "We need to ask you a few questions." Behind him, he could hear Franchi digging in her briefcase-sized purse. Getting a pen and notebook.

"You're the building super?" No response. "Caretaker?"

Hung inclined his head. "Caretaker."

"Do you have some ID?"

Hung moved his upper body forward slightly in an almost bow. "Down stair."

"There someplace we can talk?"

Again the man bowed slightly. He unplugged the vacuum and methodically wrapped the cord around the handle brackets. They followed as he pushed the machine to the stairs, then lifted it with one hand to carry it down.

On the first floor, Hung stood the machine against the wall

next to an apartment door. He unlocked it and waved them inside. Small and clean, the room smelled of cigarettes and incense. There was a couch, recliner, coffee table, console TV, and bookshelf full of French and Vietnamese books, topped by a family shrine with a black and white portrait of an older couple in formal clothes.

Hung gestured toward the couch. "Sit. Please."

Thinnes and Franchi took opposite ends of the couch.

"Get ID." Hung disappeared through a doorway across the room. He returned with a driver's license and handed it to Thinnes before perching on the end of the recliner.

The license gave his name as Minh Duc Hung. After Franchi noted the particulars, Thinnes returned it.

Hung told them his former tenant was Hue An Lee—Mrs. Lee, a widow. Her San Francisco landlord had given her excellent references. She'd lived in Chicago, with her son, for three months. She'd been a model tenant—no noise, no damage, no pets. Her rent was paid on time.

The canvass was a perfect example of *What's the use?* Everyone knew Mrs. Lee. Everyone was horrified by the murder. No one knew who might have done it. Most of the neighbors were Vietnamese, courteous and reserved. On many of their faces, Thinnes saw the same flat expression he remembered from Saigon, but not a clue to what they were thinking. And as soon as the questions got beyond, "Would you give me your name?" people's English went south. Only one woman—the neighbor who'd called the police—told them anything of substance. Mrs. Nyugen said Mrs. Lee had been a great neighbor who'd watched the children so Mrs. Nyugen could shop or attend classes at nearby Truman College. Mrs. Lee's son, Mrs. Nyugen said, was very polite, very devoted to his mother. He took her shopping and to church every Sunday. And out to dinner every week. A good son.

"Did this good son live with his mother?"

Not for the last few weeks. His mother had suspected a girlfriend. Mrs. Nyugen didn't know for sure. But maybe some young thing at the dojo where he worked . . .

"Had Mrs. Lee any enemies?"

"No. Impossible."

"Any disagreements with the super or other tenants?"

"Never."

"With anyone?"

"Only Tien."

"Her son?"

"Yes. His mother wanted to arrange a marriage for him to a young woman from a good family. He refused."

When they interviewed the "good son," Tien Lee was sitting at his mother's kitchen table, facing straight ahead, with a neutral expression on his face. His eyes were closed. He didn't look bereaved, or even upset.

Although Thinnes wasn't aware of making any noise when they entered, Lee opened his eyes.

"Lee," Thinnes said. "Isn't that Chinese?"

"It could be. Vietnam has been invaded by the Chinese many times in the last millennium. But in my case, Lee is Virginian." Thinnes blinked. Lee added, "My father's family claims to be descended from the Civil War general."

Like a guy Thinnes knew in 'Nam. Weird coincidence. But Thinnes's buddy didn't have any kids. Couldn't have.

"Who might've shot your mother, Mr. Lee?"

In the year they'd been working together, he and Franchi had developed a routine for interviews. He asked the questions if the subject was male; she questioned the females. It wasn't sexist. They capitalized on the fact that people generally feel more comfortable discussing sensitive matters with someone of the same gender. If their subject seemed uncomfortable—or they wanted to make the subject uncomfortable—they reversed their MO. Thinnes couldn't tell if Lee was uncomfortable.

"I have no idea," Lee said. "She was practically a saint."

Thinnes couldn't tell if he was being sarcastic. "You have any enemies who'd hurt her to get to you?"

"None that I'm aware of."

"Tell me about your father."

"He died five years ago."

"Did *he* have any enemies?"

"If he did, I can't imagine why they would wait so long. Or why they'd harm my mother and not me."

He might have been discussing the weather. Thinnes couldn't guess what he was feeling, if anything.

"What did your mother do for a living, Mr. Lee?"

"My father left a considerable estate. My mother's quite well off. Was." The first sign Lee was aware his mother was dead.

"What do you do?"

"I teach Tae Kwan Do."

"And where were you last night?"

FOUR

The Robert J. Stein Institute. Cook County Morgue. The smell of bleach and meat struck them at the door. The autopsy was well under way. Dr. Cutler was in blue surgical scrubs with the usual safety glasses and plastic apron. He'd finished examining Mrs. Lee's head and left it with the scalp pulled forward covering her face.

He'd opened the torso as well and was examining the organs. His assistant, a skinny black man, had a Walkman on his belt. The volume was so high that fifteen feet away they could hear the music leaking from the headphones.

Without her shapeless clothes, the victim looked younger than she had at the scene. Her delicate hands rested, half closed, on the gurney. Her wedding ring had been removed—put in the ME's safe for her next of kin.

Tien Lee.

"He must have been adopted!" Thinnes said.

Cutler grinned. "That's what my ma always said."

Franchi frowned. "What're you talking about?"

"I know this woman—knew her. Christ, I'm slow! I stayed in her house for six months in Saigon."

"And you only recognized her without her clothes?"

"I never saw her naked. She was my buddy's girl. *I* never slept with her."

"Well, somebody did," Cutler said. "She's definitely had a pregnancy."

"Yeah," Thinnes said, "a miscarriage before she married Bobby."

"So who's adopted?" Cutler asked.

"Her son. Bobby couldn't have kids."

"But *she* could," Cutler said. "They must've gotten somebody to help them out."

"Maybe, but she was a good Catholic girl who wouldn't screw around."

"When women get bit by the motherhood bug, they do a lot of things they wouldn't."

"Okay," Thinnes said, "but I doubt her son's paternity has anything to do with her death."

Franchi said, "What if he was adopted?"

Thinnes glanced at Cutler's assistant, still grooving on the plug-in drug. "What I said about her husband is off the record, right?"

Cutler grinned. "You say something about her husband?"

"Nada," Thinnes said. "We almost done here, Doc?"

Cutler shrugged. "Cause of death is GSW to the chest—tore up her heart. The other shots were overkill."

"Or insurance."

"Whatever."

Thinnes had been sweating in the cool of the morgue. Out in the parking lot, the August heat wrapped him like a wet towel in a Turkish bath. He felt like he was breathing steam instead of oxygen.

"You all right?" Franchi asked.

He didn't answer. He forced himself to put one foot in front of the other until he got to the car. He opened the door and left it hanging wide. He dropped onto the seat, started the engine, and cranked the A/C up to max as she got in. When cool air started to come out the vents, he pulled his door shut and rested his forearms on the steering wheel. He took several deep breaths.

Franchi turned sideways and tucked her left foot under her. "Maybe you didn't sleep with her," she said, "but you got close. You gonna tell me about it?"

"This heat reminds me of Saigon; Uptown reminds me of Saigon."

"You having flashbacks?"

He stared ahead and breathed in slowly. "No." Heat waves rippled the air above the parking lot, creating a mirage on the asphalt. The late morning sun laid dark shadows under nearby parkway trees. Above them, the sky was the cloudless blue-gray that measures humidity and smog more surely than do the numbers on the Weather Channel.

She waited; he knew she could wait a long time. He finally said, "Just a real strong feeling of déjà vu."

She didn't comment or put her seat belt on.

Thinnes finally said, "I met Bobby Lee at Fort Bragg; we went through basic training together. We got to be friends. He was from the South, but he was the least prejudiced man I'd ever met. We helped each other get by. After basic, I got sent to Fort Gordon for MP training; he went to 'Nam. We met again in Saigon, where he had an assignment that kept him in the city for a month. That's where he met Hue and fell for her. Hard. She was beautiful— French and Vietnamese, a Catholic, well educated. Bobby couldn't believe his luck. When he finally shipped out, he made me promise to keep an eye on her.

"I did. We got to be pretty good friends." He shook his head. "It's been more than twenty years, but I can't believe I didn't recognize her."

"Maybe you didn't want to."

"The last time I saw her, she was nineteen and pretty as a model. I guess in my mind she'll always be nineteen and beautiful." He shrugged and continued. "There was an NCO who hounded her to sleep with him. She begged me not to tell Bobby. We both knew he'd have killed the SOB.

"After one of Bobby's leaves, Hue told me she was pregnant. Bobby was delighted. He made arrangements with a local Catholic priest to marry them.

"Then he got his balls blown off—literally. He was evacked to a hospital near Saigon. We visited him there, before they shipped

13

him out. Only the baby gave him the will to live—at least he'd have one kid.

"But Hue miscarried. Bobby was out of the woods by then, on his way home. When he heard, he threatened to go AWOL, but we convinced him to wait and come back for her. I stayed with her until Bobby could get back. She was physically recovered but depressed about losing the baby. And she was missing Bobby.

"It took him months. He returned in March '73, when they were shipping the last of the troops home. I stood up at their wedding; I shipped out a week later."

FIVE

When they got back to the Area, the squadroom was empty except for a custodian emptying wastebaskets and Ferris, who was reading the *Sun-Times* with his feet up next to the coffeemaker. He said, "The boss is looking for you."

"I'll get started on the background checks," Franchi said, "while you bring Evanger up to speed."

Evanger's door was open; Thinnes tapped on the jamb.

"Come in," Evanger said. He was tall—even sitting—and fit, a light-skinned black with short hair and mustache. "Close the door." His face was expressionless. Not good.

Thinnes took the chair across the desk. "What's up?"

"You have something to report?" It sounded like he'd already gotten a report and wanted Thinnes's version.

"Mrs. Hue An Lee died of a GSW to the chest from a nine-millimeter; we didn't find any brass. Report's not back yet on the bullets. Franchi's doing background checks on her son, the landlord, and neighbors. So far, the son's our only suspect—a neighbor heard them argue, and his reaction—the son's—was odd. We've got no evidence he did anything."

"Odd in what way?"

"He doesn't seem upset."

"Anything else?"

"I—I knew Mrs. Lee."

"What do you mean, knew?"

"She was married to a guy I went through basic training with. The three of us used to hang around together in Saigon."

"And you waited until now to tell me because?"

"I didn't recognize her till I saw her at the morgue."

"Without her clothes?"

Thinnes felt himself flush. "What's this about?"

"News Affairs got a call this morning claiming the detective on the Lee murder is the natural father of Lee's son. Since you and Franchi are the only—"

"No way!"

Franchi had the file open in front of her when Thinnes came back in the squadroom. "What've you got?" he asked.

"Tien Lee. Born Étienne Quang Lanh Lee to Robert E. Lee III and Hue An Lee, née Charcot, in Honolulu in 1974. Mrs. Lee's father was Étienne Charcot, a French national who married Nhu Thi Dao, a Vietnamese. Tien Lee's a martial arts instructor. He has a BA degree in comparative religions from Stanford, and a black belt in Tae Kwan Do."

"How'd you get all this so fast?"

"Hue's and Tien's birth certificates were in that file box logged in as evidence yesterday. Along with this—"

She held up a document in French and Vietnamese with the names Charcot An Hue and Robert Edward Lee written on it in script. Thinnes recognized it—the Lees' marriage certificate. His signature was there, too, in his twenty-year-old hand. He wondered if Franchi had recognized it and was being diplomatic not mentioning it.

"I don't read French," she said. "Or—what is this, Vietnamese?" A rhetorical question, because she added, "Tien posted his résumé on the Web a while back. And—you know—once something's on the Web, it's there forever."

"Yeah. By the way, Evanger wants to see you."

"Yeah, okay." She reached for her purse and stood up.

He sat at her place as soon as she was out the door.

He was two-thirds of the way through the file by the time she came back. She stepped into his personal space and clapped the file shut, then snatched it off the table. "Nice try, Thinnes! When were you going to tell me?"

"Personnel redeployments are Evanger's purview."

"Cute."

"You weren't going to tell me anything more."

"Exactly!" She turned and stalked away.

He followed her from the room, but was forced to break off the pursuit at the door to the women's locker room.

SIX

Caleb's therapist had the same first name as Caleb's father. Arthur. Something very Freudian there, no doubt, but then, once you knew about Freud's theories, everything was Freudian. There was no confusion in Caleb's mind between the two Arthurs. It was a matter of affect. For his psychologist, Caleb felt enormous fondness.

Arthur wiped his glasses on his shirttail and put them on. He was an improbable therapist—built like a linebacker, dressed like a construction worker in blue cotton shirt and denim jeans. His size and hairy body and his red-gold beard made Caleb think of a cinnamon-colored bear. The glasses were for show, wire-rims that turned a could-be grizzly into a big plush teddy bear. "Why now?"

"A woman was murdered."

Arthur nodded. "Tell me about her."

"I only know she was Vietnamese."

"Something familiar about her name?"

"I didn't hear it."

"Okay. Tell me about the flashback."

Caleb did. As Arthur pressed for details, Caleb reexperienced the nausea that he'd felt that day in 'Nam, the horror, the self-disgust. Arthur didn't seem disgusted. He'd been in the war, too. Nothing disturbed him. "When did this happen?"

"Toward the end of my second hitch."

Arthur rested his ankle on his knee and spread his bear-paw fingers over his thighs. "You did something you had to do and you've felt guilty ever since."

"I had an epiphany that day. I saw the war protesters with

perfect clarity—the serious ones, not the druggies or the yippies—those gunned down at Kent State, and those whose heads were split in Grant Park. I finally *got* the question: *What if they held a war and nobody came?* I realized I'd let myself get drafted because my old man offered to get me off."

"And now? Have you forgiven yourself?"

Caleb smiled. "To know all is to forgive all."

"How's your life been going lately?"

"Well enough, I guess. My father's ill, but we aren't close. My lover's overextended, but that's nothing new." He shrugged.

"Tell me again about your father."

"A raving narcissist."

"Not a diagnosis. Your feelings."

"He's rigid, authoritarian, and conservative enough to make Rush Limbaugh look like Ralph Nader. When I was very young, I used to wish he would die. Fortunately, he didn't. Once I grew to understand him, I no longer cared."

"And your lover? Is he like your father?"

Caleb laughed. "He's actually more like my mother—loving and giving, only inflexible on matters of principle."

"Tell me more about this flashback."

"It was a reliving, not just a recollection. I could smell the blood and taste the dirt."

"Was this something you'd repressed?"

"I've never repressed anything."

Arthur raised an eyebrow. "How would you know—if it was really repressed?"

"Because I remember everything when I choose to. I just rarely choose to."

SEVEN

The house was deserted when Thinnes got home. There was no sign of Toby—Rob must've taken him to work. A message on the answering machine told him Rhonda would be late. He changed into jeans and got himself a beer.

He tried not to think of Saigon, but it was like trying not to think of white bears once someone's said not to. He wouldn't chance a suspension, but he couldn't sit it out while someone else—Ferris, maybe—dug into his life. What he *could* do was go at it from his tour in 'Nam.

Rhonda picked up on the third ring. "Newsome and Drees, Rhonda speaking."

"Hi. How's it going?"

"Not bad," but she sounded as if her day was going like his. Still, *she* hadn't been reassigned.

"What'd you do with the album you put together when I got home from 'Nam?"

"Good Lord, John, what made you think of that? I'll find it when I get home."

"Just point me in the right direction."

"Can't it wait?"

"No."

"Lord! Maybe in the attic."

"Thanks."

"Anytime. Anything else?"

He hesitated.

"Then—"

"Ronnie, something we gotta talk about."

"What?"

"When you get home. Love you." He hung up before she could ask him what.

He found the album in the top of a box marked VIETNAM STUFF, full of things he hadn't looked at since they moved in. He got another beer and took the box out on the patio. He started with the album. Rhonda had put the pictures he sent home in order by date—old, square prints. He'd used the white borders for writing captions. The first were taken during basic training.

At that point, he'd never been farther south than Sox Park, and basic had been a shock.

His father warned him, "Keep your head down and your tail covered . . . Don't take anything personally unless you're sure it *is* personal . . . Never volunteer." Good advice.

The sergeant—from Alabama—called all the white boys niggers, all the black boys honkies, and everyone—black or white—princess, pansy, or girl. Nothing personal.

Thinnes had been amazed, at first, by the heat. Like "a pleasant spring" according to the sarge. Thinnes was afraid to think of what he'd call a hot summer. The Chicago boy had also found the blatant racism amazing.

He'd made one friend in basic—Bobby Lee. They seemed to have the same live-and-let-live approach to life. And Bobby had a great sense of humor, defusing tense situations by cracking jokes. Then Bobby put in for medic training, Thinnes for construction. Naturally, Bobby got sent to the infantry, Thinnes to the military police.

Under the album was a loose picture that brought back Saigon: Corporal Des Drucker leaning on the fender of his jeep. Drucker was the first person Thinnes met in Vietnam.

Even coming from the South hadn't prepared Thinnes for the heat in Saigon. Stepping off the air-conditioned plane was like walking

21

into the front hallway of hell. Humid as August in Dixie, but smelling of shit and roadkill.

Thinnes was standing with his squad at the airport, adjusting, when a jeep pulled up. The driver leaned out and said, "Thinnes, John." When Thinnes stepped forward, the driver said, "I'm Des Drucker. C'mon, get in."

The trip to the MP barracks was the scariest Thinnes had ever taken. Drucker drove like a maniac through nightmare traffic: trucks and jeeps and taxis, motorbikes, bicycles, and cyclos, carts pulled by water buffalo or pushed by humans, livestock—driven or carried or dragged—and hundreds of pedestrians.

Drucker shifted to third, then drove one-handed, using the other to drag on his cigarette or punctuate his running commentary on traffic and points of interest. He didn't seem to use the brake—just the clutch, gearshift, and horn.

"Listen, kid," he'd said, though he wasn't any older than Thinnes. "Anything you need, let me know. I can get it for you." He had a faintly Southern accent. "Or if you need somethin' fixed, I can take care of that, too."

He stuck his head out and yelled something at a taxi.

"You speak Vietnamese?" Thinnes asked.

Drucker grinned. "Just 'yes,' 'no,' and 'fuck you.' But I get my point across."

"John?" Rhonda's voice banished Drucker to the distant past. "Why are you sitting out here in this heat?"

Thinnes stared at the picture as he slugged down the last of his beer. He wondered how to tell her.

Trying to get back to Vietnam.

EIGHT

They can't possibly believe that!" Rhonda said when he had finished telling her about his day.

Thinnes sat straddling the chaise lounge with the box of Vietnam stuff between his knees. God, he was glad he'd trusted her enough to tell her about staying with Hue.

"They have to check it out." He shrugged. "Cops tend to look for fire when they smell smoke."

"But sometimes smoke is just a magician's trick."

Or a smokescreen. "The question is, why now? Why did Hue move here now? And the killer could've just made it look like a burglary gone bad. Why involve me?"

"Maybe because you got the case. You *were* involved."

Which only the cops would know. He didn't say it, didn't want to give her any more to worry about.

"They wouldn't think *you* killed her?"

"The good news is I have an alibi."

"What's the bad news?"

"My alibi witness is my wife."

He slid his hand up her leg, under her skirt, feeling the silk of her skin beneath her panty hose. He pulled her against him, buried his face in the front of her dress, and breathed in her fragrance.

She pressed against him and combed through his hair with her fingers, sucking a deep breath in between her teeth. She said, "We need to go inside." She backed away, sliding her hand down the side of his face, across his shoulder, over his arm. She closed her fingers around his hand. She took the picture of Drucker and dropped it in the box, then tugged on his hand. "Come on. We need a shower." The late afternoon sun painted her skin gold. Her smile was full of light and promise.

Thinnes swung his leg over the box and stood up, dropping his beer bottle. He kissed her. Hard.

She responded as passionately as he could've hoped.

He let her go. He picked up the bottle and the box, and followed her into the house.

As he expected, Franchi was already working when he came into the squadroom next morning. And she had a pot of coffee ready. He got himself a cup and detoured past her desk to hand her his notes on the Lee case.

"What's this?"

"Some things you need to ask Tien Lee."

"Thinnes, you're off the case."

"You got the state's attorney reviewing charges?"

"Cute."

"Just look that over and think about it, okay?"

She took the paper and stared at it. The questions were fairly elementary; maybe she'd thought of them already: *You recently moved to Chicago. Why here? Why now? Did you ever hear the name "John Thinnes" before? When? From who? What did you hear about him?*

Franchi dropped the paper on her desk. "I got a few questions of my own."

"Shoot."

"When was the last time you saw Mrs. Lee?"

"March 1973. Right after her wedding, a week before I shipped out. I'd have to look up the exact date." He shook his head. "I can't believe I didn't recognize her."

"Denial?"

He reviewed the murder scene in his head. Hue's hair was gray, her smooth skin lined and sagging, but had she changed so much? Like most cops, he was good at recognizing people in unfamiliar settings. So how—?

But it was obvious! Death had changed her from the lively girl he'd known.

As if mind-reading, Franchi said, "What was she like?"

"Alive. Happy. She gave the impression she loved people. When she smiled, she made you feel she was glad to see you, not just being polite."

"The last time you had contact with her?"

"After we said goodbye in Saigon, I never saw her again. Alive."

"What about her husband?"

"The last time I saw Bobby was in 'Nam. He wrote to me when they got to Honolulu to say they'd made it out safely and were heading to California. That was the last time I heard from him. The last letter I sent him was returned—NFA. I'd just come on the job, and I had a lot on my mind besides following up on the Lees. If I'd thought about it at all, I'd've figured they'd contact me when they got settled. They never did."

Franchi leaned toward him and said, "You weren't planning on going to the wake, were you?"

"*And* the funeral. The department can't have it both ways. If I'm off the case, I'm free to pay my respects to an old friend."

NINE

Thinnes spent the next twenty-four hours working one of Viernes's gang-banger shootings. Word had it Rico Gonzales had pissed somebody off, or dissed somebody's mother, or banged someone's girlfriend. Problem was, Rico had had too many enemies. When he turned up dead, nobody knew anything. Thinnes recanvassed the neighborhood, followed up the "leads," and filed all the necessary supplemental reports. He was on his way out when he ran into Viernes.

"You calling it a day, Joe?" Viernes's given name was John, but everyone called him Joe.

"Might as well."

"Stop by the Blue Light and I'll buy you a beer."

Viernes looked skeptical. And why not? They didn't socialize, never went out drinking unless they were working a case so bad they had to decompress before heading home.

Viernes wasn't fooled. "You're off the case, Thinnes."

"No. I know. I was hoping you'd give me some pointers."

Viernes didn't look convinced but shrugged. "As long as you're buying. But I'm not talking about the Lee case."

"Fine."

"Fine."

The Blue Light was across Western from the Nineteenth District station, an unassuming fieldstone storefront marked by an old Budweiser sign. Thinnes was nearly finished with his second O'Doul's, about ready to give up and go home, when Viernes came in. The Blue Light's regulars looked up—the way they had when Thinnes arrived. Those who knew Viernes nodded and went back to their drinks and conversations; those who didn't just went on drinking.

Viernes took the stool next to Thinnes. He looked beat and Thinnes said so.

"This sucks," Viernes said.

The bartender put a coaster in front of him and waited.

She was middle-aged, with dark hair. She wore wire-rimmed glasses, gold cat earrings, and lots of silver rings.

Viernes jerked his head toward Thinnes. "Whatever he's having."

Thinnes said, "Heineken," as the bartender removed his empty. She nodded. She served two bottles, paid herself from the cash on the bar, and moved away.

Viernes held up his beer. "Here's to dumb crooks."

They drank, then just sat for a while. Eventually, Viernes said, "What's this problem you're having?"

"Nothing much—just I don't know the players, don't know their associates, don't speak Spanish worth a damn."

Viernes laughed. "My money's on Arcángel." A flashy lieutenant in the local chapter of the Latin Kings. "But good luck getting someone to talk—even if you did speak the language." He sipped his drink. "Too bad Evanger split you and Franchi up. She speaks Spanish better than me."

A third-generation Mexican, Viernes had grown up on the North Side. He'd learned "book Spanish" in school, picked up street Spanish on the job, and now counted himself trilingual.

Thinnes asked him, "How do you like working with her?"

"Beats the hell out of working with Ferris."

"How'd *he* get back working days?"

"Same way he got on the job." Ferris was a "merit promotion"—whose chief "merit" was his connections.

"I'm stuck, too," Viernes said after another swig.

"You got *any*thing?"

"Naw. The woman was a solid citizen."

"What about her son?"

"He has a degree from Stanford," Viernes said, "and a résumé that's too good to be true. But it checks out."

"A model son, too, according to the landlord."

"So unless you believe the neighbor, Mrs. Nyugen, Lee never had a quarrel with anyone but the model son."

"You check the neighbor out yet?"

"Do you know how many Nyugens there are in Uptown?"

Thinnes laughed. "When you recanvass, ask about her. Somebody always resents the neighborhood busybody. Better yet, have Franchi do it. She's good at that. And you got to keep her busy or she gets in trouble."

"Her first name really Don?"

"Yeah."

"What's the story behind that?"

"She'll tell you when she wants you to know."

TEN

The funeral home was in Uptown, on Lawrence. When Thinnes got there, the lot was full. He had to park a block away. Yesterday's heat was back with interest, and a haze of smog blurred the building edges on the skyline. The streets were gridlocked. There were lots of Asians among the crowds on the sidewalks. Thinnes got out of the car. He took off his jacket and slung it on his shoulder.

He had the feeling there were things going on around him he couldn't quite connect with. People sitting in doorways or chatting outside stores seemed to watch him as he passed. While he waited for the walk signal, a black Jeep sailed through the intersection, long after the light turned red. The squeal of tires, cars braking, the chorus of horns took him back to the Paris of Indochina.

"How the hell do you do it, Drucker?" he'd asked.

Drucker laughed. "It's the ultimate game of chicken. Guy with the most balls—or the biggest truck—wins."

"Yeah? What if no one blinks?"

Drucker laughed again and reached over to tap the crossed pistols, the MP insignia, on Thinnes's collar. "You'll see."

Four men were talking outside the funeral home. Vietnamese. They stopped as Thinnes got near. Impassive faces. He fought the urge to shiver in spite of the heat.

Then one of them—a man in a gray suit and white open-necked shirt—nodded, maybe acknowledging a fellow mourner. Thinnes returned the gesture. The man turned back to his conversation. Thinnes put his jacket on and went inside.

The visitation had been going on for half an hour. There was already a line, and the first two pages of the book were filled with names. It seemed like a lot of attention for a woman who'd only been in the city three months. Thinnes added *John Thinnes, Chicago, IL,* to the list and slipped one of the prayer cards in his pocket.

He didn't see Viernes, but Franchi was there. Good. She'd note who didn't sign the guest book and get the names of those who did. In her conservative suit with its midcalf skirt, she looked like one of the mourners. She made eye contact, but gave no other sign of recognition.

The room was crowded, mostly women, mostly Vietnamese. He knew from the canvass that many, including Mrs. Nyugen, were Hue Lee's neighbors. He noticed Mr. Hung.

Tien Lee stood in front of a group that seemed to be part of the same family—parents in their forties, twenty-something daughter and son or son-in-law, two teenage girls, and three small boys. Dressed in a white suit, Lee seemed as unaffected as he had been at the crime scene. In fact, he seemed to be the one providing comfort. Thinnes noticed that when the family moved along, Lee studied the men. His eyes swept past Thinnes as if the detective weren't there, but his gaze paused briefly on each of the adult males. An elderly woman approached him and he seemed to give her his complete attention. Then he fixed on something behind Thinnes.

Thinnes turned. He smelled the man before he saw him—a tall, thin white male in a shabby suit too short in the sleeves and legs, and a shirt that was clean but wrinkled. He bypassed the line, hugging the perimeter of the room, and wandered over to the casket. By the time he took the flask from his pocket, he had everyone's attention. He unscrewed the cap and held the flask up in a silent toast to the corpse, then took a long pull.

When he headed for the door, the crowd parted to let him

pass. No one challenged or spoke to him. The odor of his un-washed body lingered like a bad feeling.

Thinnes looked at Franchi, who shrugged and shook her head. He turned around to find himself facing Tien Lee.

"You knew my mother well," Lee said. Not a question.

"Your father, too. We served together in Vietnam."

"You were at their wedding."

The wedding pictures, of course. Or maybe Hue had talked about her wedding like his mother did, fondly, often. Thinnes said, "Yes."

"But you didn't keep in touch. Why *was* that?" Lee seemed to have an agenda, like a cop grilling a suspect.

Why was *that*?

"They never sent me a forwarding address."

ELEVEN

Mr. Maharis, if you are joining us, you'll have to shower."

As Arthur spoke, Caleb watched Maharis's face. There was no sign of anger or embarrassment. He was a tall, thin man with skin burned dark by the sun, which made his sky-blue eyes even more striking. His graying hair was crew-cut, his beard neatly trimmed. His suit and wrinkled shirt appeared clean, but Arthur was right. Maharis smelled as if he hadn't bathed in weeks. Maharis was schizophrenic.

Arthur polished his wire-rims on his shirttail while Maharis thought it over. Finally he nodded, and Arthur pointed down the hall. "There are towels and washcloths in the closet behind the bathroom door. Use soap."

Arthur turned back to the group seated around his coffee table. Besides Caleb, they were Joe, a veteran fighting Gulf War Syndrome; Butch, another Vietnam vet; and Alec, a twenty-something computer nerd who'd seen three coworkers mowed down by a disgruntled fellow employee.

"Jack," Arthur said. "Have you had any more flashbacks?"

Caleb caught a sharpening of interest in the others. "No, just a few ordinary recollections."

"From before or after the incident you described?"

"A few weeks before."

"*You?*" Butch said. "A flashback? Mr. Control Freak?"

Caleb ignored him. "They had us in a hard spot." For Alec's sake, he added, "That's a position outside a secured perimeter. I think we were supposed to be bait—to get the VC to open up on us so the artillery could get a fix. We'd dug in and set out claymores. We were waiting for dark, trying to get a little sleep. It was the dry season, as hot as it was here the summer we had all those heat deaths.

"Of the eight in the squad, Froggy and Preacher and I were the only survivors of our original platoon—all the others had been killed or wounded or rotated out, to the rear or back to the world. Froggy was a French-Canadian who'd never say how he came to be in the U.S. Army. His real name was Gervais; I'm probably the only one he'd told that. He was teaching me to speak French. The other guy we called Preacher because he'd take off his helmet to observe a moment of silence for the dead—VC dead, too. Froggy and Preacher were short-timers, so much alike, they'd hated each other when they first met. We didn't know the FNGs—fuckin' new guys—didn't want to.

"Once we were set for the night, there wasn't much to do except smoke or talk and watch for VC. We knew they wouldn't come until after dark, so some of us tried to get in a little nap while it was quiet. I'd just nodded off when Froggy and Preacher woke me arguing about a sociopath killed a few weeks earlier, a guy called Ears because of his collection of human body parts. Smart money had it someone in the squad did it. Every one of us hated him.

"Froggy asked Preacher if he'd pray for the soul of the man who killed Ears. Preacher said, 'Sure, but I ain't prayin' for Ears 'cause he didn't have no soul.'"

"You had a honest-to-God fraggin'?" Butch asked.

"Not really. He wasn't an officer. And he may have been killed by the VC." ⋅

Maharis came in, wearing the same clothes but smelling acceptable. "What are we talking about?" He sat down.

"Fragging," said Butch.

Joe said, "Jack was telling us about a time he was stuck in a hard spot. How did that come out?"

"After the conversation about Ears, we watched a blood-red sun seep into the western treetops. We were short on water. We ate our rations, then the sergeant assigned watches and told us to maintain silence.

"With the moon down, it was really dark that night. At first, fear would keep you awake, but . . ."

"Incoming mortar rounds woke me. Our bunker was pretty well protected. We hadn't spared the sandbags, but one of the grenades opened a hole in the wall. A second hit right outside the breach, just as Froggy was stepping up to plug it. The force of the concussion blew him back against the far wall. He landed on a metal ammo box; I could hear his ribs crack. Then the sergeant called in our coordinates, and artillery began lighting up the night.

"I started doing triage. Two of the men were dead. Froggy was close to it. The only other casualty had a severed artery. By the time I got that patched, Froggy'd regained consciousness. Preacher and I made him comfortable as we could, but he wasn't going to make it."

"So what happened, Jack?" Butch leaned forward like a sports fan at a game.

"He died."

"What about the fragging?" Joe asked.

"Yeah, Jack," Butch said. "Give."

They waited for details. But Caleb had had enough. "We found Ears with his throat cut. It could've been VC."

"But you don't think so."

"There was no sign of Charlie. Everyone hated Ears."

"You kill him, Jack?"

"Of course not."

"But you think one of your buddies did?"

"No one claimed credit."

"Bless me, Father, for I have sinned . . ." Froggy's grip tightened on Caleb's arm.

Froggy was dying; Caleb had seen too many deaths to harbor false hope. His eyes teared up, and he blinked to keep from crying openly. He started to protest that he was no priest. But, if there *was* a God—and he'd wondered about that since he'd been in country—under the circumstances He'd surely accept a medic's absolution.

What do you do when the damage is beyond your skill to mend?

34

You do whatever's needed. The sergeant's voice sounded in his head from a lifetime ago.

Froggy needed forgiveness; Caleb was determined he would get it. He wished he knew the formula. Catholics had prayers for all occasions. Comforting rituals. What was the proper response? Froggy was waiting.

"Go ahead, Gervais."

"It's been so long since my last confession, I can't remember when . . ." He seemed distressed.

"God knows, Gervais. Don't worry about it."

Froggy was bleeding out internally; blood was pooling in his lungs. There was a long silence as he struggled to breathe. He finally managed, "Father, I killed a man."

Caleb stifled a laugh. "It's war, Gervais. God won't hold it against you."

"You . . . don't . . . understand. Father."

"That's true, Gervais, but God does."

"Are you going to absolve me?"

"I absolve you, Froggy. God forgives mistakes." He could hear Preacher behind him, feel him listening.

"Aren't you going to give me a penance?" Froggy asked.

As if being here, dying here, weren't penance enough. "Say the Lord's Prayer, Gervais."

"Say it with me?"

"Our Father, who art in heaven," Caleb said. Preacher joined in. If God wouldn't listen to Preacher, no one had a chance.

Caleb went on, "Hallowed be Thy name . . ."

Froggy was dead by the time Caleb got to "Lead us not into temptation," but he finished anyway. It occurred to him that he hadn't recited the prayer since his mother was dying. It hadn't helped her, either.

"What made you think of that particular incident, Jack?" Arthur asked mildly.

"I don't know," Caleb said. "An unsolved murder?"

TWELVE

Thinnes didn't make it to the funeral. His pager went off as he was leaving home. When he called in, the sergeant gave him an address on Western Avenue. "This one's a cluster fuck, Thinnes. Boss said get everybody on it."

"Viernes, too?"

"Everybody."

Viernes was on the scene already, acting like the primary. Good. Let him. He'd been with Gang Crimes before he made detective, and his Spanish—judging by the crowd that had gathered—would be a requirement for clearing this one.

Northbound Western was closed off at either end of the block by blue and whites with Mars Lights flashing. A beat copper directed traffic; his red face suggested he was losing it with the gapers.

Not that they could see anything. Yellow POLICE LINE tape marked the scene perimeter. Outside it, dicks and tac cops stood watching the crime scene techs do their thing.

The lot next to the scene had been commandeered for emergency vehicles—squad cars, ambulances, squadrols, and the crime lab van. Thinnes pulled in and parked.

Two bodies, one in the parking lot of the commercial building east of Western, the other in the street. Young. Male. Bloody. Dead. Spent cartridges surrounded them, marked with numbered cards. A tech was taking pictures. Thinnes walked up to Viernes and said, "What's happening?"

Viernes pointed to the body in the lot. "That guy came out of his place of employment—he was off today, just stopped in to get his check—and he was gunned down. The other one"—he pointed to the second body—"far as we can tell, was just a passerby who tried to warn the first victim and got killed for his trouble."

"We got any clues as to why?"

Viernes shrugged. "Gang business? We got pictures of the people standing around after it happened. I'll have Gang Crimes try to identify the players. Meanwhile, we're taking names." He pointed to a tall cop in street clothes who was interviewing a woman out of earshot of the onlookers.

Thinnes recognized Jaime Azul, a tac cop from the Nineteenth District.

"Work with Azul," Viernes said.

"Yeah, okay." He walked to the perimeter to get his own impression of the scene.

Bendix, the senior crime-scene tech, was supervising just inside the perimeter. He had his hands on his hips and a cold stogie between his teeth. Legend had it he chose cigars on the basis of their nasty smell. He never smoked anything that wasn't stronger than a week-old corpse.

"Pity they're all such rotten shots," he offered to no one in particular. "If they were just offing each other, who'd care?" He noticed Thinnes and said, "Hear you got demoted. Whose wife d'you get caught banging?"

It occurred to Thinnes that Bendix was a pretty shrewd judge of people, always managing to push the right button. "I'd never get caught, Bendix," he said. "You better leave the interviews to the smart squad."

Working with a new partner was a pain in the ass, but Azul wasn't bad. A draftee in the War on Drugs, he'd been conscripted because of his Spanish and acquaintance with the local homeboys. Thinnes let him question anybody who didn't speak English—all but a half dozen. After taking names and checking IDs, Thinnes asked what happened and noted responses. Then he either sent the "witness" home or back to the Area with the beat coppers. By the time he and Azul were finished, the bodies were being loaded into a squadrol, and Bendix and his crew were packing up.

"You two can go back to the station," Viernes told them. "Take statements and write up your reports,"

"Where's Franchi?" Thinnes asked

"I sent her to cover the Lee funeral," Viernes said.

So much for everybody working the heater case.

When they got back to Area Three, Evanger was huddled with Deputy Chief Keller. Thinnes wondered what would get the brass out to the boonies. As soon as Keller left, he asked.

"Apparently certain leaders of the Asian community have expressed the concern that we're not moving on the Lee case because one of our own may be involved."

"Did you tell—"

Evanger held up a hand. "I told Keller if these community leaders have information, they need to talk to us.

"That's it. Back to work."

The box of Vietnam stuff was still in the kitchen. Thinnes put it on the table. He took out the album and set it aside. His dog tags were next, and brassard. He tossed an old can of C-rations in the trash. He found his uniform shirt with the MP insignia on the collar and, under it, a few postcards he'd sent Rhonda and a bundle of his letters to her. She seemed to have kept every one.

Thinnes untied the string and started reading.

Dear Rhonda,

This morning I landed in Saigon. The place is unbelievable. It's hotter than in the South and palm trees grow right in town. In some places, the streets look like pictures of Paris, but others are like the dirtiest alleys in Chicago, only not as well paved.

They don't have any traffic regulations here. Every-

body seems to be trying to run other drivers off the road. And they have water buffaloes and farm animals right in the city. Most people don't have indoor plumbing, which you can tell by the smell. The Saigon River is pretty much a giant sewer. The water's full of sewage (and other things you don't want to know about), but people still live on it in boats. At night, you can't see the filth and the river is really beautiful with all the boats lit by lanterns.

Well, that's all for now. If you write every day, I can make it through this tour.

All my love, John

Thinnes skimmed the rest of the letters, noticing they got shorter and less formal, noticing he'd censored his reports more and his feelings less as the realities of Vietnam set in. He'd told Rhonda about meeting Bobby Lee and Hue, and how the three of them palled around until Hue and Bobby got serious and moved in together. He always signed the letters, "Love, John," but "Dear Rhonda" became "Ronnie Dear," then just "Ronnie." Gradually he wrote fewer details of his work—"Had to search some bars in Tu Do Street last night for deserters"—and more of how he felt—"Today's Thursday and it's raining. I can't tell you how much I hate being here. So many things happen that aren't right, that I can't do anything about." And, "During the day I keep busy. Night's the only time I have to think. At night I REALLY miss you." On Christmas, he wrote, "Days like this I miss you most of all."

His letters went into more detail about Hue's pregnancy— "Bobby's walking on air and plans to marry her his next leave"— and about Bobby getting shot—"By the time I got the news, Bobby was out of the woods, but crazy with worry about Hue. He's being shipped home. He made me promise to take care of her until he can get back."

Dear Ronnie,

Bad news. Hue had a miscarriage. I talked to her doctor—she's gonna be OK, but she's really down. I

didn't find out about it for two days because I was out of
Saigon helping guard some stupid "fact finding" group
from the States. Most of what they were told—about how
well the war is going—is BS, but I think they bought it.
I'd like to give them a tour. Vietnamization is a joke.
Without U.S. troops to back the government, it's a matter
of time before the NVA takes over. Most ARVN soldiers
were drafted. They're about as happy to serve as U.S.
draftees, maybe less because some of them have family on
the other side.

One of Hue's girlfriends is staying with her for a
while. Good thing. She's going to be out of it a while, and
I don't think I'd make a very good nurse.

Meanwhile, I'm counting off the days until I see you.

Love, John

The letters after that were newsy without saying much. He'd
taken Hue and her girlfriend to Mass at the cathedral on Sundays,
and once to lunch at the Hotel Continental, where the foreign
newsmen hung out. When the girlfriend left the city, he'd moved
in with Hue because young women living alone were considered
whores and fair game.

Bobby returned two weeks before Thinnes was due to come
back to the world. Thank God.

"I'll be able to stand up at their wedding," he'd written in his
last letter. "I'll tell you all about it when I get home." Back in the
world, he'd called long distance when he felt the need to connect.

THIRTEEN

Thinnes was halfway through his first report when a man whose strut and suit pegged him for a lawyer came in the squadroom and asked to see the guy in charge. Asian. In his thirties—as near as Thinnes could tell, five-six, maybe 140 pounds.

The desk sergeant pointed at Evanger's office; the lawyer nodded curtly and headed toward it.

Curious, Thinnes got his mug and went to the coffee setup—the better to hear what was happening. Someone had replaced the beat-up BIOHAZARD decal on the coffeemaker with a diamond-shaped sticker announcing, POISON. The warning didn't stop Thinnes from filling his mug.

The lawyer, meanwhile, walked right through Evanger's open doorway. "I understand you're in charge." He didn't seem to be shouting, but his voice carried.

Evanger's voice carried, too, and Thinnes knew he must mean for anyone in the squadroom to hear his response: "What can I do for you Mr. . . . ?"

"Andrew Duong. I represent Étienne Lee."

Evanger said, "Maybe you'd better close the door."

Duong left; Evanger came out of his office with his BIG DOG mug. When he walked past, Thinnes said, "Trouble?"

Evanger helped himself to coffee, creamer, sugar. He stirred the mix. He looked around the room—empty except for the two of them—then leaned against Thinnes's table. He tried his brew and made a face Thinnes interpreted as, *Too hot*.

"Franchi called Mr. Lee," Evanger said, "to ask him to come in and give a statement. Apparently he told her he didn't have anything to add to what he told the two of you at the scene, and he saw no reason to waste our time or his coming in. He also asked why *she* called him. She told him you were off the case."

"She tell him why?"

"Please!" Evanger took another sip. "That's what he sent Mr. Duong to find out. Also to protest your removal. Apparently Mr. Duong made inquiries about you and was told you're the best homicide dick in the Area."

"What did *you* tell Duong?"

"The official line: You knew the victim. So to avoid any conflict of interest, you were reassigned."

"He bought that?"

"Not quite. He wants you back on the case. Which doesn't jibe with Lee being a killer."

"Unless he knows the more he pushes for my reinstatement, the more the department will resist. Hell, if he killed his mother, he might have made that *anonymous* phone call himself."

"I thought of that. Which is why I told Duong about the call. Told him his client would have to submit samples for a paternity test to get you back in it. That shut him down. He said he'd have to confer with his client." Evanger swirled the coffee around in his cup, then stood up. "When they get back, tell Viernes and Franchi I want to see them."

FOURTEEN

Thinnes finished his reports and turned them in, then refilled his coffee mug. He was trying to decide whether to make a few more calls on the Gonzales case or take a crack at digging up more on the Lees, when Franchi and Viernes brought in a suspect. The detectives looked happy.

The male Hispanic they had with them looked bored. In his mid-twenties, he had the cold stare of a hard guy. His T-shirt was sweat-soaked, his Air Jordans bloodstained.

"Good news, Thinnes," Viernes said. "We got our shooter. We caught Mr. Rodriguez red-footed, so to speak."

"Good news for you, too, Thinnes," Franchi added. "Word on the street is Rodriguez also killed Gonzales."

Rodriguez said, "I want a lawyer."

"In good time, Rodriguez," Viernes said. "You know the drill."

Judging from the crude tattoos on his forearms, Rodriguez had been through it many times, though the Latin Kings logo on his left biceps was a professional job.

Viernes pulled on a pair of latex gloves and pointed to Rodriguez. "Sit down and take off your shoes."

"These mothers cost me a fortune, man," Rodriguez said. "You gonna take 'em, I want a receipt."

"Sure thing," Viernes said. "Thinnes, show our guest to the interview room and watch him for us, will you?"

"My pleasure."

• • •

Rosario Rodriguez, a.k.a. Arcángel, had saved them the trouble of an interrogation by lawyering up. They left him hanging on the wall in the interview room while they got the assistant state's attorney to approve the charges; filled out the case reports, arrest reports, and complaints; and got the watch commander's okay. The ASA wanted them to hold a lineup, so before they took Rodriguez to the lockup, they had to locate four Hispanic males fitting Rodriguez's description and round up two sets of witnesses. Since many of the witnesses didn't speak English or weren't comfortable with it, Viernes and Franchi did most of the work.

Thinnes was able to go home at the end of his regular shift. He'd even had time to start a list of people he remembered from Saigon. He wasn't sure if any of them were still alive or, if they were, how to find them.

But it was a start.

FIFTEEN

How are you feeling today?" Caleb couldn't bring himself to say "Father," and "Arthur" seemed disrespectful.

"Like hell. They haven't got my pain meds right."

Caleb looked at the chart. He wasn't an expert on pain management, though he'd consulted on the care of terminal AIDS patients. Arthur's treatment regimen seemed reasonable, but pain is relative. "I'll speak to them."

"They won't listen to you. What does a shrink know?"

A rhetorical question. Caleb let it go.

Arthur reached for the remote and turned on the TV. A rerun of *M*A*S*H* lit up the screen. He watched for a minute; it seemed to take him that long to recognize what he was seeing. He fumbled to aim the remote, lost it down the side of the bed. Annoyance crossed his face.

Caleb picked up the remote and offered it to him.

Arthur shook his head. "Just turn it off. Making a joke of it. It's obscene." He had been a surgeon in the Korean War, like Caleb, a draftee. "We didn't have time for nonsense. We didn't even have time to sleep. We didn't have time to do anything but cut and sew—sometimes thirty-six hours straight."

Caleb didn't argue. If they actually made realistic movies, people might not be so quick to start wars. "Is there something else you'd like to watch?" he asked.

"No, shut it off." When Caleb did, Arthur said, "You've always been my favorite. It's not fair, and I know Robert, for one, resents it. But there it is."

As a child, Caleb had been intimidated by his father's bullying. He was scorned as a wimp when he obeyed and disapproved of if he disobeyed—*Tails I win, heads you lose.* But he'd rejected his father's actions, though he hadn't been able to interpret why, when he'd accepted most other adult behavior as appropriate for adults. Adults were, after all, the ones who made the rules. In retrospect it was because he'd decided that if there was no pleasing the man, he might as well please himself.

When he'd first begun to study psychology, Caleb had had a series of epiphanies. Reading about narcissistic personalities illuminated his father's character in a way that was both satisfying and liberating. Arthur had become someone to be studied and pitied rather than fought.

In later years, impatience with his father's unpleasantness and their lack of anything in common kept Caleb from making frequent contact. And his father would never risk showing vulnerability by making the first call.

It was Caleb's brother, Robert, who'd alerted Caleb to Arthur's condition. "Pancreatic cancer. Metastasized. Come immediately if you want to make your peace."

Caleb didn't particularly.

When his father learned Caleb had been drafted, he'd said, "Serves you right. Should have stayed in school."

They had never written when Caleb was in 'Nam.

Even graduating cum laude from Northwestern Medical School hadn't earned his father's approval. *You should have been a surgeon.*

Now he said, "I don't want to end up in that mausoleum you run down on Wilson. I'll stay here until it's over. I can afford it. There'll still be plenty left for the three of you to divvy up. It won't be long. A month at most."

"If that's what you've decided."

"That's what I know. Textbook case. Abdominal pain, lower back pain, weight loss, nausea, enlarged liver—If you'd stuck with medicine . . ."

Caleb said nothing.

"Good Lord, boy, you've just been insulted. You haven't got the sand to be angry?"

Caleb smiled. "I'm no longer seventeen."

Arthur chuckled.

Caleb waited.

"Your brother's a sentimental fool."

"What's your point?"

"I want you to do something for me."

"It's too late for me to study surgery. I'm too old."

Arthur laughed mirthlessly. "You were too old when your mother died. Shouldn't have made you go to all those operas.

"That was a joke," he added when Caleb didn't reply. "You're not as sentimental as your brother."

Caleb continued to wait.

"When the time comes, I don't want him to countermand my DNR. That's why I gave you power of attorney."

"I'll see to it."

"Good. Now get out of here and let me sleep."

"Good night, Arthur."

" 'Night." Caleb was halfway out the door when Arthur called out, "James!"

Caleb stopped and turned. Arthur closed his eyes and took in a breath that he let out slowly. He seemed to have aged thirty years while Caleb's back was turned, to have become, suddenly, frail. He didn't open his eyes, but his voice carried clearly.

"You were right about Vietnam."

SIXTEEN

When they came into the squadroom together the next morning, Tien Lee had on the same white suit he'd had on at the wake; his lawyer was wearing sharkskin. Fitting.

Franchi signaled Thinnes to let Evanger know about them, then showed them into the conference room. Viernes followed, pen and notebook in hand.

Evanger opened the blinds that usually camouflaged the two-way mirror in the conference room wall. "Don't you have something to do right now?" Thinnes shrugged. Evanger shook his head but didn't press the point.

In the room, Franchi offered the visitors seats facing the mirror and sat with her back to it. Viernes parked at the end of the table, where the others would have to turn to see him. The lawyer glanced at his reflection and frowned. Lee faced it and Franchi with no apparent emotion.

"Mr. Lee," Franchi said, "where were you the week your mother died between nine P.M. Tuesday and noon Wednesday?"

"I was at my place Tuesday night, conducting classes in the dojo and doing paperwork Wednesday morning."

"Can you verify that?"

"Only the classes."

"What did you and your mother fight about?"

"We had a disagreement."

"What did you disagree about?"

"I believe I've answered that question."

"Humor me."

"My mother wanted to arrange a marriage for me. I prefer to select my own mate."

Thinnes noticed that Lee held Franchi's eyes until she looked away. Not good, Franchi, he thought.

Judging by his expression, Viernes noticed, too.

Franchi said, "Your mother seems to have been well liked." Lee didn't respond. "In fact, you seem to be the only one she ever had a fight with."

"A disagreement is *not* a fight."

"Who stands to gain from your mother's death?"

"No one."

"Don't you inherit her estate?"

"That implies that her estate would compensate me for her loss. Not so."

Franchi blinked, seemingly at a loss.

Her timing was off. Thinnes wondered why. He didn't know much about her personal life; by mutual agreement, they kept their conversations to business.

In the year they'd worked together, he'd never noticed the time of month affecting her performance. She didn't drink much; the few times they'd gone out to decompress after work, she'd stuck with O'Doul's. But maybe she'd been partying last night.

Ferris came up behind Thinnes and said, "Think she's being too hard on junior?" Dammit!

"Shut up, Ferris!" Thinnes glanced around. The only others in the room were Evanger, the sergeant, and the custodian.

Evanger said, "That's enough!"

In the conference room, Franchi said, "I checked. You could've gone anywhere. Why move here? Why now?"

"My father's estate was finally settled," Lee said. "I didn't want to follow in his business, but it made sense to invest in one of my own. This dojo was available. Chicago is a cosmopolitan city. Why not here and now?"

In the squadroom, Evanger said, "What do you think?"

Thinnes shrugged. "If he's telling the truth, I'll bet it's not the whole truth."

"The inscrutable Asian," Ferris chimed in.

Evanger turned sharply. "Ferris!"

"I'm going. Hang in there, Pops," he told Thinnes.

In the conference room, Franchi asked Lee, "Did you kill your mother?"

"Of course not!"

"You don't have to put up with this," Duong said.

Franchi ignored Duong, kept talking to Lee. "If you're innocent, you can't have any objection to answering questions that will help me catch her killer." Lee shook his head. "Would you be willing to submit DNA samples?"

"Mr. Lee's parentage has long been established," Duong interrupted. "This is a pathetic attempt to get something you have no probable cause to ask for!"

Franchi whirled and got in Duong's face. "But what's his objection to submitting DNA?"

Lee answered. "Beyond insulting my mother's honor, what would it do?"

"It would help nail your mother's killer."

"How? Would it eliminate me as a suspect?"

"Of course it wouldn't," Duong snapped. "We're through here."

SEVENTEEN

As Thinnes unlocked his car after shift change, Ferris came up behind him. "*That* is a *nasty* car, man. You could almost leave that running with the lights and radio blaring—any neighborhood in the city—nobody'd steal it."

Thinnes's old Caprice was the original, with squared-off profile and taillights, not the rounded version Chevy tried to put over on the public by redefining *classic,* the so-called watermelon car. A classic Caprice was to a watermelon car what original Coke was to generic cola.

"What do you mean? It's a classic."

"Nah." Ferris pointed at a beautifully restored sixties Mustang convertible parked where the Western Avenue overpass rose above the Belmont-Clybourn intersection. "*That* is a classic. What you're driving's a piece of crap."

Thinnes hadn't noticed the Mustang, though it was bright red and in mint condition. He just shook his head. But he exited the parking lot onto Belmont and turned under the overpass, slowing so he could take another look. The car reminded him of Bobby Lee.

A red '67 Mustang convertible had been Bobby's dream car. He'd worked all through high school to save up for one. He'd had to leave it behind when he was drafted, but he'd brought a picture of it with him to basic.

Bobby's car haunted Thinnes all the way home, or maybe it was Bobby. Thinnes thought he spotted it when he turned onto Lincoln, then again on Peterson. Superstition, he decided, a cop's natural paranoia. He concentrated on traffic and fought the urge to right-turn around the block.

When he got home, he went straight to the box of Vietnam stuff. An old photo near the bottom showed Bobby, nineteen, skinny, in a T-shirt and fatigues, relaxing against a jeep with a cigarette dangling from his mouth. He was holding the picture of his car with one hand, a beer in the other. The photo had yellowed, the car faded to orange, but Bobby's pride was still unmistakable. Weird, how that red Mustang brought his buddy back.

When Thinnes came downstairs next morning, Rhonda had already left for work. Rob was wolfing down Cheerios as he studied the *Sun-Times*. Toby waited hopefully under the table. Rob didn't look up. "Morning,"

"Morning."

"Someone hit the Lotto." Still without looking up.

"How's that?" Thinnes asked.

"There's this awesome old Mustang parked at the end of the block—mint condition. It *had* to cost a fortune."

"How old? What color?"

"Sixties-something. Red ragtop."

"What's the plate number?" A game they'd played when Rob was small was memorize the license. It kept him from getting antsy on long trips. He'd gotten very good. Now he closed his eyes as if reading something off the insides of his eyelids. He rattled off a plate number.

A familiar number.

Before Rob opened his eyes, Thinnes was out in the hall. He paused to reach his holstered .38 down from the closet shelf. He flew out the door, charging toward the street with the gun in one hand, the holster in the other.

No red cars in sight. He stepped to the center of the road to look all the way to the corner. Nothing.

Rob was waiting when he got back to the porch. "Dad, you okay? You look like you just saw a ghost."

Thinnes didn't believe in ghosts. Or coincidences. He did believe in stalkers.

"I'm fine," he said. "But I want to know right away if you see that car again."

"Why? Who was it?"

"I don't know. That plate number belonged to a man who's been dead a long time."

Rob looked surprised. He grinned. "Maybe *I* saw a ghost."

EIGHTEEN

The group members were all there, all in their usual places. Maharis looked ready to nod off, Alec nervous, Joe bored. Arthur, as always, seemed interested.

Butch laced his fingers and stretched, cracking his knuckles. "You never did finish your fragging story, Jack."

"You seem particularly interested in fragging, Butch," Arthur said. "Do you want to explain?"

"What's to explain?"

"You ever do it?" Joe asked. He seemed more interested, suddenly. Maharis came wide awake.

"If I did, would I tell you? What about it, Jack?"

Alec said, "Fragging is murder?"

"I'm sure some of the fraggings were seen as self-defense," Caleb said. "Enlisted men served a year in country, a year of jeopardy if you were sent to a combat position. They rotated the officers out after six months. So about the time your CO figured out what he was doing, they sent him somewhere safe. And sent us an FNG CO."

"Yeah," Butch added. "A guy who'd survived six or seven months in country would suddenly find his ass in a sling because his CO didn't know a RPG from a ladyfinger. So if that CO wouldn't listen to reason . . ."

"Why'd they call it fragging?" Alec seemed equally fascinated and repelled. It made him seem younger—as young as Caleb had been when he was sent to 'Nam.

"I suppose because most cases were committed with grenades," Caleb said, "usually fragmentation grenades."

Butch chuckled. "You use what ya got."

"Care to expand on that, Butch?" Arthur asked.

"Nope."

"Continue, Jack."

Caleb addressed Alec, since *he* knew nothing about military service. "They called the infantry 'legs' because we marched all over Vietnam. Sometimes they'd drive us to the end of the pavement, so to speak—there really weren't many paved roads—and drop us off. Most often they'd airlift us to our AO—area of operation—by helicopter. And we'd walk around looking for the enemy."

"Yeah," Butch added. "From the air, all you could see would be treetops or rice paddies. Or flashes from tracers or rockets or whatever."

"Were you in the infantry?" Alec asked him.

"Nah. That was work, man. Way too much work. I was a door gunner on a Huey 'til I got my Purple Heart. Then I was a REMF—that's a rear echelon motherfucker." Before Alec asked, he added, "Combat support, you know, base camp duty. But enough about me." He gave Caleb a wolfish grin. "You're not getting out of this by changing the subject."

They all looked at Caleb.

He sighed. "As Butch said, it was physically hard work. The heat was exhausting—it was always hot. We walked around in a perpetual state of dehydration, soaked with sweat. We had to carry everything we needed—equipment, food, and water. After seven or eight hours of humping in the heat, frequently up- or downhill, we had to dig bunkers to protect ourselves from shelling during the night. Most of us were draftees or boys who had no idea what they were signing up for. Even with bunkers we didn't get much sleep; we took turns standing watch. Sometimes it rained—up to eight or ten inches a day. The mosquitoes were voracious. In smaller base camps or forward observation posts—any semipermanent installation—and anywhere near rice paddies there were rats . . ."

"Yeah," Butch said. "You know why they don't have cats in 'Nam? The rats eat 'em."

"There were snakes, spiders, centipedes, and insects—unbelievable insects. Out in the jungle there were wild animals—pigs and monkeys, parrots, deer, even the occasional panther or tiger. Most of them made some kind of noise, but you couldn't see anything, so you spent a lot of time lying awake listening, trying to determine if what you just heard was coming to get you."

"Then, of course, there was Charlie," Butch chimed in. "Charlie was always out there. But he would come to get you in his own good time."

"So," Caleb continued. "We were always sleep-deprived and irritable, bored by day, terrified at night. Most of us were physically ill with dysentery, anemia, malaria, infections, funguses. We all suffered—to a greater or lesser degree—from post-traumatic stress. Young men impaired by disease and exhaustion, fueled by rage and testosterone. It was like living the *Lord of the Flies*."

They'd been sent on a recon patrol with a strac lieutenant and a new sergeant. The sergeant was new to the unit, not to the war. He'd come back off injury leave assigned to Caleb's platoon.

"We were undermanned as usual, and to make things worse, the CO split us up. He'd set up a rendezvous just an hour before dark. Our AO was near the Cambodian border, mountainous. Not like the Rockies. These mountains were smaller and covered by jungle. In the places where we hadn't bombed recently or dumped Agent Orange, it was rough going. We'd been out for days and hadn't seen any sign of Charlie—not even booby traps. There weren't any villages around, just an abandoned Buddhist shrine, overgrown with vines and orchids. It was like a tourist spot.

"*My* squad stayed with the lieutenant and the radio man. The lieutenant kept the new sergeant with us, I think so he could assess his judgment before trusting his life to him. The rest of the squad consisted of Froggy, Preacher, Ears, four other guys, and me.

"About an hour after we split from the rest of the platoon, we came to a small clearing—just big enough to park a six-by, too small for a dust-off. We swept it for booby traps and sat down for a smoke while the CO reported in. I fell asleep immediately. Most of us did that whenever we stopped.

"The sergeant woke us with the order to move out. We got up and were just stepping off when the sarge said, 'We're short one.' He didn't know all our names, but he could count. 'Who's missing?'

"We looked around and noticed Ears's pack. No Ears. The lieutenant had us fan out to look for him. We took our time. Figured he was sleeping somewhere. Or Charlie got him. Either way, finding him could be hazardous. He was on his second tour—came awake locked and loaded. And if Charlie'd gotten him . . .

"Soon the sergeant called out, 'Here!'

"We all went. Ears was lying in his own waste with his throat slit and his pants around his ankles. Whoever killed him had cut off his ears and stuffed them down his throat.

"The sarge told us all to fall in. When we were lined up, he inspected us carefully, looking—I'm sure—for Ears's blood on whoever had killed him. He didn't find any.

"The lieutenant told Froggy and Preacher to wrap him in his poncho and bring him along. They refused to obey.

" 'I'm not risking my life for that piece of shit,' Froggy said.

"Preacher just said, 'No, sir.'

"The lieutenant knew how they felt about Ears, so he said, 'I'll deal with you two later. Doc, you and him.' He pointed to one of the other guys. 'Pack him up.'

"I felt a surge of rage. Ears had been no good; Froggy was right. We didn't have room for a dust-off without cutting a lot of trees, which would take time. And we'd kill ourselves trying to carry him to the rendezvous point. So I said, 'I respectfully decline, sir.'

"I thought the CO was going to burst a blood vessel. The sarge walked up to the body, removed Ears's dog tags, and handed them to the CO. 'We can report he was KIA.'

" 'We can't leave his body here!'

" 'You're right, sir,' the sarge said. He took out a grenade and pulled the pin. Everybody scrambled to get away. The sergeant dropped the grenade on the body and dived for cover. The grenade went off.

"It was the sergeant, not the lieutenant, who told the radioman to call in and report that Ears had been completely blown away. He said the lieutenant could write Ears's family that he died like a soldier. The lieutenant swore he'd have us all court-martialed. Not to worry, we said—to a man—at least we'd be outta there.

" 'Don't we have a mission to complete?' the sergeant asked.

"So we picked up our gear and headed out."

NINETEEN

The dojo, on Broadway, was a two-story brick commercial building with a large front window. Lettering on the glass announced: MARTIAL ARTISTS JUDO, KARATE, TAE KWON DO, TAI CHI. There was no sign of the red Mustang, but inside, Thinnes could see Tien Lee drilling a squad of junior high kids. Students and teacher were dressed in identical outfits except for the colors of the belts. Lee's was black. The class shouted in unison as they lunged forward and back. Lee moved among them—fourteen boys and a girl—wordlessly repositioning a foot or moving a hand, arm, or elbow.

Inside, a young Asian woman sat behind a counter by the door. "May I help you?"

"I need to talk to Mr. Lee."

She smiled. "He'll be done shortly." She pointed at a row of chairs along one wall. "You're welcome to wait."

When the class was finished, the students bowed. Lee bowed in return. Then the students transformed from disciplined martial artists into normal teens, laughing and trading punches. Except the girl, who hung back talking to her "sensei." Thinnes could see a serious crush in progress.

Lee bowed and called the girl's attention to his visitor. Her disappointment was obvious, but she returned the bow and followed the boys out.

Lee seemed amused as he crossed to greet Thinnes. "Detective Thinnes, what brings you to my humble hall?"

"If you're planning a career as a stalker, you'd better get a less conspicuous car."

"Stalker?" He seemed to think about it, then said, "Of course I was curious. Wouldn't you be?"

Before Thinnes could answer, a phone rang.

"Maybe we should discuss this in private." Lee gestured toward a door near the locker rooms.

His living quarters occupied the floor above the dojo. Lee let them in through a battered metal door secured with a hasp and padlock. Thinnes noticed he closed the lock on the staple. Smart. No one could lock him in.

They were greeted by a large cat, marked like a Siamese but stockier and dark brown in color. The cat rubbed against its owner's legs and stared round-eyed at Thinnes. Lee picked it up. "You bothered by cats?"

"Not usually."

The cat climbed onto Lee's shoulder and draped itself around his neck like a stole. He stroked its dangling tail and hind feet, then put it down.

"Excuse me a moment. Make yourself at home." He crossed the room and disappeared through a doorway.

"Home" took up a good third of the second floor. Tall windows faced east, south, and west, and a small jungle of exotic plants occupied the center. Others were tucked in corners or suspended from massive ceiling beams. A giant flat-screen TV hung above a killer entertainment center. There was no couch; matching love seats faced each other across a glass-topped coffee table. Thinnes recognized the plant on it as a white moth orchid because he'd scored points with Rhonda when he got her one for Christmas. The orchid shared space with a chess set, a kaleidoscope, several books, and high-tech cat toys. Everything said taste and money.

Thinnes was petting the cat when Lee returned.

"Méo likes you." Lee's hair was wet and he was dressed in street clothes. He gestured toward a love seat. Thinnes sat down; Lee sat across the table.

"We were discussing stalking," Thinnes said.

"As you pointed out, a stalker would drive a less conspicuous car."

"The question remains, why'd you follow me?"

"The answer remains curiosity."

Thinnes waited for him to explain.

"My attorney seems to think you are the best homicide detective in the district, but you were taken off the case." Thinnes nodded. "Why?"

"Your mother was my friend. The department sees that as a conflict of interest."

"It's been alleged that you were more than friends."

For the first time, Thinnes could see a sign of emotion, one he couldn't identify.

"What kind of man are you?" Lee persisted.

"More to the point," Thinnes said, "who'd make such an accusation? And why?"

"Maybe to get you off the case. Detective Viernes doesn't seem particularly anxious to find the killer."

"He's uncomfortable because he's unfamiliar with Vietnamese culture and doesn't speak the language. But he'll do his job. And he'll have help."

"Detective Franchi," Lee said. Thinnes nodded. "She seems more determined to find my mother's killer, but I doubt anyone will talk to her."

"She'll do whatever it takes."

"I seem to be the only one the police suspect."

Thinnes shrugged. "We were told you had an argument with your mother."

Amusement softened Lee's face. "Mrs. Nyugen."

Thinnes neither confirmed nor denied it.

"You have children?" Lee asked.

"A son."

"You and he never disagree?"

"Not often. What did you disagree about?"

Lee showed no sign of annoyance at being asked the same

question yet again. He said, "The oldest son in a Vietnamese family has the responsibility of caring for his aging parents. Since most of the actual work will fall to his wife, his parents usually arrange his marriage to a compliant woman who won't balk at becoming a virtual slave. My mother defied tradition to marry for love but for some reason expected me to ignore her example. I think she wanted the security of a compliant daughter-in-law.

"My father was good at business. He left enough money to assure her comfort, so there was no reason I should marry a servant. I prefer a woman with spirit." He paused for a long moment, then added, "It seems to me that you have as much reason to find her killer as I."

"How's that?"

"Does your wife know of your alleged affair?" Lee seemed to be amused.

Strange response to the *allegation* that Thinnes was his natural father. Why no outrage or curiosity or bitterness? Thinnes tried to imagine how he'd feel if someone accused his mother of infidelity, if the man he'd grown up believing was his father wasn't. But maybe Lee had always known he was adopted.

He noticed Lee was waiting. What was the question?

Oh, yeah. Rhonda. He said, "Yes."

"And?"

"She wouldn't get bent out of shape over a rumor about something that *might* have happened years ago."

"But if it were *true*?"

"It's not." Lee waited, and Thinnes was aware he hadn't answered the question to the other's satisfaction. "But if it was," he said, "so what?" He watched Lee closely as he added, "Lots of guys left bastards in Vietnam."

Lee laughed.

It was not what Thinnes expected. He felt they were playing a game and he didn't have the rules.

Lee put his inscrutable expression back in place and said, "Maybe *you* killed my mother."

"Before the day she died, I hadn't seen her in twenty-four years."

62

"Prove it!"

"I can't prove a negative."

"You can prove you didn't kill her by finding out who did. In fact, you and I ought to work on this together."

"Not possible. It's a police investigation. I could be fired and you could be jailed for interfering. Anyway, even if we closed it, any evidence we found would be attacked by the defense."

"The alternative is my mother's killer gets away."

Lee was so totally different from his mother. Maybe he *was* adopted. Maybe Hue and Bobby had smuggled an orphan out of Saigon. Amerasian children were as common as fleas before the end. Children of the dust, they were called, a dime a dozen. Birth certificates had been forged before.

But it was irrelevant now. Hue had raised him. She was his mother, and it was unlikely that he'd killed her.

"I tell you what," Thinnes said. "If you come up with anything that might help catch the killer, give it to Detective Franchi. I'll do the same."

TWENTY

Caleb's patients always made appointments—that was the rule, but his friends and family had the annoying habit of just showing up. Caleb was at his desk when his receptionist called on the intercom to announce, "Detective Thinnes."

Caleb sighed. "Send him in."

Thinnes closed the door behind him and stood for a moment, inspecting the room. Caleb guessed that he was trying to tell what was different from his last visit. The office had recently been redecorated, but in deference to those of his patients who abhorred change, Caleb had made the modifications subtle. The floor was refinished, the drapes a bluer shade of slate, the couch a bolder pattern. He'd traded the Jason Rogue lithograph of a cat for a watercolor of two felines curled in sleep like Yin and Yang.

Thinnes was observant about people, but Caleb would have bet he'd never studied the decor. He finally fixed on the watercolor; he stared it a moment, then relaxed as if it explained any differences from his recollection. He finally said, "Jack."

Caleb gestured toward the couch and followed as Thinnes moved to it. When Thinnes was seated, Caleb took the chair opposite. "What can I do for you, John?"

He could tell that Thinnes still wasn't at ease discussing personal matters—his body language fairly screamed it. He perched on the edge of the couch and leaned forward, resting his forearms on his knees.

Caleb said, "Coffee?"

"Yeah, sure." He seemed relieved by the reprieve.

When Caleb had set a mug on the end table beside Thinnes, he resumed his seat and waited.

Thinnes squirmed, then took a folded paper from his pocket and handed it over.

It was a memo quoting the allegation from an anonymous source that Thinnes fathered a murder victim's son. Caleb glanced at his friend. Was he blushing?

"Is this charge true?"

Thinnes's discomfort was his only answer.

"Could it be?"

Thinnes seemed at a loss. "I don't know. You know how it was. You could get drunk and lose weeks at a time."

"Did you?"

"Just once. The day my friend Bobby Lee got married."

"You were alone with the woman at some time that day?"

"Damned if I remember. It's been almost twenty-five years."

Caleb recalled the newscast that had triggered his flashback. "Mrs. Lee was the woman murdered recently in Uptown?"

Thinnes nodded. "I stood up at her wedding. We celebrated afterwards. I woke up on their floor the next day. To save my life I can't remember what happened."

"But if you avoided trouble up to that point, what makes you think *anything* happened?"

"I woke up dreaming I'd been making love to Rhonda."

"And you'd never made love to her before?"

"Yeah, but she was in Illinois. We were in Saigon."

"What did you think I could do for you?"

"Help me remember?"

"Why not just have a paternity test?"

"Franchi suggested that. Lee's lawyer practically threatened to sue. As far as the law's concerned, Bobby Lee was Tien's father. I've got no standing to claim paternity, even if I wanted to—which I don't. And the department wouldn't risk offending her son by asking unless there was enough evidence to get a court order."

"I still don't see how I can help."

"Hypnosis? Drugs?"

"We're friends. It wouldn't be appropriate."

"I couldn't talk about this with a stranger. Besides, no one would understand who wasn't there."

"There are excellent therapists who were there."

"Look, I'm not asking to have my head shrunk. I just need help remembering the details of a single day."

"This is pretty important to you. What haven't you told me?"

"I don't remember how I got there, but when I came to on the floor, I was buck-naked."

"In order for this to work," Caleb said, "you have to relax completely." He was already smoothing his voice. "So get into a comfortable position and loosen your tie."

Thinnes complied, but the rigidity of his posture told Caleb that the control freak hadn't yet abdicated.

"Close your eyes." Thinnes did. "Now imagine that you're walking along a deserted beach. It's your favorite time of year. The sun is warm; the temperature is just right. The air smells of spring. A gentle breeze stirs the surface of the water. The water washing over the sand makes a soft swishing sound."

From the way Thinnes sank into the couch, Caleb knew his suggestions were taking effect. He continued. "You lie down on the sand and stretch out. Perhaps you clasp your fingers behind your head. You take a deep breath. You let it out slowly. Your eyelids are getting heavy. You close them. You relax your eyes. You relax your arms. You relax your shoulders. Every part of your body is relaxing. You feel lighter, as if you're floating . . .

"I want you to go back in time. To Saigon. Tell me what you see . . ."

"It's early March, a week from my DEROS. Bobby and Hue are getting married. My CO gave me a three-day pass.

"We're all inside the cathedral—Notre Dame. It's dark and cool, all high ceilings and stained-glass windows, and religious statues and paintings with lots of gold. It's huge—room for three hundred people. There's maybe twenty sitting in the front pews.

Two of 'em are guys from Bobby's old unit. The rest, mostly women, are Hue's friends from the bank or her school. The church is dressed up, too—some kind of pink flowers and lots of candles.

"Hue's boss is walking her down the aisle. She's wearing a red satin dress, traditional, with long sleeves and boocoo embroidery. And a carved jade pendant on a string of freshwater pearls. Good luck, she told me.

"It's hot as hell, but I'm in my dress uniform—the closest I could come to a suit. Bobby's standing next to me, looking like a GI on his way back to the world. He's wearing a baby-blue Nehru jacket and a navy silk shirt. And his dog tags, even though he's been a civilian a month.

"Hue's boss is putting her hand in Bobby's now. Bobby leads her up to the altar where the priest is waiting. The priest's outfit is gold. It hits me that there isn't any white to speak of in the church—except the tablecloth on the altar. It's weird. Usually you expect white with weddings—when the bride's young, even if she's not officially a virgin.

"Hue is so beautiful, she's glowing. She looks like she could've stepped right out of one of the windows.

"God, I wish Ronnie was here. She'd eat all this up—the flowers, the dress, the romance. Bobby's so fucking lucky!"

Thinnes was silent, reliving the experience, until Caleb said, "Tell me what's happening."

"Hue and Bobby are kneeling in front of the priest at the altar. The priest is talking, but I can't understand him. It's not French. Latin, maybe?"

"Okay," Caleb said. "I want you to think ahead. The ceremony is over and you leave the church. Tell me what's happening."

"It rained while we were in church. It's hot. We're all in cyclos on the way to a restaurant. Traffic is gridlocked as usual—cars and trucks, cyclos, motorbikes, and carts. The kid pedaling the cycle is sweating; he looks ready to drop. Hue's boss is hosting a reception for her and Bobby—paying for it, too. He has money."

"Okay," Caleb said, "I want you to remember what happened after the reception."

"Bobby and Hue went back to their place."

"And you?"

"Me, too."

"Now you're inside the Lees' place. Tell me what's happening . . ."

"Hue's pouring something into sake cups. Absinthe. It was a wedding gift. She calls it liquid happiness.

"I'm making a toast. Health, wealth, and joy.

"We drink it down and Bobby refills our cups. 'We're gonna finish this sucker off before you go,' he says.

"The absinthe tastes bitter, but gives a great buzz.

"I must be getting *really* drunk! Hue and Bobby are starting to get it on. They're taking off their clothes. It's like a porn film.

"This isn't right. I'm fucking getting a hard-on."

"Tell me what's happening," Caleb said.

"Ronnie's here."

" 'John, do you want to make love with me?'

"Jesus!"

"What?" Caleb asked.

"She's undressing me. Oh, God!" Thinnes started breathing fast and groaning. "Oh, God, Ronnie! Oh, God!"

He relaxed. His slow, even breathing signaled that he'd fallen asleep.

"John," Caleb said softly. "Tell me the next thing you remember."

"Birds singing outside in the garden. I can see light through my eyelids, but I don't want to open them. It's already too bright. I can feel tightness at the base of my skull. It'll be a headache if I move. I know I must be on the floor; I can feel it under me. It's hard and cold. I don't remember how I got here. I can't remember where 'here' is. I'll look in a minute. I'm wearing—

"Jesus Christ, I'm buck-naked!"

"Open your eyes," Caleb commanded. Thinnes complied. "What do you see?"

"Hue and Bobby are asleep across the room. Shit! This is their place. I don't know what the hell I'm doing here. The last thing I remember is toasting them with absinthe."

68

"Very well. I'm going to count to three and when I do, I want you to come fully awake. You will feel rested and alert. You will remember everything you just told me without feeling embarrassed.

"One. Two. Three."

Thinnes blinked and sat thinking for several moments.

"Do you remember what you did next?" Caleb asked.

"Yes."

"What?"

"I grabbed my clothes and beat feet," Thinnes said.

"Well?"

"That's all there is. Properly done, hypnosis only works if you have a memory to recall."

"That's good, isn't it? It means nothing happened."

"Not necessarily. It could mean that whatever happened never got transferred into long-term memory, or that it never made it to your conscious awareness."

TWENTY-ONE

Thinnes had to testify in an aggravated battery case. He spent an hour driving to the Criminal Courts Building at Twenty-sixth and Cal, another hour going over his notes.

The assistant state's attorney handling the case was Anthony Shiparelli, a.k.a. Columbo because of his old raincoat and habit of playing dumb to throw opponents off. Today he was dressed like a public defender. Camouflage. You bought his act at your own risk. He was laid back at the Area, but he was quick and vicious in court, with a memory like a supercomputer.

Thinnes was ready to testify when Columbo came in to report, "Faced with a truckload of evidence and a roster of witnesses, the defendant's decided to plead. You can go."

It was too early for lunch; Thinnes went back to work.

The detective's squadroom was nearly deserted, as usual at lunchtime—just the sergeant, the custodian, and Evanger and Ferris huddled in front of interview room's one-way window. The room was intentionally stark—blank walls, bench for the subject, chair for the interviewer. Thinnes got coffee and went over to watch the show.

Inside the room, Viernes was facing the man who'd drunk a toast from his pocket flask at Hue Lee's wake. The witness was sitting on the bench. Under the bright lights, he looked even skinnier than at the funeral home. His eyes shifted wildly. His uncombed hair and week or so of beard made him look like Thinnes's idea of John the Baptist.

"Sometimes I confuse them," he was saying. "You know?"

"What's that?" Viernes said.

"The voices inside and the voices outside." He didn't look at Viernes.

Thinnes got the impression of mental disorder rather than dishonesty. He wondered how the man smelled. Viernes was in his personal space, but if the subject was unpleasant to be near, Viernes didn't show it. "Maybe I could help you sort them out."

"You're not a doctor."

"No," Viernes said. "But I'm pretty good at puzzles."

"Oh, yeah? What's black and white and red all over?"

"A newspaper."

"No. Nobody reads the news. They get it on CNN now."

"Okay, you tell me."

"I can't tell. I'd like to help you, but I promised."

"Who'd you promise?"

Maharis stared at him for a moment, then said, "You're very good. But it won't work. I won't tell, not even if you cut off my nuts and keep me in the Hilton forever."

"The Hilton?"

"You know. The Hanoi Hilton. Hilton, Milton, Chilton. Hilton built hotels. Milton wrote poetry. Chilton fixed cars. What did they have in common?"

"I give up."

"Nothing. Just like what we accomplished in country."

"Maybe you just don't know," Viernes said.

"What?"

"What *is* black and white and red all over?"

"Nothing's black and white. It's all gray. All cats are gray in country, now and forever. Amen."

"Okay, what's red all over?"

"That's easy. Hands. We all got 'em good and bloody over there. And we came from all over."

"Are you talking about Vietnam?"

"What else?"

"The war's been over more than twenty years."

"Now that we're back in the world, we're all over it with our

71

bloody hands. We came from all over. Now we're back with our hands bloody, blood's getting all over."

"Do you know what day it is?"

"I lose track. Not that it matters. One day's just like the rest."

"Do you know who the president is?"

"Washington, Adams, Jefferson, Madison . . ."

"No, who's the current president?"

"President Clitoris." Viernes laughed. John the Baptist continued. "He likes 'em well enough. And tits. And asses. President Tits-and-Asses. Or we could call him President Hoover. He likes to be hoovered well enough. That's what they call it over the pond. Instead of 'suck my dick,' they say 'hoover my prick.' "

"What's the president's name?"

"What's the difference? They're all the same. Interchangeable parts." His eyes widened and he stared Viernes in the face. "And they all lie."

Viernes stood up. "Hang tight. I'll be back."

He came out and looked from Evanger to Thinnes to Ferris, then asked, "Is this guy faking?"

"I think we should send him to Ravenswood," Evanger said, "for a professional opinion."

Ferris couldn't resist saying, "Why not let Thinnes work on him? He's been all hot to get back in the case."

Franchi walked up with a stack of computer printouts just in time to hear. "That won't be necessary. Mr. Maharis has been in the system."

TWENTY-TWO

Lieutenant," the sergeant said, "there's a guy downstairs claims to be Maharis's shrink. He's threatening to get a lawyer if we don't let him see him."

"Bring him up," Evanger said. "Maybe he can help us make some sense of Maharis."

The visitor was five-ten or -eleven, and stocky, with thinning red-blond hair. He was wearing wire-rimmed glasses and a suit he'd gotten too fat for. He looked familiar, but Thinnes couldn't place him.

When he said, "I'm Arthur Doherty. I run a therapy group for men with post-traumatic stress disorder," Thinnes remembered where he'd seen him before—taking Dr. Caleb home after a meeting. Four years ago.

"I'm Mr. Maharis's therapist."

"You here to tell us Maharis is a wacko?" Ferris said.

Doherty whirled on him and said, "Define *wacko*!"

"That's enough, Ferris!" Evanger said. He turned to Doherty. "Does the fact that he has a therapist mean Maharis has a problem we need to know about, Doctor?"

"As a matter of public record, Mr. Maharis is schizophrenic, not a *wacko*. If he's gone off his medication, he may be psychotic. I'd have to speak with him to make a determination. Why are you holding him?"

"So far, a parole violation."

"What?"

"He hasn't checked in with his parole officer in a month. We may be able to cut him loose if he's not dangerous and he's willing to help us out."

The shrink looked suspicious. "That sounds like extortion."

"What're you, a lawyer?" Ferris demanded.

"Ferris," Evanger said, "find something to do."

Thinnes hadn't been sent to find something to do.

"We're investigating a murder," Evanger told Doherty. "Mr. Maharis may have information that could help us."

Thinnes noticed how Evanger changed his vocabulary to fit his audience. Doherty looked like he thought Evanger's intentions were suspicious. "Mr. Maharis needs his rights protected by an attorney while he's helping you."

Thinnes wanted to ask, *What does he need a lawyer for when he's got you?* He kept quiet, though. No sense reminding Evanger that he wasn't supposed to be in on this.

Evanger looked resigned. "Does he *have* an attorney?"

"Jack, Maharis is in police custody." Even over the phone, Arthur sounded stressed.

"What's he supposed to have done?"

"They claim he may be a witness in a murder case. But I'm afraid . . ."

"I'll see if my attorney can recommend someone."

"Great. One other thing. Maharis is probably off his medication. He may have to be hospitalized. I can't get back to the police station until late this afternoon."

"I'll take care of him."

Thinnes knew it wasn't coincidence when Caleb showed up. Caleb was Doherty's friend; Doherty was Maharis's shrink.

Evanger headed Caleb off. "Sorry, Doctor. Maharis hasn't given us a statement yet."

"Mr. Maharis is in need of medical intervention."

"You know this how?"

74

"I've been advised by his therapist that he's having problems and was asked to examine him."

Evanger shook his head.

Thinnes couldn't resist getting into it. "Maybe Dr. Caleb could persuade Maharis to cooperate."

Evanger nodded at Caleb. "Once he gives us a statement, he's free to go. With you, if he wants."

"Have you advised him of his rights?"

"Unnecessary," Evanger said. "He's not under arrest."

"But he will be if he implicates himself in this."

"If questioning becomes accusatory, we'll Mirandize him."

"How 'bout it, Doctor?" Thinnes said. "We need to know how Maharis is connected to the victim and when he saw her last. He may even know who had it in for her."

As soon as Viernes asked about the wake, Caleb remembered the day and Maharis's appalling odor. He tried to remember his friend's demeanor. He hadn't seemed upset or even saddened, the way people usually are when faced with the fact of death. But then, Maharis wasn't usual in his response to anything.

"Did you know Mrs. Lee?" Viernes asked him.

Maharis was sitting on the edge of the bench in the interview room, arms crossed, hands tucked into his armpits. He was rocking forward and back.

"No. No. No. No Mrs. Lee. Who?"

"The dead woman. At the wake," Caleb said softly. "The day you came to the meeting and Arthur made you take a shower. Do you remember going to the wake?"

"Nobody woke."

"Did you know the woman?"

"No. Never saw her before. Never saw her since."

"Then why did you go to her wake?"

"Pay my respects. She was respectable. She was a peach or an apple. Maybe an apple flower. I forget."

"If you never saw her before, how do you know she was respectable?"

75

"I can't tell. I promised."

"Who?"

Maharis just rocked back and forth.

"Can you tell us anything about the dead lady?"

"She had friends in low places and enemies at the zoo."

"What kind of enemies?"

"Lions and—" He hesitated, and Caleb could tell he was dissembling.

"And what?"

"Bears!"

"Bears? You're sure?"

Instead of answering, Maharis rocked faster, refusing to meet Caleb's gaze.

"Did you and Mrs. Lee have a mutual friend?"

Maharis glanced up at him, then looked down at the floor and rocked faster. "That's no fair, Jack. You're reading my mind."

"Just a guess," Caleb assured him. Maharis was getting more agitated. "Did your friend kill Mrs. Lee?"

"No. No. No. They were friends."

"Was your friend afraid to go to the wake? Afraid of someone else who might be there?"

Maharis stared. "No reading thoughts, Jack." He put his hands over his ears and rocked furiously.

Caleb touched his forearm gently, waited until the rocking slowed. "Who's threatening your friend?"

"I don't know!"

"Then tell us who your friend is. We'll protect him."

"Can't. Shan't. Plant." He rocked faster.

Caleb kept his hand on Maharis's arm until he stopped. Maharis cupped his hands over his ears. Caleb waited, looking him straight in the face.

After a while Maharis put his hands down and said, "What?" He started rocking again.

"Your friend may be in danger from the same person who killed Mrs. Lee. The police can't protect him if they don't know who he is."

"He can take care of himself."

76

"How do you know that?"

"He made it back to the world."

"Who?" Viernes demanded.

"I wasn't talking to you! You keep out of this!"

"Are you afraid of someone?" Caleb asked.

"God."

Caleb hoped Viernes'd have the sense to keep quiet.

Rocking faster, Maharis finally said, "The devil." A wait elicited, "*My mother.* Jack, can I ask you something?"

"Of course."

Maharis crooked his index finger in a come-nearer gesture, all the while rocking. As Caleb moved closer, he was aware of Viernes bracing for trouble.

Maharis whispered, "Jack, I gotta pee."

"Okay. Detective Viernes will show you where."

"You won't leave me here?"

"I'll wait for you and take you back to Arthur."

Thinnes, Franchi, and Evanger were standing in front of the mirror-window when Caleb walked out.

"I hope you have what you need," he told them. "Mr. Maharis has had enough."

"We don't have a name, Doctor," Evanger said.

"You're detectives. You can figure it out without driving him over the edge. Unless you're going to charge him with something, he'll be leaving with me."

TWENTY-THREE

John Thinnes was leaning against his car, parked in the CTA bus stop, when Caleb stepped out of his office building into the Michigan Avenue heat. Thinnes was still wearing his suit jacket, though he'd removed his tie and unbuttoned his collar. His badge and gun were concealed, but Caleb doubted anyone paying attention would fail to recognize a cop. He walked over to the car.

Thinnes said, "Need a ride?" He had had the old Chevy Caprice as long as Caleb had known him.

"Have I a choice?"

Thinnes held his hands up. "I'm off the case." He pushed off the car and opened the passenger door. The front seats were covered by a clean sheet. The folds creased into it were undisturbed, as if it had just come from the package. Caleb waited for an explanation. He got none. Thinnes just waited for him to get in, then closed the door and walked around to get behind the wheel.

As Thinnes started the engine and headed south, Caleb inspected the car. The back seat was piled with the debris men collect—a pair of boots caked with dried mud resting on a yellow newspaper; empty fast-food containers; a crumpled shirt and coffee-stained tie; a gym bag; an empty plastic wrapper; a lap rug covered with fur. Obviously the mysterious seat cover was to protect Caleb's suit.

The car's A/C was marginal, but Caleb had endured worse. Funny. Lately, everything reminded him of Vietnam.

As they crossed Jackson Boulevard, Thinnes said, "Coffee? Or a beer?"

"I have an appointment. Why not just take me home?"

Thinnes signaled left and changed lanes like a professional chauffeur. Once they were headed north, Caleb said, "What can I do for you, John?"

"I need a translation."

"What makes you think there is one?"

"Maharis was afraid of something—besides God and his mother. I need to know the devil's name."

"His name is Legion."

"I need his *current* alias. Also Maharis's friend."

"You did a background check on Mr. Maharis?"

"Sent home from 'Nam on a Section 8. In and out of hospitals and institutions, including County. Apparently he doesn't have a family."

Caleb tried to recall if Maharis seemed friendly with anyone in the group. He usually came and left alone. "He said his friend made it back to the world. That's obviously someone he served with. The VA might know."

"Franchi's on it. What do *you* know about him?"

"Depressingly little."

"You mentioned a meeting. Who was there?"

"I'm sorry, that's privileged."

"How's that?"

"It's a therapy group."

Thinnes's jaw clenched but he didn't argue.

"I've thought about it," Caleb said. "I honestly don't think anyone in the group could be involved. Maharis comes and goes by himself. He doesn't socialize."

"What was he saying about peaches or flowers?"

"I don't know. Was the victim's given name Vietnamese for a flower or fruit?"

"I'll check it out. What about the zoo?"

"He said 'lions and—.' Then he hesitated before he said 'bears.' I'll bet he was going to say lions and tigers. It's a common association with the zoo. Or if he was thinking of the phrase 'lions and tigers and bears, oh my,' it's significant that he left out tigers."

Tiger rang a bell, but Thinnes couldn't quite recall the tune. He'd have to think about it. "He didn't seem as crazy as some of the schizophrenics we've had in custody," he said. "But what was with the rocking?"

"He rocked faster when I was getting warmer. I don't think he wanted to lie, but he obviously didn't want to break his word to his friend."

"You think he doesn't know who threatened his buddy?"

"I'd say he was telling the truth about that."

Thinnes stopped the car in front of Caleb's building. "You got my number if you think of anything else."

It was probably eighty degrees inside the squadroom the next morning, but it seemed cool compared to outside. The place was bustling—three Violent Crimes dicks interviewing a witness; two Property Crimes detectives wrestling a bass fiddle across the room; a custodian emptying trash; and the desk sergeant talking on the phone with hand gestures. Someone had recently made coffee, leaving a dusting of grounds on the table. Thinnes filled his LONE STAR mug.

Franchi was at her usual place, drinking iced cappuccino. "Thinnes, we caught a break on the Lee case." As if she'd forgotten he was out of the loop.

"How's that?"

"Maharis got arrested with another Vietnam vet. Theodore Ragland. *He's* got an extensive sheet. And an outstanding warrant."

TWENTY-FOUR

I'm tired all the time," Joe said. "No energy. I get headaches, rashes, and diarrhea. I can't sleep; I wake up in a sweat from nightmares I can't remember. My wife's ready to call it quits."

Another sweltering afternoon. They were all in their usual places. Half-closed blinds sliced the August sunlight, barring them with tiger camouflage. Arthur polished his glasses with the tail of his shirt. Maharis wore a sleeveless undershirt, but smelled acceptable. Butch scowled.

"You've been to your doctor?" Arthur asked.

Joe nodded. "He did every test he could think of. I've had CAT scans and MRIs. He finally said it must be Gulf War Syndrome. They can't find what's wrong with me physically; they think it must be all in my head. Told me to see a shrink. So here I am."

"When did you start having symptoms?"

"Right after I got back to the States."

As Joe expanded on his problems, Caleb's mind wandered. He found it hard to be sympathetic. His generation had had headaches and rashes and diarrhea while they were still in country. Many of them were having nightmares and flashbacks decades later. In 'Nam, he'd been on patrols longer than the whole Gulf War.

"Jack?" Arthur had noticed his woolgathering.

Caleb was brought back abruptly to 1997. "Sorry."

"It's okay," Joe said. "It's gotta be pretty boring for someone who survived 'Nam."

"No," Caleb said. "What you said reminded me of something." When he didn't elaborate, Butch demanded, "Give."

"The distance from Hanoi to Saigon's about the same as from Chicago to New York City. Along the coast, the land is flat and fertile—rice-farming land. Inland it's mountainous and wooded. If you look at a map, it's not a stretch to see the country as the silhouette of a dragon.

"At the start of my second tour, we were sent on a recon patrol somewhere along the dragon's backbone—on the Cambodian border. It was hilly and forested, a bitch to traverse because it was all up- and downhill. It was monsoon season; some days we got ten inches of rain. We'd been out two weeks without ever getting dry. In all that time, we hadn't had a hot meal or more than four hours' sleep a night. So many of the men had dysentery I'd run out of medication and was giving them powdered ginger. Two of them were limping so badly I was afraid to look at their feet. I think we were just slogging around in circles, frustrated by our lack of progress—though damned if any of us would've recognized 'progress' if we'd tripped over it.

"We'd stopped to make camp for the night midafternoon when we stumbled across a nearly level spot with half a dozen live canopy trees missed by the defoliants. There were plenty of dead and dying trees as well. One had fallen across two giant stumps. We threw tarps over it and used it for a tent ridge, then built a raft of branches underneath to keep us above the puddling water.

"By dark, the rain was coming down so hard, it was like camping under Niagara Falls. When lightning and thunder started, Preacher swore we'd camped in God's artillery range.

"Some of the men were exhausted enough to fall asleep immediately. I unpacked my kit and asked if anyone needed help. Seven lined up. Preacher had an infected blister. I'd run out of antibiotics, so I cleaned the wound and packed it with Corona salve, a home remedy my sister'd sent me. I gave him my second-to-last pair of dry socks—also compliments of Rosemary. One of the others couldn't keep anything down; I hooked him up to an IV. Rain dripped on him as the fluids dripped in.

"My next patient had foot rot, a fungus that flourishes in hot, wet conditions. Kid hadn't taken his boots off in a week. When I pulled off his socks, half the skin came with. He got my last pair of socks. I commandeered the lieutenant's hip flask to disinfect his boots, and we dried them over a fire made from the last of our claymores.

"I don't recall what ailed the next three men, but the final patient in my makeshift waiting room was Ears. He was covered with a rash that looked like scarlet fever, but he didn't have the other symptoms. I knew he'd been exposed to Agent Orange, so I dried him off as best I could and had him smear Corona on the rash. Few of us got any sleep that night.

"It rained the next day, not hard but steady. We kept moving through it. About two hours before dark, we came to an area of flatter terrain along a small river. There were bombed-out farms on either side; scrub and weeds had grown in the abandoned fields. One farm farther downstream had somehow escaped destruction. It was just a couple huts, a few paddies, a vegetable patch, half a dozen fruit trees, and a bed of rice seedlings. We got closer and saw pigs and chickens, smoke from a cooking fire, but no people.

"We used to say that you could watch the rain fall down in country, then watch it fall back up. The sun broke out as we waited for the farmer to return. Mist steamed from the surrounding paddies like the souls of their ancestors traveling heavenward. For a moment it was beautiful and mysterious.

"Then the sun disappeared. I had a bad feeling, and I could tell the others did, too. Except for Ears, who was always spoiling for a fight. Even though the lieutenant wouldn't let him add to his collection of body parts, he was always looking for a chance to kill the 'enemy.'

"Our lieutenant was a textbook sociopath. He'd have us march into a village, trample the fields and gardens on the way in, toss the houses, rough up the people, and help ourselves to whatever we liked. Sometimes we'd shoot the livestock and torch the hooches on the way out.

"Our victims never said much, just stared. If they weren't VC sympathizers when we arrived, they surely were by the time we left. I doubt they could have hated the lieutenant more than we did.

"He gave the order to move in and search the hooches. We spread out and surrounded them. Ears went in one, fortunately empty. Before he could hit the other, Preacher ducked inside. He came out dragging the oldest woman I'd ever seen. She was wrinkled as an elephant, and so thin he got his whole hand around her biceps.

"He let go, and we surrounded her. She wasn't afraid.

"The lieutenant knew a few French phrases. He and Froggy, who spoke French fluently, started questioning her. Her answers were too fast and—I suspect—too angry to be understood. But one of the men reported finding a large pot of steaming rice—far too much food for the woman and the one or two others who probably lived with her. That was proof enough for the lieutenant that she was VC.

"He said to take her prisoner and torch the hooches. He ordered the RTO to call for transport and me to search the woman ''cause you're the doc.'

"I'd been out too long; the order was too much. I turned to the woman and asked her if she had any weapons. By then I knew the culture required respect for old people. I called her 'aunt,' and tried to seem respectful.

"The woman understood me enough to say she had no guns—search enough for me.

"Not for the lieutenant. 'We can't take her word for it,' he said. 'If you're not gonna search her, shoot her.' He grabbed the RTO's M16 and held it out to me.

"I put my hand up to deflect the gun; it fell to the ground. The lieutenant drew his sidearm. I tried to get between him and the woman so he wouldn't shoot her.

"The RTO scrambled to retrieve his M16. We watched. We lost sight of the woman. When the lieutenant fumbled and dropped his gun, she didn't waste her opportunity. She grabbed it with the agility of a girl and opened up on him.

"He fell. He looked amazed. Then he looked dead.

"The woman aimed at the RTO, who froze. She could have killed him. And me. But she took the gun and vanished.

"I ran to the lieutenant, though I knew he was beyond hope. The RTO recovered and fired after her as the rest of the platoon came running. They all fired, sprayed the area with bullets. They fanned out and took the huts apart, straw by straw, then torched the rubble. They flattened the rice bed, ringed the fruit trees, and took machetes to the garden. By the time the dust-off came, the farm was wasted. But there was no sign of the woman, or the people that she'd planned to feed. After we lifted off, they bombed the farm into a moonscape."

"How did the Gulf War bring all that to mind?" Arthur said.

"The contrast, I think. Between the two wars. Or maybe Joe made me think of how what you do comes back around." He looked at Joe. And thought the veteran seemed disturbed.

TWENTY-FIVE

Evanger came out of his office with his BIG DOG coffee mug and a telephone message slip. He handed the slip to Thinnes. "It seems Theodore Ragland turned up."

"Where?"

Evanger pointed to the paper. "Take Viernes and Franchi. They already sent Bendix, so step on it."

The street was paved with garbage, lined with decrepit cars and trucks. Thinnes steered the unmarked Crown Vic past inhabited buildings with broken and boarded-up windows, sagging porches, peeling paint, and piled-up trash. There were no residents in sight. The scene was in the middle of the block. Heat waves rose above gravel and demolition rubble in empty lots across the street and to the east and west. Blue and white flowers—weeds—bloomed between the piles of garbage dumped there.

A beat car parked at the front curb had its hood up, its windows closed. The copper inside was reading the *Trib*. Behind the squad, a board-up company truck had its A/C cranked so high Thinnes couldn't see through the condensation on the windows. The Major Crime Scene van and an empty squadrol were parked behind the truck.

Thinnes curbed the car across the street. Reluctant to go out in the heat, he left the motor running. Next to him, Franchi took her star and weapon out of her purse and shoved it under the seat.

Behind her, Viernes said, "Well, the canvass should be easy."

From the look of it, the building had been burned by a pro. Black soot rose above the boarded-up basement windows. The oriented-strand boards covering them were gouged at the edges, riddled with holes, and dimpled with indentations from hammer blows. You couldn't see for sure from street level, but soot patterns above the third-floor windows suggested the roof had been destroyed. Squatters could live without heat, light, and plumbing, but once the roof went, the elements invaded. Only rats lived here now.

Viernes echoed Thinnes's speculation. "Five bucks says the back stairs and porches were torched."

"No takers," Franchi said. "The only mystery here is why anyone would bother breaking in."

"Scavengers," Viernes said cheerfully. Thieves who stripped the wires and pipes, even bricks, for scrap. "Don't know why we bother running 'em off."

"So we don't have to do death investigations," Thinnes said, "when they bring the buildings down on themselves." He shut off the engine.

Viernes said, "But here we are."

Thinnes got out. He took off his tie and jacket, and draped them over his seat back. Viernes followed suit. Franchi, who wasn't wearing a jacket—just a short-sleeved shirt and slacks— got out and clipped her star on her belt. She slipped her gun into a small holster on the waist of her slacks. Thinnes locked the car.

The front entrance was still boarded up, so he crossed the street to ask the beat cop what was up. The copper hitched his thumb toward the building's west end.

"Follow your nose."

"Thanks." As he led the others around back, Thinnes noticed that the fire had burned out so long ago the burned-building smell had faded.

They smelled death long before they got to the opening under the charred skeleton of steps and porches. The stench of putrefaction warred with smoke from Bendix's ever-present stogie. Flies swarmed in and out of the darkness.

"I gotta start taking summers off," Viernes said.

Inside, the basement was black on black. The Crime Scene team had set lights up on stands. They didn't help. The charred debris seemed to soak up the illumination.

Wearing Tyvek coveralls and old rubber galoshes, Bendix was supervising his photographer, pointing with a half-smoked cigar. Just inside the doorway a patrolman watched, arms folded. And two beefy uniforms—the squadrol crew—stood outside the circle of light next to a body bag. Neatly folded coveralls and gloves were piled on top. The men were already wearing their boots.

"What's the story?" Thinnes asked the beat cop.

"Board-up crew smelled trouble when they came by to rese-cure the place. Called us."

"I hate working these burned-out holes," Bendix announced to no one in particular.

"You hate working anywhere," Viernes told him.

Bendix gave him a disgusted look.

Franchi started picking her way through the perimeter of the space. The men watched as she stopped to roll her pants legs above her ankles.

"You almost done?" Thinnes asked Bendix.

"Yeah. Knock yourselves out."

Franchi said, "Any way of telling who this guy was?"

"Theodore Ragland," the beat cop said. "We called that in. We had a bulletin he was wanted for questioning in Area Three. You, right? They shoulda told you."

Thinnes picked his way through the shit to the bloated mass that had once been human. Its slimy surfaces reflected light. Mag-gots writhed and squirmed over it.

"How the hell could you tell?"

The copper pointed at the corpse. "Dog tags. His name's on 'em. Pretty considerate of him." He pointed to a .22-caliber re-volver next to the body. "Must've decided he'd had enough."

Before Thinnes could say it, Franchi said, "Or that's what someone wanted us to think." Good for her, though the copper was probably right.

The cop hitched a thumb toward the outside world. "If one of those assholes shot him, they'd've taken the gun."

To head off an argument, Thinnes said, "Any guess how long he's been here?"

Bendix shrugged. "The ME'll get his bug guy to look at the maggots—tell you within an hour or so."

"What's your guess?"

"More than twenty-four." Helpful.

"Why hasn't the city razed this eyesore?" Franchi asked when they were walking out.

The beat cop leaving with them said, "Word has it the owner's claiming it can be salvaged, and he's suing the insurance company for the money to do it."

"Yeah, sure," Viernes said.

"He's probably holding out for more from the developers that own the rest of this prime real estate." The copper gestured toward the surrounding dump sites. "When it's all worked out, they'll put up condos worth half a mil apiece."

Viernes shook his head. He pointed to the board-up truck. "Wonder how often they get sent back."

Franchi said, "You can ask them, Joe."

Viernes hitched his thumb toward the building. "When was the last time you guys boarded this up?"

"A week ago. Someone's been checking regular, an' callin' every time there's a break-in. Used to be every day, but lately . . ." The man shrugged.

"You notice anything besides the body?"

"We did'n see no body."

"We don't get paid enough to go in somewhere like this," his partner added. "Jus' to board it up."

"We yell for anyone inside to come out. After five minutes or so, no one does, we close it up."

"So how'd you know there was a body?" Viernes said.

"You shittin' me?"

"Smell that bad *had* to be somethin' big."

"Coulda been a dog," Viernes said.

"That broke in?"

"Later."

"What dog'd be stupid enough to wander in there?"

Viernes shrugged. "So you figured it was a body and dialed 911. Then what?"

"Nine-one-one told us to wait for the *police*."

"Can we go now?"

Thinnes shook his head. "Wait 'til they bring the body out, then do what you came here to do."

In the car, Franchi put her gun and star in her purse, then leaned back and closed her eyes. "Is assigning this to you Evanger's way of letting you back in on the Lee case?"

"What do you think?"

She didn't answer. She had already.

"What we *gwon* do now, boss?" Viernes asked.

"Ragland did time in Stateville," Thinnes said. "See if he had any dental work done there."

Viernes nodded.

"If not, he was a vet. See if the VA has any records."

Franchi said, "What are *we* going to be doing?"

"Checking out Ragland's place."

TWENTY-SIX

When Thinnes and Franchi got to the two-flat where Ragland had lived, a hearse was parked in front, an old classic fifties Caddy with the big fins. It wasn't there for Ragland. Lettering on the side said EZEKIEL GODSENT, LICENSED PLUMBER. A thin, bearded old black man was loading tools and boxes of copper T's and elbows into the hearse's rear at a pace slow enough to drive a customer postal. Reluctant to abandon their A/C, the detectives watched from the car.

The neighborhood was a collection of middle-class residences on the edge of the slum they'd just come from, one of those areas that could go either way. The two-flat was sided with gray shingles and had a steep-pitched roof covered by red roll roofing. Tall basement windows flanked the front porch steps. The paint was peeling from the porch and the gateless picket fence.

They got out of the car and climbed the steps.

Neither of the names next to the doorbells was Ragland. The two entrances were mirror images—wooden screen doors over green-painted outer doors. The windows on both floors had identical A/C units dripping water.

Thinnes pushed the bell labeled OWENS. They could hear it ring inside the first-floor apartment.

The green door was opened by another tall, thin black man with the same curly beard as Godsent. This guy had his head shaved, though, and wore a dingy sleeveless undershirt. He didn't open the screen. Before they even identified themselves, he said, "What that boy do now?"

Franchi said, "What?"

"You here 'bout Theo?"

"Theodore Ragland?" Thinnes said. The man nodded. "He live here?"

"He do."

"You a relative, Mr. . . . ? Owens?"

"Yeah. Shadrack. Theo's my nephew."

Franchi took her cell phone to the edge of the porch—calling for backup and the Crime Lab van.

Thinnes pointed to the bells. "I don't see his name."

"Oh, he don't live with me and Zeke." Owens pointed to a basement window. "He got a room in the cellar."

"Just one room?"

He pointed again. "Right there."

"Does he have a storage space or shed?"

"Nope."

"When was the last time you saw him?"

"What this about?"

"Can we go inside?"

"That bad?" Owens thought about it briefly, then nodded and pushed the screen door open.

His parlor was tidy and sparsely furnished—matching end tables flanking a fat sofa, an old console TV, a rocking chair on the middle of a braided rug. The walls were bare but for family portraits and a framed eight-by-ten of Ragland in his dress uniform. Smiling. Before the war wolfed him down and barfed him out.

Owens offered them seats on the sofa and planted himself in the rocker. He crossed his ankles and rested his palms on his thighs. He began to rock. "Tell me."

"Some workmen found a body in a burned-out building," Thinnes said. "It had your nephew's dog tags."

"It! What you tellin' me?"

"I'm sorry, sir. He'd been dead for some time."

"Oh, Jesus! My poor sister!" He clasped his fingers together and rested his forearms on his knees.

"Could you tell us when you saw him last?"

" 'Bout a week ago. He don't always stay here. Didn't."

"Tell us about him," Franchi said gently.

"A good boy. Never got in trouble 'fore he went to Vietnam. Didn't do drugs." Owens nodded. "An' he was smart. Spoke Vietnamese. Coulda been a interpreter 'cept he had a record. Wouldn't nobody hire him for that.

"He came back from the war mad. Brought hisself a lotta grief 'cause he couldn't keep it in. Couldn't keep a job 'cause he'd lose his temper an' go off. But there wasn't a mean bone in 'im. He just couldn't keep it in."

"Was he depressed lately?"

"No, just mad."

"About anything in particular?"

Owens shook his head.

"Joe's here," Franchi said.

"Mr. Owens, we need to look at Theo's room."

The old man nodded. "I'll get the key."

After unlocking the basement door, Owens stepped away. Thinnes pushed it open. He could see the whole room from where he stood. The ceiling and walls were a uniform white. A canvas cot and chest of drawers were the only furniture, a Gideon's Bible the only personal property in sight. No use trampling through it before the techs had had a crack. Thinnes stepped aside to let Franchi look.

"I've seen more cheerful jail cells," she muttered.

"Yeah." He turned to Owens. "Without going in, sir, could you look and see if anything's missing?"

The old man stood in the doorway a long time, then backed away. "Pi'ture. Theo had a pi'ture of his girl. Now it's gone. But he mighta took it away with him."

"We'll look into that."

"Guess mebbe I'll go break the news to his mother."

"We'll take care of that, Mr. Owens," Franchi said. "We need to talk to her anyway."

The old man nodded. He turned to go, then stopped. "I be needing somethin' to do."

"Is there a minister you could call?"

. . .

Ragland's mother, Mrs. Maitland, lived in the second-floor apartment. She took the news as if she'd been waiting for it all her life. "My baby," she said. "Gone home to Jesus." She sat in a chair in her homey kitchen and rocked herself back and forth and sighed. She didn't know who'd killed him. When pressed, she said he was afraid of cats. She wouldn't or couldn't elaborate. They stayed with her until the reverend showed up with ladies from the church.

When Thinnes and Franchi went back downstairs, Bendix and his assistant were hard at work. "Place's been searched and sanitized," he pronounced. "What'd you expect me to do?"

"Luminol?" Thinnes said. "See if he was killed here."

"You sure know how to make mountain ranges out of anthills. Why'd anyone kill him here and drag him over to that dump? And how'd they do it without someone seeing?"

Ezekiel Godsent's hearse came to mind, but Thinnes didn't say so. "Well, why would he go there on his own?"

"To shoot up, of course," the assistant said.

Thinnes and Bendix both told him to butt out.

Bendix said, "To shoot himself. He wouldn't want to do it here, with all his family."

Thinnes shook his head. "From what I've heard so far, he'd be more likely to shoot someone else."

When Bendix was finished, Thinnes went over the room. Apart from subtle clues that it had been searched, it was neat as a Marine barracks before inspection. No dirt. No dust. No personal touch unless you counted the shadow of the girlfriend's missing picture. Ragland seemed to have bought most of his clothes at an Army surplus store, but they were clean and neatly folded in the dresser. A winter coat hung on a hook behind the door. There was a paperback copy of Dante's *Inferno,* annotated, in one of the pockets. Thinnes bagged it for evidence. He paged through the Bible and found Ragland's discharge papers. Evidence, too.

The church ladies were quite helpful, supplying the history of Ragland's entire clan. Thinnes hung back and took notes while Franchi quizzed them. Owens and Godsent were half-brothers, having had different fathers. As did their sister, Ragland's mother. When she was sixteen, she'd borne Ragland out of wedlock and given him her maiden name. She'd married later, but had had no more kids. Theo was the apple of her eye and his stepfather's pride and joy before the stepfather passed. Shame what they did to the boy in the war.

Thinnes left Ragland's family homestead with a list of references—people Ragland had worked for and folks who'd known him all his life. God-fearing churchgoers all.

Before they started the neighborhood canvass, he called the Area and asked to have Maharis picked up.

The canvass and the reports it generated took up the rest of the day. They hadn't found Maharis by quitting time. Thinnes asked the desk sergeant to call him at home if he turned up. Then he called it a day.

Franchi insisted on accompanying him to the autopsy the next morning, though she could have begged off. They tried to arrive late enough to miss the opening act. They put on blue plastic gowns before they went into the room reserved for "stinkers," but even the negative ventilation couldn't keep the stench of death from penetrating their thoughts and sinking into their clothes.

The bloated remains didn't smell better for having rested in a cooler overnight. The body had been cleaned, the maggots flushed away. Putrefaction couldn't be as easily banished. Ragland's dark skin couldn't hide the color changes caused by decomposition.

Dr. Cutler was probing the mush that had been the man's brain when they came in. He nodded to acknowledge them but skipped the usual banter, grimly reciting his observations to his tape recorder. When he recovered the fatal bullet, he held it over the body until Thinnes produced an evidence envelope.

Cutler finished his examination of the victim's head, then started on the torso. He seemed to be working faster than usual. Duh! It still seemed like a week before he said, "We're done." He waited until they'd shed their protection and were out in the relative fresh air of the hall before he announced his findings. Cause of death: GSW to the head. Manner of death: homicide.

"How do you know it wasn't suicide?" Thinnes asked.

"I'll show you."

They followed him into an office that had an X-ray viewing unit above a stainless steel counter, and waited while he fetched the films and put them up on the viewer. The hole in Ragland's skull was obvious.

"It's highly unlikely a suicide would shoot himself in the back of the head." Cutler pointed to the hole above and a little behind the right ear. "The bullet entered here." He traced what looked like a scratch inside the skull. "It ricocheted off the inside here."

The slug was a .22-caliber, probably from the gun found near the body. Small-caliber rounds often bounced around inside a skull like a cue ball on a pool table, macerating the victim's brain in the process, which was why .22s were the professional's choice.

When they got back to the Area, Franchi announced that she was going home to change. Thinnes didn't argue. He got clean clothes from his car and hit the shower in the men's locker room. Half an hour later, he had the case spread out in the conference room, a picture of Ragland's sad life.

Born and raised in Chicago, he had never been in trouble until he was arrested in 'Nam for dealing drugs—a month before Thinnes arrived in country. He'd been caught with enough stash to land him in Long Binh Jail, where he stayed until he was shipped home and dishonorably discharged. His life had gone downhill from there. He'd been arrested for battery, aggravated battery, and attempted murder. Interestingly, never for drugs.

He'd spent time in Cook County Jail and Stateville. Arrested again and paroled, he'd simply dropped out of sight.

The canvass reports took up the story. Ragland had taken odd jobs for people in his mother's church, every one of whom said he would hire Ragland again. He hadn't stayed more than a year anywhere. One of his former employers gave the cops Ragland's job application, listing half a dozen previous jobs. Three of those employers had Vietnamese surnames and addresses in Uptown. Small world. Thinnes put them on his list of people to see.

Ragland's jobs became poorer and less frequent as time went on. He'd stayed out of jail until recently, but hadn't had steady work. Thinnes wondered if he'd reverted to selling drugs to support himself.

Another thing that jumped out was that while he was in Vietnam, his family had lived in the building where his body was found. It could've been a weird coincidence, but Thinnes didn't believe in them. He made a note to find the owner, then called his contact in Bomb and Arson

When he heard the address, Art Fuego confirmed that the fire that finished off the building had been set. "Most likely for profit. Definitely a professional job."

TWENTY-SEVEN

When Franchi got back, she was wearing a pantsuit Thinnes hadn't seen before. She came into the conference room and handed him a manila envelope. "Sarge asked me to give this to you. Said the Crime Lab sent it over. Something they found in Ragland's pocket." Her short dark hair was still wet, and she smelled like vanilla. Must be trying to get the morgue stench out of her head.

He realized he didn't notice how she smelled or dressed as often, lately, as he had when they first worked together. Just as well. The times he *did* notice, he was *too* aware of her. For a married man.

He opened the envelope and took out a photocopy and the Polaroid snapshot of a crumpled, stained note. A Post-it stuck to the copy said, 'Found in right pants pocket.' The RD number for the Ragland case was printed on the back.

He felt another wave of déjà vu. He put the Polaroid in his pocket, then scooped up the photocopy, envelope, and reports, and shuffled them back in the case file folder.

"Let's go to lunch."

"Now?"

"Yeah. I got a taste for something different."

The Thai Binh Restaurant, east of the Red Line stop on Argyle, was nearly deserted. Between the lunch and dinner crowds, Thinnes guessed. He'd driven past but never stopped in before. At his request, the young Vietnamese hostess showed them to a table against the back wall. She gave them menus, served tea, and disappeared.

He didn't usually drink tea, but he was trying to bring back Saigon. And in Saigon, he'd drunk a lot of it.

"So what did I miss?" Franchi asked.

Thinnes showed her the list of Ragland's employers. "We got a few leads." He looked around.

There were only four other patrons, all Asians. Two men in suits puffed away over tea in the smoking section, their empty plates pushed to the side. Sharing the nonsmoking section with Thinnes and Franchi, a young man sat opposite an older woman wearing a skirt that showed off nice legs. She'd slipped one shoe off and was stroking his ankle with her toes. They were holding hands across the table, oblivious to everything except each other.

From Franchi's expression, Thinnes knew she was watching the couple, too. He wondered what she was thinking. When they'd started working together, there was talk that they were an item. Not that he wasn't tempted, but they'd kept it professional.

A waitress came, an even younger woman in the traditional long-sleeved Vietnamese dress with slit sides. He and Franchi ordered.

Eventually, she brought their entrées and put a large bowl of rice and a bottle of nuoc mam on the table between them. Like salt in American restaurants, it wasn't labeled.

Franchi picked it up. "What's this?"

"Fermented fish sauce. Vietnamese use it like the Chinese use soy sauce."

She unscrewed the cap and sniffed. "Yuck."

"Don't knock it 'til you've tried it."

She pushed a forkful of rice to the edge of her plate and shook out a few drops. Thinnes waited while she tried it. She shrugged noncommittally.

"Some vets get sick from the smell," he said. "It brings Vietnam back."

From habit, he reached for the chopsticks. More than twenty years after mastering the art, it was like riding a bike. Franchi watched him eat without comment.

The flavor brought him back to Saigon. In spades. He'd eaten in so many restaurants there with Hue. She was as beautiful, then, as Franchi, and even more alive.

Franchi pushed her plate away and swallowed the last of her tea. She waved away the waitress hovering with refills. "What's this about, Thinnes?" she asked. "Why all of a sudden you like Vietnamese?"

"What do you know about the war?" he asked her.

She shook her head. "Hardly anything. One of my brothers was there, but he won't talk about it. One of my cousins was killed, but we weren't close."

He nodded. About what he'd expected. Those who'd been through it wouldn't talk; those who hadn't usually didn't want them to. He said, "My dad fought in Korea; he never talked about it. When I got my draft notice, all he said was, 'Wouldn't think less of you if you headed north.'

"We were pulling out of 'Nam by the time I was sent over, which really sucked. The poor SOBs still stationed there resented it like hell unless they were profiteering. But there were still a few active bases, with American advisors and contractors, 'technicians,' helicopter pilots, embassy personnel. They still needed MPs to guard them. And it wasn't publicized, but we were still hunting MIAs and deserters. There were thousands in Saigon alone. Depending on how long they'd been AWOL, deserters were sent back to their units when they were caught, or sent to Long Binh Jail. MPs provided escort service.

"When I got there, Saigon was going to hell. The city had always been the most corrupt place in the country, but there was a fuck-it-all attitude toward the end, and the feeling that you'd better take what you could get while you could get it. MACV used to have daily briefings that the press corps called the five o'clock follies. Nobody believed any official pronouncement. How could you? Whole provinces were falling, but the official line was, 'Vietnamization is succeeding.' Lots of people saw our pullout as rats leaving the sinking ship. Plenty of Vietnamese were leaving, too—the ones with money on planes, the poor pouring out of areas in immediate danger, jamming into already overcrowded cities. Cholon, the sector of Saigon where we spent so much time, had more people per square mile than Hong Kong or Tokyo.

"By the time I'd been in country a month, I'd heard every possible excuse for why a soldier was doing what he shouldn't, or hanging out somewhere off limits. After two months, I was ready to cut anyone some slack who could tell me a story I hadn't heard."

"What's this got to do with anything?" Franchi asked.

He held up his index finger. "I'm getting to it.

"I'd only been in country a few weeks, I for sure hadn't adjusted to the god-awful heat, when they put me undercover. The company scrounger came into the MP office one day with the ugliest Hawaiian shirt I'd ever seen and one of those paper leis you get when you land in Hawaii. The captain told me to put on jeans and the ugly shirt and lei because he had a special detail for me.

"They sent me to a bar on Tu Do Street, Saigon's red-light district. Only, like everything else over there, it was bigger and badder. There'd been complaints about Americans being rolled. It was the monsoon season and it was pouring. I had an umbrella, but it didn't help much.

"It was dark and very crowded inside, mostly with Vietnamese—lots of ARVNs still in uniform. There were plenty of Americans, though, civilians, and a few Aussies, and mercenaries from God knows where who placed their orders in French or Vietnamese. Plenty of B-girls, too.

"The smoke from cigarettes and marijuana was so thick you could barely see the bar from the door. The bar had every kind of booze that you could think of. I worked my way over and asked for a Lone Star. And it was cold!

"I'd never worked undercover before, so I was nervous as hell and excited—probably stood out like a sore thumb. But that worked. If I'd really been a cherry—that's military for virgin—I'd have been just as nervous. I knew somebody was undercover

101

watching my back, so I just followed orders—drank"—Thinnes wiggled his fingers to indicate quotation marks—"too much. Tried to make time with the bar girls who were crowding around, urging me to leave with one of them. I must've aggravated every serious drinker in the place. When I finally staggered out with one of the women, I bet half the guys in there would have paid to see me mugged."

Thinnes paused to slug down half his remaining tea.

It was late, still raining. Saigon had a curfew that was pretty strictly enforced. He'd bought eight or ten beers for himself and the girls, though he hadn't swallowed any because they were re-filling the empties with formaldehyde in a lot of places. You had to be careful. Still, he had a fair contact high by the time he left the bar.

It was close to midnight but it was probably eighty-five de-grees. It was still pouring and too dark to see anything clearly, though he could make out shapes crouched in the shadows. The city was so jammed that people slept anywhere—doorways, alleys, sidewalks. You didn't know until sunup which of the bodies were still breathing. He walked out with the umbrella in one hand, the girl in the other.

They got about a hundred feet from the bar before someone stepped out of a doorway and tried to brain him with a bottle. He dropped the umbrella and let go of the girl. She took off. He ducked in time to save his head, but caught it on the shoulder. For some reason, the bottle didn't break. But it was heavy. And it hurt like hell.

The assailant smelled like sweat and fish sauce. Thinnes could hear someone else splashing toward them; he got a whiff of Old Spice. He had no idea if it was his backup or another mugger. He concentrated on disarming the guy who'd hit him. He grabbed the hand holding the bottle. The mugger was small but tough, and Thinnes could only see his outline. He kept slipping out of Thinnes's grasp. They fell together, rolling in the mud—or God knows what. The bottle broke. Thinnes figured he'd be cut but couldn't see to stop it.

The person he'd heard approach was in it, too, grunting, snarling English.

Thinnes heard a shrill whistle. An American voice yelled, "Cops!"

Someone screamed; the guy Thinnes was holding went limp. Thinnes smelled shit. Footsteps splashed off in the darkness. How the hell could anyone see where to run?

He was afraid to let go of his captive's wrist. He got his lighter out. He clicked it on.

Two Americans stood over him, one in civvies with an umbrella, the other—an MP—in uniform and a slicker.

Just then, rain drowned the lighter. But the MP had a flashlight. He turned it on and said, "You must be Thinnes. I'm your backup. Doesn't look like you needed it, though." He didn't introduce the other man, but aimed his light at the guy Thinnes had hold of a young Vietnamese. He'd dropped the bottle, and was trying to hold his guts in with his free hand. His accomplice had fucked up in the dark.

"Do you speak English?" Thinnes asked him.

He looked up and said, "Yes."

"Who you working for?"

"He's not gonna talk," the MP said.

"Does he understand he's dying?"

"Probably. But he's got family; all these people got family. He won't put 'em at risk by talking."

"He did, though," Thinnes said. "He pulled me toward him. I didn't think he was still dangerous, so I put my ear near his mouth, and he told me who'd stabbed him."

"Thinnes, why are you telling me this?"

He held out the Polaroid, let her read the message: *Cọp Trắng*. "Because of this. This is what he said."

"What's it mean?"

" 'White Tiger.' The cat even the white mice feared."

"White mice."

"What we called the Vietnamese cops in Saigon."

"That was twenty-five years ago. So what!"

"Because a few months later, a deserter I arrested told me he knew Cọp Trắng by sight, not by name, but he would finger him for me if I'd just let him go. He said the white tiger had a piece of all the action in Saigon. He didn't say how he knew, but I believed him."

"Did you let him go?"

"No."

"I repeat. Why are you telling *me*?"

"Because you're still working on Hue Lee's murder. This is connected."

She shrugged.

"And you're better at quick-and-dirty research than me. I need you to find that deserter, if he's still alive. And Drucker. I gotta talk to Drucker."

"Who's Drucker?"

"In Saigon, he was my Chinaman."

TWENTY-EIGHT

The Tai Nam Market on Broadway had an air about it that reminded Thinnes of Saigon. The market's fish were too fresh to smell really fishy, and there weren't any live animals. But there were other exotic things. Like the display of durian facing the door as they came in. He knew from the lack of odor that the fruit wasn't ripe. Durian smelled like shit when they were ready to eat.

Midafternoon on a weekday, there weren't many customers. All were Asian, all filling their carts with things you couldn't get at Dominick's. With Franchi in tow, Thinnes did a quick recon of the place. The aisle to the far left had dried beans and nuts and more kinds of rice than Jewel stores had breakfast foods.

In the next aisle over, there were imports from Hong Kong, Cambodia, and Korea, cans of fruits and vegetables, exotic things Thinnes had never heard of, and staples he hadn't seen since Vietnam. There must have been two dozen varieties of soy sauce and at least six kinds of nuoc mam, as well as dried mushrooms and dried shrimp. Freezers held more kinds of aquatic animals than the Shedd Aquarium.

Behind the frozen offerings and in front of the butcher case displaying cuts of meat, rows of five-gallon buckets kept fish of every description fresh on ice. Farther to the right, a produce counter offered green onions, five varieties of yams, ginger roots the size of Thinnes's hand, bunches of cilantro, and vegetables Thinnes couldn't identify. The rest of the store seemed to be given over to shelves loaded with cookies, candies, and pastries, as well as dishes, teapots, and miscellaneous.

"How come you never mentioned this place before?"

Thinnes shrugged and asked a man unpacking bunches of odd-looking bananas for the manager.

Mr. Trinh was Vietnamese, about five-eight, medium build. The sleeves of his white shirt were rolled, his tie loose. White Nikes showed below his pants legs. He took Thinnes and Franchi to his office, a tiny, cluttered room in the back. There was no place to sit. Trinh hitched his rear up on the desk, on top of a scattering of papers, and crossed his arms.

"We'd like to know about Theo Ragland." Thinnes showed him Ragland's graduation picture.

"Ah," Trinh said. "Ragman. What do you want to know?"

"He worked for you?"

"What is this about?"

"We're not here to find out if your W2s are in order," Thinnes said. "Ragland was murdered."

"Oh, no."

Thinnes waited. Franchi poised to take notes.

"Sometimes he would ask for work," Trinh said, "not hand-outs. He was very helpful. He would do anything—stock shelves, wait on customers, clean the toilet. He even worked in here. He was a good typist. Sometimes he entered orders. He was good with the customers—polite and he spoke Vietnamese."

"So why didn't you keep him?"

"He wouldn't stay. He'd only work if he needed money. Then he'd go. Never any notice." Trinh shrugged. "You can't run a business with employees like that."

"He have any problems with anyone?"

"Not that I know of."

"He ever tell you about his friends or family?"

"No. He had a girlfriend. He carried her picture around. But I don't remember him saying much about her."

"Anyone here he was friendly with?" Franchi asked. "Who might remember her name?"

Trinh shrugged again. "I don't know. You can ask."

. . .

It was nearly shift change by the time Thinnes finished writing reports on the market interviews. The employees had been as helpful as possible, but Theo Ragland hadn't been an outgoing man. And his appearances were too infrequent to make for close personal friendships. To a man—and woman—fellow workers said Ragland was quiet, polite, and helpful. Not the usual profile of a violent ex-con. He'd never lost his temper at work, so no one could say how he'd be under stress. The only useful tidbit they'd gotten was that Ragland had shown his girlfriend's picture around. She was young and beautiful. Vietnamese.

Evanger was on the phone when Thinnes went to report before leaving. He motioned Thinnes in and pointed to a chair. Thinnes sat; Evanger said, "Yes, sir. I'll do that," and hung up. "What've you got?" he asked Thinnes.

Thinnes summarized: A murdered felon with a curious history. A grieving family clueless about why he'd turned up dead. A huge disconnect between the man known to law enforcement and the one his friends and family claimed to know.

Thinnes was beginning to wonder if they were all talking about the same guy.

TWENTY-NINE

When Caleb arrived for the meeting, Maharis was standing in front of Arthur's door, hugging himself as he rocked back and forth. "What's wrong?" Caleb asked.

"Ragman's dead."

"How?"

"White Tiger got him."

"Who the hell is that?" Butch demanded.

Maharis shook his head. As usual, he was sitting on the floor between Butch and Joe, with his knees pulled up to his chest—ankles crossed, and his arms wrapped around his legs. He was staring straight ahead. "I don't know."

"What the hell *do* you know?"

Caleb thought Butch's upset was disproportionate. To the best of his knowledge, Butch and Ragman had never met. And Butch wasn't close enough to Maharis to be suffering vicariously.

The blight man was born for, Caleb decided, quoting Hopkins. Apparently it was Butch Butch mourned for.

Echoing Caleb's thought, Arthur asked Butch if he'd known Ragland.

"*No.*"

"You seem quite upset over the death of a stranger."

"He was a vet." As if that explained it.

"How'd you find out?" Arthur asked Maharis.

"Mr. Trinh told me." Arthur waited. "He's a guy me an' Ragman used to work for. In Uptown."

Arthur kept looking at him. They all waited.

Maharis continued. "He told me the cops came. Asked him about Ragman. They wouldn't do that if he died of cancer." Maharis began to rock forward and back.

The suggestion of murder put a pall on the group. Except Butch, whose rage seemed fueled by it. "How'd you know he was killed by— Who's White Tiger? That a tag from 'Nam?"

"I guess so. Ragman said better I don't know. So I don't."

"You guys've lost me," Alec said. "What's a tag?"

Caleb explained. "We all went by nicknames over there. Nobody wanted to know anyone well, especially a new guy, who had the shortest life expectancy."

"Like in *Platoon*?"

"I don't know. I could never bring myself to see that. If you lasted six months in 'Nam, you'd proved yourself, but by that time you *were* your nickname. I was the platoon medic, so they called me Doc."

"That's why he was called Ragman," Maharis said without raising his head. "It's what they called him in country."

Alec persisted. "But why'd they call him that?"

"I don't know!"

Joe put an awkward hand on Maharis's shoulder.

Maharis's arms shot up. "Don't touch me!"

"Sorry," Joe said. He looked more scared than repentant.

Maharis scrambled sideways, out of the circle, out of reach. He curled up and glared at Joe.

Arthur put his hands up in a hold-everything gesture. For one long, uncomfortable minute, nobody moved.

A soft pat, pat, pat sound broke the bad spell as a huge gray cat trotted into the room and sat down.

"Is anyone bothered or allergic?" Arthur asked.

Everyone but Maharis responded with no or a shake of his head. Maharis stared at the cat.

Arthur said, "C'mere, Carl."

Silly man, Caleb thought. Cats don't come when they're called.

As if to prove Caleb's point, Carl walked toward Maharis, tail in the air. Everyone held his breath.

Maharis laughed and scooped the cat up, holding it like a baby. Everyone relaxed. Arthur seemed the most relieved.

Maharis started to rub the cat's face. "When I was in country," he said, "I had a cat. She kept the rats out of our hooch, so no one messed with her. We called her Cobra 'cause she was deadly as a gunship."

A twinge of sadness shivered through Caleb like a premonition. So many stories of 'Nam that started like this—'I had a pet . . .' or 'I had a friend . . .'—ended tragically.

"So what happened to it?" Butch demanded.

Maharis rubbed his face against the cat. "I don't know. We got orders to move. I gave her to a kid that used to hang around. They're both probably dead."

Caleb looked around. Alec seemed surprised, Joe saddened.

Butch said, "This touching tale have a point?"

"Nothing connected with the war had a point."

Caleb stayed after the others left.

"What is it, Jack?" Arthur asked. "Your father?"

Caleb shook his head. "I remembered something."

Arthur sat back down and waited. Caleb perched on the edge of the chair opposite. "I went to the Gay Rights March in Washington in '93." He laughed ironically. "Not much of a march. Contrary to what was reported on the news, it was huge. The Mall, the parade route, and all the streets leading up to it were so jammed, there was no room to march. We all just stood where we were and talked.

"My flight back wasn't until the next day, so afterward I stayed to see the Wall. It was late afternoon, still very warm, though shadows were overtaking the path. There were many people sharing the experience—mostly men my age. It was quiet. Even the groups of teens spoke with hushed voices.

"The monument rises from the earth and—the way it's

designed—invites you to run your fingers over the names, to share the grief of others by observing their reflections on the polished stone. There were so many names . . .

"As I stood in the last of the light, I remember thinking of that line from 'Dust in the Wind'—*Nothing lasts forever* . . . "

Caleb felt tears building. He swallowed and blinked.

"I stared at my reflection and realized I couldn't look up more than a handful of the men I'd watched die. I never knew their names, only the tags we gave them to avoid getting close, to kill the pain we'd feel when we zipped them into body bags."

THIRTY

Theodore Ragland's funeral was held at his mother's church. Baptist, an old red brick building in serious need of tuck-pointing, in a neighborhood in need of renewal. The street in front was lined on both sides with cars. Thinnes parked in the upstream end of a CTA stop.

When he and Franchi got out of the car, Ezekiel Godsent was standing in front of the church, smoking with three men who had the predatory look of gangbangers.

The old man had cleaned up pretty well. With his beard and fringe of hair trimmed, and in a suit, he looked like a successful businessman. The younger men gave the cops dirty looks. Two of them dropped their cigarettes and walked into the building. The other gripped Godsent's shoulder and shook him gently.

Thinnes told Franchi to go on ahead. When Godsent's remaining companion followed the others, the old man turned to Thinnes. "You find out who killed my nephew yet?"

"We haven't ruled out suicide."

"You wouldn't be hangin' 'round here if you thought Theo killed hisself." Thinnes nodded. "Think you'll catch the peckerwood?"

"If I don't, it won't be for lack of trying."

"Why'd you care 'bout a daid ex-con?" He didn't say "black" but his tone implied it.

"I think the same bastard killed a friend of mine."

Godsent nodded. "What kin ah do?"

Thinnes handed him his card. "If you think of anything that might help us—anyone with a grudge; anyone he might have threatened or who threatened him; anyone he owed money to or who might have owed him; or anything odd—call me. Sometimes the smallest things are the most important."

Inside, the church had wooden pews and a linoleum floor patterned with abstract designs by sunlight glowing through stained-glass windows. There was a lectern in front, no altar. A framed eight-by-ten of Ragland sat on the casket, which was surrounded by floral arrangements—lots of red roses and white carnations. There was no A/C. Old-fashioned ceiling fans turned lazily overhead. It was hot. Most of the people used their program books as fans.

The church was packed, blacks mostly, but quite a few whites and a surprising number of Asians. Vietnamese. Ragland had had plenty of friends in Uptown.

The obituary had been published in both the *Trib* and the *Sun-Times*. It was impressive. Ragland's military service wasn't mentioned, but his academic record was. Before being drafted, he'd graduated high school at the top of his class and earned a BS in political science at UIC.

It didn't make sense. Not that there weren't plenty of guys who'd gone to 'Nam and ruined their lives by getting hooked on drugs. But Thinnes had read all the reports; he hadn't discovered any evidence of Ragland using drugs after 'Nam. And while thousands of guys used drugs in country, most quit cold turkey when they came back to the world.

Not Ragland. He'd been arrested a dozen times—but never for drugs. Shadrack Owens had said anger was the monkey on Ragland's back. Maybe he was right.

An organist opened the service with a processional. Then the pastor read from the Twenty-third Psalm. A hymn from the choir followed. The pastor gave the eulogy.

Thinnes had been to too many funerals over the years, for everyone from infants to hardened felons. Often, when the deceased was the family's black sheep, the minister had to dig deep for something good to say. Not this pastor. Either he'd known Ragland or he'd

113

heard enough good about him to speak well of him with conviction. He likened Ragland to Job—tested by God with trials and tribulations, loss, and false accusations. His delivery made Thinnes think of Martin Luther King's "I Have a Dream" speech, and members of the congregation responded with heartfelt amens and 'I hear that!'

"In the end, God has called Theo to his heavenly reward! *God* has made a place for *him* in His heavenly kingdom! Reunited him with loved ones who have gone before . . ."

Who, exactly, were they? Thinnes wondered. And what happened to Ragland's girlfriend? For that matter, why hadn't they found her picture?

After the last hymn, the pallbearers rolled the casket down the center aisle, and everyone filed out after it, front pews first. It gave Thinnes a chance to see who he'd missed while talking to Godsent. Somehow it didn't surprise him to see Jack Caleb, Arthur Doherty, and Maharis there.

Tien Lee was a bit of a shocker, though. Thinnes made a point to ask how he knew Ragland.

"He did odd jobs for me," Lee told him. "He didn't show up regularly, but he worked well when he came."

Lee couldn't add anything about who would kill Ragland or why, so Thinnes sought out Maharis, found him just as Caleb and Doherty were putting him into the back seat of Caleb's Jaguar. "I need to have a word with Mr. Maharis."

The two shrinks blocked Maharis from view like bodyguards protecting the president.

"This is not a good time, John," Caleb said. What he didn't say—though Thinnes heard it clearly—was that he would make trouble if Thinnes pushed it. Thinnes knew he had the connections to make plenty.

"I have your card," Doherty said. "I'll call you as soon as he's sufficiently recovered from his friend's death to speak with you. I promise."

There wasn't anything Thinnes could say but, "You do that."

. . .

When Thinnes pressed her, Gramma Rags remembered Ragland mentioning the news report of Hue Lee's death. Hue had been a good friend of Theo's girlfriend. He'd wanted to go to Hue's wake, but he'd had an outstanding warrant and worried that the cops would get him. Which was why he'd sent Maharis.

"Tell me about Theo's girlfriend," Thinnes said.

"Oh, she died a long time ago. I don't know much about her, but Theo never got over it—made him crazy."

"What was her name?"

"Nahy."

The girl whose picture hung in Ragland's room. Someone removed it. Ragland, for some reason? His killer? Why?

Thinnes listened to the old woman's reminiscences until Shadrack Owens came to put her in a car.

Thinnes didn't get any more out of Mrs. Maitland, Ragland's mother, than he had the last time they spoke. She alternated between staring blankly ahead and sobbing hysterically.

The graveside service was hot but mercifully brief. And moving, but Thinnes learned nothing new. The reverend finished with an invitation to join the family for a meal back at the church.

Thinnes watched Doherty and Maharis get in a cab. He caught up with Caleb as he was getting in his Jag.

"Are you going back to the church?"

"Yes."

"Keep an eye out for the killer, will you?" Caleb nodded. "But if you see him, call for backup."

THIRTY-ONE

The church basement had been painted in the bright pastels favored for kindergarten classrooms, accented with flowers and butterflies and children's handprints. Caleb supposed they used the space for Sunday school.

Today, the child-sized furniture had been pushed into a corner, replaced by folding tables clothed in white. Someone had brought the vases of white chrysanthemums from the church and set them on the buffet table, among plates of fried chicken, potato salad, stewed greens, and deviled eggs—soul food. Vietnamese food, too. Caleb recognized *pho* and spring rolls and sticky rice with peanuts.

Another table held a huge coffeemaker flanked by rows of polystyrene cups, a large sugar bowl, a quart of Half & Half. And desserts—cakes, and pecan pie and apple, and peach cobbler. Two-liter bottles of pop and gallon plastic jugs of milk and iced tea chilled in tubs filled with ice.

More long folding tables had been covered with plastic cloths, surrounded by folding chairs. Caleb went to the end of the food line and watched the show.

The woman introduced to him as Gramma Rags was small and frail and shaking with age. She had a dark face seamed with wrinkles, and hands that curled into talons from arthritis. She sat across the table from Caleb, ramrod-straight in her pink flowered dress. The white gloves and hat with token veil were out of a Eudora Welty story.

There was something maddeningly familiar about her. As she visited with several teens, he stared, trying to remember.

A search-and-destroy mission. They'd rousted two old men and an old woman, a boy about ten, and a little girl. The lieutenant told Ears to fire the hooches, and Froggy, Preacher, and Caleb to shoot the animals—a few chickens and dogs, a pig and a water buffalo. He told Caleb to shoot the buffalo, then stalked away to watch the arson.

The animals scattered. Froggy and Preacher aimed low when they pointed their guns at the pig. Neither soldier seemed to believe his orders included hunting down the strays. The chickens were harder to miss, Caleb surmised as he watched some fly off squawking. A few lost feathers as they scattered. Half a dozen were too stupid to flee and ended up fricasséed.

Which left the buffalo. Even if he'd wanted to, Caleb couldn't have shot the animal. The old woman parked herself in front of it and made it plain he'd have to shoot her first. She was tiny and wrinkled, burned nearly black by the sun, with arms and legs as thin as matchsticks, and gnarled arthritic hands. Her black peasant clothes hung on her loosely.

A good shot could have aimed around her; she was scarcely big enough to cover the beast's head. He wasn't a good shot, and he understood that the buffalo meant the difference between getting by and starving. Even if that hadn't been the case, there was no point in killing it.

He spoke no Vietnamese. She, apparently, spoke no English. But they had some French in common. And they had Froggy. With Froggy translating, Caleb told the woman they were going to fool the lieutenant.

He cracked his med kit and laid out his supplies, working as quickly as if he had a man down. It took most of his remaining morphine to get the beast to play dead. There wasn't any blood. The old lady caught on and salvaged some of the slaughtered chickens. Caleb wrung the blood out of them, all over the buffalo.

117

Their ruse worked. The lieutenant glanced at the gory mass, surrounded by wailing villagers, and gave the order to move on. The village lay in ashes. But the damned buffalo survived.

When they finished eating, the young relatives who'd been visiting with Gramma Rags left, and Caleb cleared her plate away, along with his own. He returned to sit across from her.

"Were you a friend of Theo's?" she asked.

He thought about it. He and Ragman had been in therapy together, years ago. They'd had similar issues with anger. They'd both made an effort to help one another. "We were friends."

"In Vietnam?"

"No. We met after the war. Here in Chicago."

She nodded. "Police say he killed hisself. You believe that?"

He tried to remember the last time he'd seen Ragman—at Arthur's. Ragman had been teed off about something. As usual. Arthur had probed for a reason, but it seemed anger was Ragman's habitual response to life. Since 'Nam. Then Maharis tossed in one of his word salads, and Ragman laughed. Heartily. He'd turned to Arthur and said, "Jus' when you figger you got stuck with the short straw, you find someone's got one shorter."

Caleb could imagine him working himself into a frenzy, goading the cops into shooting him. But not shooting himself. To answer Gramma, he said, "He'd never do that."

She patted his arm. "You *were* his friend."

They sat in companionable silence for a while. Then she said, "Theo ever show you a picture of his girl?"

Caleb shook his head. He'd never mentioned a girl.

"Han' me my pocketbook." She pointed with twisted fingers.

He gave her the old-fashioned black leather purse. She opened it, using her thumb and the side of her index finger to grip. She took out a checkbook/organizer, from which she removed a three-by-five photo.

"This his girl."

Caleb studied the picture—Ragman with an exquisitely beautiful Vietnamese woman in a red *ao dai*. The photographer had captured his pride, the girl's adoration. Portrait of a couple hopelessly besotted.

Caleb had never seen Ragman happy before. He turned the picture over. *Nhài January 1972* was printed on the back.

"What happened to her?"

"Don't know. Theo got arrested an' never seen her again." The old woman stretched her arm across the table, flattening the hand as much as she could on the white tablecloth. Her elbow was swollen. Even resting on the tabletop, her hand shook. "He was gonna marry the girl. Bought her a ring. His momma didn't approve, but the rest of us was all glad for him."

"Mrs. Ragland?"

"Call me Gramma."

"Gramma, may I borrow this? I'd like to have it copied."

"Copied?" For a fraction of a second, he thought she seemed afraid. Of what? Perhaps just of losing the only happy picture of her grandson.

"I'll guard it with my life," he said, cringing at the melodrama, but meaning what he said.

"Well . . ."

"If you like, I could make an enlargement for you."

"Can you do that? Without a negative?"

"At almost any drugstore."

"Well, I s'pose . . ."

Caleb put the picture in his inside jacket pocket. "I'll go right now. I'll be back before you've finished your coffee."

She nodded, staring past him. "Guess the war kilt him sure as all those boys got they names on the Wall."

Her eyes filled with tears; Caleb handed her a napkin. He put his large, soft hand over her tiny, knobby one.

She patted his forearm. "I'll be fine. You go get that picture copied. Least he'll be live as long as his friends don't ferget 'im."

There was an Osco Drug nearby. Caleb made three four-by-six copies of Ragman's picture, one each for himself, Maharis, and Arthur. He blew the image up to eight-by-ten and played with the adjustments until he'd achieved the maximum resolution. Then he printed it for Thinnes. He cropped the sharpened image to enhance its composition and printed the resulting enlargement for Gramma Rags.

When he got back, the church ladies were just clearing away the cake plates and coffee cups.

THIRTY-TWO

Gary, Indiana. Thinnes pulled up at the address on Franchi's note and told himself, This can't be right. A sign on the door, right below the number, said ST JUDE'S RECTORY. The building didn't look like a rectory, but the number on the door matched the number on the paper. And the sign on the storefront window next door said ST JUDE'S CATHOLIC CHURCH. So maybe Drucker was using the church for some scam.

Drucker opened the door himself. In a Roman collar.

Thinnes waited, wondering how much he himself had changed in twenty-four years.

"I know you!" Drucker said. "But I'm sorry—"

"John Thinnes. Saigon."

Drucker thought a moment. "Sure," he said, "the strac MP. Come in." He stepped backward, holding the door.

The interior—Drucker's living room, Thinnes guessed—was a major contrast to the hooch Thinnes remembered in Saigon. Drucker's digs there would have put many Gold Coast apartments to shame, with Oriental rugs and mahogany furniture. This room looked like it was furnished from an alley. The couch was faded and worn, the reclining chair patched with duct tape, the TV had a cracked case.

Thinnes looked for signs of drugs. There was a table against the wall with an old computer and an older printer. Stapler, tape dispenser, a ream of cheap typing paper. Stacks of flyers were spread out on the tabletop.

"Have a seat, John. Tell me what I can do for you."

"You really live here?"

"Three years now."

Thinnes didn't know what to say.

Drucker smiled. "It's not what you expected."

"You used to have a hand in every game."

"I didn't do or know as much as I got credit for. Sometimes you've just got to keep your mouth shut to seem smarter than you are."

"You weren't even Catholic. How'd you get to be a priest?"

Drucker laughed. "People change."

A dive on Tu Do Street. Dark. Noisy. Crowded. Thinnes was off duty, but he'd been in country long enough to keep his guard up. He made his way to the bar and pushed in between two guys in uniform. To his surprise, one of them was Drucker.

They weren't supposed to frequent bars in uniform. Drucker didn't seem worried. He introduced the other guy as Mike. The name on Mike's shirt was CORSO. *His* greeting was guarded. Obviously Thinnes had interrupted something.

"Buy you a drink, John?" Drucker asked.

Corso looked annoyed.

Thinnes had the sudden urge to hang around and see what was going on. "Sure."

"Lone Star for my friend," Drucker told the bartender. "The real thing. Anytime he comes in."

The bartender, an Amerasian, nodded and fished the beer from an ice chest under the bar.

Drucker dropped a fifty-dollar bill on the bar—a real fifty, not the military scrip they were paid with. Without looking at either Thinnes or Corso, he said, "Keep an eye on my drink, will you guys? I gotta see a man about a dog."

Thinnes followed where Drucker had been looking. A powerfully built Asian disappeared into the can. Chinese? "Yeah." He held up his bottle. "Thanks for the drink."

Walking away, Drucker said, "Think nothing of it."

Corso turned to the bar and hunched over his drink. Thinnes didn't try to make conversation. He watched the men's room door. After a while, Drucker came out, looking relieved, not—Thinnes would have bet—in the usual sense of the word. And Drucker didn't strike Thinnes as the kind who jerked off in public restrooms.

Drucker came back and took up where he'd left off, though talking a little too fast, laughing a little too heartily. Corso kept sulking.

Two Vietnamese in suits went into the can; came out. Two Asian thugs dragged in a third man, also Asian. The third man staggered out alone, bruised and bloody.

Curious, Thinnes started toward the can.

Drucker caught his arm. "You're not leaving?"

"Just going to see a man about a dog."

Corso said, "Shit!"

Drucker said, "Give it a minute. Or go in the alley."

"Just tell him to stay out of there," Corso said.

"I've been watching him. John's not the type to follow unauthorized orders. It'd just make him curious."

Thinnes didn't comment.

"I don't think I have to *tell* John anything. I think he's smart enough to leave things be."

"But you didn't come all this way to ask about my Damascus experience," Drucker said. "What can I do for you?"

"What do you remember about White Tiger?"

As he'd done so often in Saigon, Drucker ran his fingers through his hair. "Lord," he said. He thought for a while, then shrugged. "He had a piece of just about every dirty game going in Saigon, but I never met anybody who'd admit to knowing his real name, or what he looked like, or even his nationality."

Thinnes waited.

Drucker thought some more. "He might've been Chinese. He did a lot of business in Cholon. Why the sudden interest after all these years?"

Thinnes handed him the Polaroid of the note found on Ragland. *Cọp Trắng.*

Drucker stared at it. "It's got to be a coincidence."

"A woman I knew in Saigon moved here from the West Coast. She must've known something, because she's dead."

"Is that where you got—?" He nodded toward the note.

"It was in the pocket of another murder victim, an ex-serviceman who was arrested in Saigon for dealing."

"You know how many men we arrested for dealing?"

"Thousands."

"At least."

"This guy swore he was framed."

That seemed to surprise Drucker, but he shrugged.

"What?" Thinnes said.

"Nothing."

Thinnes waited.

"There was a guy—about a month before you arrived—a black guy. I can't remember his name, and I don't know where he was from, but he was better educated than most. He swore he was framed because of a woman."

"Theodore Ragland?"

"Yeah, as a matter of fact."

"You remember the woman's name?"

"No. Sorry. I think she was Vietnamese."

"It wasn't Hue?

"I don't think so."

"So what happened to Ragland?"

Drucker shrugged. "We dropped him at LBJ. Last I heard, he was court-martialed and shipped to Leavenworth."

"Why were you such a cynic?"

Drucker laughed. "You remember how it was. The war was a crock. There was no front. There was nothing to gain. All the time we were chasing Charlie, we were chasing our tails—a dance with the devil. Sometimes we'd lead, sometimes Charlie did. On the days the town was off-limits, Charlie was having his turn with the local whores.

"I was sure that there couldn't be a God. If there were, He'd have wiped humans off the planet. So good and evil had to be sub-jective, right and wrong a matter of getting caught."

"So Damascus?"

"It wasn't really Damascus, and a gasoline tanker hit my car broadside, not lightning. Shoulda killed me, but it didn't. Broke my back but saved my soul."

"How's that?"

"I was laid up a year, so I had lots of time to think. When the doctors told me I'd never walk again, I made a deal with God—if He'd give me another chance, I'd use it.

"I can hear confessions now, because I know what's being confessed. When I give absolution, I know what I'm absolving."

"You remember anything else about Cop Trắng?"

"There was a guy who bragged he knew him. Ended up with his tongue cut out. Cop Trắng didn't kill him, but the guy never mentioned him again. That was a long time ago."

"Yeah." Thinnes handed him his card. "If you think of any-thing else, call me."

"Sure."

Thinnes was unlocking his car door when Drucker called out, "The girlfriend's name was Jasmine."

Thinnes's next stop was a belated courtesy call on the local PD. After they'd exchanged pleasantries, the Gary detective said, "What can I do for you?"

"What can you tell me about Father Des Drucker?"

THIRTY-THREE

It was weird consulting Caleb for a personal problem once, but twice in two weeks was off the chart. Still, Caleb was good and could keep his mouth shut. Thinnes dialed his number and tried to think how to explain the problem.

Caleb was still reluctant to get involved. "I belong to a veterans' therapy group. I'm sure you'd be welcome."

"Thanks, but with my luck one of 'em'd turn out to be a guy I arrested."

"Then let me give you the name of someone you can meet with one-on-one."

"I don't need therapy. I just need help remembering details. Hypnosis, like you did before. The murder happened twenty-five years ago; it's not like an open case would be compromised. I was assigned to the case; I got pulled off. I thought at the time it was because I might be getting too close to someone with connections. I think he was military or connected with the U.S. government because my informant called him *Cọp Trắng*—White Tiger. He was terrified of him. He quoted an old Vietnamese proverb: *When a cat steals a piece of meat, we chase it; when a tiger takes a pig, we stand wide-eyed and say nothing.*

"The little I could find out about Cọp Trắng was that he was some kind of underworld kingpin. The dead woman must have known too much about him.

"My friend Hue and I had only Saigon in common, so I'm hoping that if I can figure out who killed the woman in Saigon, I might know who killed Hue."

· · ·

The call had come in a half hour before curfew. Trouble on Tu Do Street. Surprise!

The sergeant took the call and told Thinnes, "You're with me, and we're it. No one available from CID. Bring your camera. We'll meet Captain Bành at the scene."

Bành was the only one of the white mice who spoke English and wasn't corrupt or stupid. He was still single and seemed to put all his energy in his job. Thinnes had never seen him take anything from anyone. Drucker and the other MPs called him the White Knight. He had lots of enemies, but he must've had some pretty good connections because no one had put a knife between his ribs.

Bành pulled up behind the MPs' jeep. He ordered the men he had with him to watch the vehicles while he and the sergeant and Thinnes went inside.

The bar was cooking. The light was bad, the music loud. Smoke and incense hung in layers below the ceiling. There was a mixed crowd—mercenaries and civilians—Caucasians, mostly; B-girls and hustlers; and the few beggars willing to risk pissing off the management. Men were waiting two deep at the bar. Kibitzers surrounded the pool table, and the stakes were pretty high, judging by the fistful of greenbacks held by an older Asian man standing off to the side. At two of the tables, poker games were in progress.

People began to notice the police; the noise level dropped. Many of the patrons stared like wildebeests at a water hole when the lions arrived, but no one panicked.

A man in a dingy white suit jacket materialized at Captain Bành's side and muttered something.

As Thinnes followed the others to a hallway across the room, the crowd parted to let them pass—grudgingly, it seemed—then closed again behind them. He could feel his back-hairs standing up. He kept a hand on his sidearm.

The hall was lit by red electric bulbs under which the wood

floor and woven bamboo paneling looked gray. Doorways on either side were staggered so no one faced another. None of the openings had doors, just beaded curtains. Most of these semiprivate rooms were dark or lit by candles.

The man in the white coat led them down the hall, to a doorway on the left, and pulled the bead curtain aside.

Captain Bành looked into the room and said something in Vietnamese. The man nodded and let go of the bead strings. He went back the way they'd come. The three of them waited awkwardly until he returned with a lantern.

Bành took the light; he spoke Vietnamese. White coat pulled the curtain strands aside and looped a few around the others to hold the curtain back. He stepped away and let them enter.

The room was typical—Thinnes guessed—of a more expensive class of brothel. A double bed with red satin sheets. A tall wardrobe. Candles. Flowers. The room smelled of incense and piss.

A young woman lay face up on the bed, arms and legs splayed. She was Vietnamese, slightly built and pale-skinned, almost white, naked from the hips up. Black trousers, pulled below the slight mound of her belly, were soaked with urine. Her silk top lay crumpled on the floor.

No question she was dead. The knife buried to the hilt between her flawless breasts had a carved handle like a cat's paw, claws bared. The blood pooling on the sheet looked black, reflecting lantern light.

Thinnes'd seen nasty sights since he arrived. This was his first murder. He wanted to run, to shoot the bastard who'd done it. He forced himself to stay and pay attention.

"Why are we here?" the sergeant asked Bành.

"Mr. Thach thinks Americans did this. You start. I find room to interview witnesses."

The sergeant nodded.

Before leaving, Bành set the lantern on the wardrobe. The harsh light made everything look unreal. But the smell of death was genuine enough.

"You want to get the job done quick," the sergeant said. "Because it's horrible. It seeps into your head the way the smell sticks to your clothes. You know you'll take it home with you, and it'll stink your life up.

"But you can't hurry. God's in the details, and if you don't study the scene, you'll miss 'em. Then the asshole who did this gets away."

Thinnes started taking pictures. The girl seemed to be surprised by death. Her face was a smooth oval, full red lips and eyes seductively half closed. Her hands were soft, feet smooth—not those of a displaced farm girl. Her finger- and toenails were glossed in Chinese red. A large diamond flashed from her left ring finger.

Following the sergeant's lead, Thinnes felt the body, which was still warm, and looked around for clues. There was no purse or ID, no personal items but her clothes and ring. The wardrobe was empty. Most of the things they usually found investigating in brothels were absent—condoms, liquor, drug paraphernalia, sex aids. The flowers were white carnations. The sergeant pointed to them and said, "This means something."

"Think we can get an autopsy?" Thinnes asked.

"We can ask. You got enough shots?"

Thinnes shrugged. "How many's enough? I got most of a roll." The film was black and white, but he wouldn't forget the bright red color of the blood.

"When you left the murder scene, what did you do?" Caleb was sitting back in the chair opposite the couch.

Thinnes couldn't read his expression. Afternoon sun warmed the treetops in Grant Park across Michigan Avenue. The trees hid the Art Institute from view.

"Bành interviewed the staff—manager, bartender, madam, other girls, and cleaning guys. The dead girl's name was Jasmine. The madam found her when she didn't come to get her next client. Conveniently, nobody remembered who she'd gone in the room with. Nobody saw anything. Nobody heard anything. Nobody told us anything resembling the truth, except Bành said he heard one of them muttering that Jasmine's crazy boyfriend once threatened to blow up the place with a grenade. Nobody remembered his name."

"When was this?"

"A month earlier.

"Bành took the knife for evidence and had his men deliver the body to the morgue. He said he'd ask for an autopsy. I never saw a report of one. He told us later the cause of death was the knife through her heart.

"The sergeant and I spoke to the English-speaking patrons. Of course, nobody knew anything. We made out our reports and put them in the file with the photos. A couple days later, someone requisitioned the file. I never saw it again. When I asked, the sergeant said forget it."

"And?"

"I checked with a guy I served with in Saigon, a pretty savvy guy. He said he arrested a black soldier on drug charges in Saigon who had a girlfriend named Jasmine."

"Theo Ragland?"

"Yeah."

"I have something for you." Caleb took an eight-by-ten photo from a desk drawer. "Theo's grandma gave me this."

Thinnes recognized Ragland from the portrait in his uncle's living room. And he'd seen the woman before. Dead. In the brothel in Saigon.

THIRTY-FOUR

The group's mood mirrored the weather—overcast and muggy.
Arthur's study seemed gray without the sunlight leaking in. As
usual, the A/C wasn't keeping up. Maharis's absence cast a pall over
them. Caleb happened to know he was taking his friend's death so
hard that Arthur had checked him into a hospital. They started the
session listening to Butch complain about his domestic problems.

"Somebody got up on the wrong side of the bed today," Joe
observed. He sounded bored.

"It's this weather," Butch said. "It makes you want to jump
out of your skin."

"We'd have killed for a few days like this in the Gulf, it was so
damn dry and dusty."

"It was like this all the time in 'Nam—when it wasn't pouring
rain. It drove a lot of guys crazy." Butch stared at Caleb. "You got
that look, Jack. What?"

"Ears," Caleb said, "was crazy before he got in country. Too
crazy for the Marines!"

At the beginning of his second tour, Caleb was serving under a
butter-bean lieutenant who was going to save the gooks from
communism. Caleb was at the top of his shit list because he
wouldn't carry a gun.

The lieutenant was a week from his DEROS. Caleb was
glad—some FNG just out of OCS had to be better for the platoon.
They'd pulled back to base camp for a week stand-down. Showers. Cold beer. Trips to the brothels in town.

Caleb heard his squad sergeant was taking a deuce-and-a-half to Long Binh to pick up supplies and replacements.

In 1970, Long Binh was one of the largest military bases in the world, with good security by Vietnam standards. Charlie may have controlled the night, but by day the road to Long Binh was as safe as any in country. And the nearby town was big enough to have a market.

The market was where you could get fresh produce, rice and beans, animals—alive and dead—and black market items, from AK-47s to the latest *Hit Parade* single. Caleb got a lot of medical supplies in local markets. Sad, because at base camp they had fresh milk and eggs and ice cream, cigarettes, and all the beer the men could drink. But sometimes they'd run out of morphine or antibiotics, or the amount they were issued would be limited so they wouldn't be tempted to trade the surplus.

So Caleb asked if he could go along to score a few extra medical supplies. The sergeant brought Froggy and Preacher because—he said—Caleb was worthless in a fight.

The weather was decent for a change—relatively low humidity, temperatures below ninety degrees. They took turns driving, with the sarge up front. The others rode in back. They made good time. After they got past the MPs at the gate, they parked the truck, and Sarge went to see about the personnel. Caleb headed for the supply depot. He arranged to pick up what they would give him, then rounded up Froggy and Preacher, and they headed into town.

The new lieutenant was waiting when they got back. It was obvious he was career Army, a control freak who started by quoting regulations. Verbatim. And by chewing out the sarge for his uniform and for Caleb's long hair.

"You?" Butch interrupted. "Long hair?"

"I actually *had* hair back then," Caleb said. "Though at that point it wasn't below my collar. The lieutenant ordered us to get haircuts as soon as we got back to base. That was the last haircut I had for five years."

. . .

Sarge didn't say anything to the new lieutenant but "Yes, sir," and "No, sir."

The next morning, when they were loaded up, the sarge asked, "Ready to go, sir?"

"We've got to pick up a couple of replacements."

Long Binh Jail was where they sent deserters, rapists, murderers, and the seriously insubordinate—anyone serving less than six months. The lieutenant directed them to the intake area, and they waited while he did the paperwork on their *replacements*. The MPs marched two men out in handcuffs. They looked like bums and smelled almost as bad as if they'd just come in from the bush.

One of the MPs told the lieutenant to watch his back around the two. He spoke softly, but not softly enough.

The prisoner they came to know as Ears turned on him and snarled, "What would you rear-echelon motherfuckers know about anything?"

The MP didn't rise to the bait. He just unlocked the handcuffs and officially turned the prisoners over.

Back at base camp, Ears and Watt, the other new guy, got off on the wrong foot with the rest of the platoon by bumming cigarettes and sharking at pool. After a week or so, they relaxed enough with their new buddies to let their true natures show, bragging—just short of a chargeable admission—about the havoc they'd wreaked since coming in country. Ears brought out his necklace and grossed the others out by making it clear how he'd gotten his name.

Not to be outdone, Watt tried to entertain them with stories of his sexual prowess. No one believed a word—he was crude, rude, and as subtle as an APC. As much as he bragged about getting it for free, they suspected he had to pay the local whores extra just to put up with him.

"Ears never got over that the Marines wouldn't take him," Watt told them one day.

"Why's that, Ears?" Froggy demanded.

"He's full of shit! Who'd want to be one of those crazy motherfuckers?"

"You," Watt said.

"You callin' me a liar?"

Watt just laughed. "Naw, just sayin' you're too soft for the Corps."

Ears turned red. "There's nothing soft about me!"

Froggy'd had enough by then. He turned to Ears. "What you would call soft, most people would call human. And you're right. There's nothing human about you."

"Cu Chi District," Caleb told them, "was originally a fertile agricultural area, covered with orchards, farms, and rubber plantations. Because it was near Saigon and most of the terrain was above the water table, the Viet Minh had built networks of underground tunnels during their war with the French. When the Americans came along, the Viet Cong used the same tunnels. Because the Americans couldn't tell Charlie from the civilians, most of the peasants were forcibly removed from the district to strategic hamlets—essentially concentration camps. And by 1970—between the H&I with artillery fire at night and saturation with bombs and Agent Orange by day—most of the district was a dead zone."

"Don't forget the Rome plows," Butch said. "Big motherfuckers just scraped everything bare—trees and all."

"True, but in a few places vegetation had started to return, and a few villagers drifted back. Their existence was centered on the land. Farming was all they knew. Most of them combined Buddhism with a form of ancestor worship, and their ancestors were buried there. So preserving their land was almost a part of their religion.

"And as soon as we pulled out of an area, the VC would rebuild the tunnels. They were like red ants—they'd come swarming out and sting like hell."

"They were fuckin' *fire* ants," Butch insisted, "only they built their nests underground where you couldn't spot 'em."

134

Caleb smiled. "They sent us out on recon. Patrols were usually limited to a squad or two, depending on transport available. Choppers could only take on nine or ten men. We were supposed to look for VC, weapons, tunnel entrances. We found out early on that we'd been given Watt and Ears because they were tunnel rats—men crazy enough to go in after Charlie, ruthless enough to kill anyone they found there. But there weren't many tunnels left, so they just humped with the rest of us and complained constantly.

"When we searched a ville, we'd get all the residents out and check them for weapons. Then someone would keep an eye on them while the rest of us searched the hooches. I noticed that when Watt was assigned guard duty, he would grab his crotch and thrust his hips forward and back—never in front of the sergeant, of course. He used to call his penis 'Snake,' and it didn't take us long to start calling *him* Snake.

"We lost him the day we were sent to 'pacify' a hamlet—just a dozen huts separated from the surrounding rice fields by the usual hedgerows."

Caleb closed his eyes. He could see sun filtering through thin clouds onto the rice paddy along the river . . .

Tiny, newly planted rice seedlings showed green above the water, gray silt below. Raindrops splattered on the surface, creating overlapping patterns of concentric circles. The light changed. The soft squish-splash of carefully placed feet, and the gentle swish of cloth brushing grass made him feel anxious. He was aware of decaying vegetation, the sour smell of unwashed bodies, the aroma of cigarette smoke. Danger. There was a soft hiss as a cigarette hit the water. Caleb looked down. The wakes of wading boots stretched and distorted the busy pattern of raindrops. A dragonfly choppered across the surface, airlifting its catch out of range. There was the click and rasp of a Zippo, and—in keeping with the motto of the land: *Hurt me, I'll hurt you worse*—a hiss, a plop, then the sickening odor of singed leech flesh.

One of the FNGs. Old hands didn't bother with the leeches. They'd drop off when they'd had their fill. It seemed everything in country wanted their blood—leeches a taste, Charlie enough to put them out of commission, the war all the rest.

The rain stopped before they got to the ville. It was temporarily deserted, but there were dogs and pigs and chickens. The lieutenant told them the gooks must be out working the fields.

They went house to house. The only weapon found was a rusty rifle—probably fifty years old—with no ammunition. So the lieutenant told Caleb and Preacher to stay by the hooches and watch. "The rest of you spread out."

The two watchers were killing time, smoking, when they heard a woman scream. The sound stopped abruptly, as if someone had struck the victim midcry. The men dropped their smokes and ran.

They found Snake on top of a young girl—perhaps twelve—with his pants down, pumping away. Thin and tiny, she lay beneath him still as death.

They pulled him off. Her shirt had been ripped open, her pants torn apart. Mud coated the pale skin of her torso, blood the insides of her thighs. She'd stopped breathing, her throat abraded, as if she'd been punched in the larynx. Caleb grabbed his kit and started laying out what he needed to do a tracheotomy.

Preacher started calling Snake every insult ever heard in country. He held his M-16 over his head and pounded Snake with his boots.

Snake curled up, protecting his head and genitals.

"Calm down!" Caleb yelled.

The rest of the platoon came charging back, the lieutenant in the lead. "Preacher, knock it off!"

Preacher complied reluctantly. The lieutenant grabbed Preacher's rifle and tossed it to Caleb, who dropped it and went back to work on the girl. He glanced up often, following the action.

Snake rolled on his back and propped himself up on his elbows. He lay there with his tongue hanging over his lower lip, breathing hard through his mouth.

"What the hell's going on?" The lieutenant was white with rage.

"He tried to kill me, sir," Snake sobbed.

Preacher started yelling again, calling Snake baby-raper and motherfucker.

"Shut up, both of you!" The lieutenant put enough rage behind his words to silence them. "Doc, what happened?"

Caleb had the trach tube in by then and was taping it in place. He didn't look up as he answered.

The story didn't improve the lieutenant's mood. "You're going to Leavenworth!" he told Snake.

Caleb glanced over to see the lieutenant turn to Preacher. "I'll deal with you later!"

Snake took a grenade off his flak jacket.

Caleb screamed, *"No!"* though he wasn't sure what Snake was going to do.

The lieutenant drew his pistol. Faster than you could say, *Don't shoot!* he drilled Snake through the head.

Ears raised his M-16. Out of reflex, Caleb guessed.

The lieutenant pointed his gun at Ears. "Drop it!"

For fifteen seconds it was a standoff. Then Ears backed down. The lieutenant looked around. "Anybody else?" Nobody moved. "Call in a dust-off."

The villagers faded back as soon as they realized the soldiers were more danger to each other. The girl's father was a slight man, middle-aged. He stood holding his young son, looking shell-shocked. The mother started screaming when she saw her daughter.

"She was still wailing when we moved out. Her daughter was alive when we put her in the chopper. I don't know what happened to her. I think they classified Snake as KIA."

"What happened to the lieutenant?" Butch demanded.

"Nothing. Twenty-seven of us saw Snake threaten him. So the JAG investigation found his action justified."

"And Preacher?"

"Nothing at all. As far as I know, no one said a word."

"And Ears?"

"The lieutenant let it drop, but he should've shot him."

"That's weird for a conscientious objector to say."

"I didn't say kill him. But he should have enforced his authority and gotten that psychotic out of the field. It might have saved them both."

THIRTY-FIVE

In Saigon, one of the duties Thinnes had been assigned early on was writing up traffic accidents involving U.S. personnel. Driving in the capital was pretty much as Drucker had described—a giant game of chicken. And when somebody miscalculated, or nobody blinked, the result was carnage. Which was why Thinnes got to know the ER staff at most of the hospitals. And why he asked Franchi to locate Bea Gardner, Faith-Hope Hospital's head ER nurse on the graveyard shift.

As soon as he crossed the threshold, Thinnes knew why she'd asked him to meet her where she did. The Café Francais could have been time-warped from Saigon in the early seventies, across the street from L'Hospital d'Espérance et de la Foi. Le Chat Gris had been one of those French bistros where—if you knew the proprietor—you could read your overseas paper and get cognac in your coffee.

Café Francais greeted him with the aromas of baking bread and brewing coffee. Truckers had replaced hospital staff, and the mangy Persian cat had been replaced by a clean, sleek calico. But the walls were covered with the same hand-painted tiles, the tables with the same snowy cloths, the floors with the same red tiles in the same herringbone pattern. A little ceramic pitcher on each table held black-eyed Susans and something frilly and blue.

The man wiping down the stove was identical to the Vietnamese chef who'd baked croissants and whipped up omelets behind the counter in Saigon. Only he hadn't aged in twenty-five years. The illusion dissolved when he said, "Good evening," with an Indiana drawl. "Help you?"

"I'm supposed to meet someone."

The man pointed to a table near the windows.

Bea Gardner—Bea—closed the book she was reading as he got near, and gestured to a chair opposite. She was an older version of the tough woman he remembered from the long nights in the ER. Her off-blond hair was more gray than gold, the furrows in her brow deeper. She'd gained a few pounds. She was wearing jeans and Reeboks, and a Rude Dog T-shirt under a linen jacket.

When he was settled and had ordered coffee, she said, "Mind if I smoke?"

He shrugged. She took Marlboros and a Zippo out of a pocket and lit up. She took a long drag, letting it out slowly like a character in a movie.

"For a long time I had a problem with booze," she said. "I think I got it under control." She studied the smoke rising from the glowing tip. "But I can't seem to get free of these."

There wasn't anything to say to that.

"*You* quit," she observed.

"I didn't want my son exposed."

The waiter interrupted with their coffee. They were silent until he'd finished serving and moved away.

Bea stubbed out her cigarette. "People forget women served in country. Until recently, there weren't even any programs . . . How did you manage to get yourself straight?"

"An understanding wife and a job that kept me busy."

"The Army should've prepared us."

"You never complained," Thinnes said. "You never talked about things—except bullshit stuff."

"By the time I met you, I'd grown a shell like an APC." She shook her head. "When I first got over there, I used to cry all the time—whenever I wasn't working. I was sure I'd never cope. By the end of my tour, I was pretty good. No! I was damn good. I was making decisions only doctors would make back in the world. But I was addicted—you know how it could be—to the adrenaline.

"When I got home, I felt useless. Nobody needed me like they did in 'Nam. Everything was trivial. The things people obsessed about seemed so stupid. And people treated vets like shit.

"So I re-upped. Twice. When they wouldn't let me do a fourth tour, I got out and went back on my own. The hospitals always needed nurses. And in Saigon . . .

"But you didn't look me up after all these years to hear my problems. What's up?"

"When you were there, did you ever hear of Cọp Trắng?"

Her eyes widened. "The Bogeyman? Bạch Hổ? White Tiger?"

Thinnes nodded.

"I heard him mentioned from time to time. Why?"

"I have reason to believe he moved here."

"People turning up dead?"

"Yeah. Did you ever hear his real name?"

"Word was that nobody who did ever lived to tell it."

"What do you remember?"

"Just that he got blamed for half the evil in Cholon—what couldn't be accounted for by the Chinese or the government."

"Nothing specific?"

"No. Sorry."

"Do you remember a hooker named Jasmine?"

"Are you kidding? Do you know how many hookers there were in Saigon?"

"Thousands."

"Counting amateurs and homeless women, tens of thousands. Every whorehouse in Saigon had one. I'm sure Jasmine was a position—manned twenty-four/seven by a rotating shift of girls."

"Point taken." Thinnes took out Caleb's picture of Jasmine and Ragland. As he pulled it from the envelope, Hue's picture came with and dropped on the tabletop. Before he could retrieve it, Bea picked it up.

She studied it, then said, "*Her* I remember. But she wasn't a hooker when I met her."

Thinnes let his surprise show. "She wasn't a hooker."

Bea shrugged. "She was having a miscarriage when she was brought in. I guess I just assumed . . . She was screaming in

French and Vietnamese. I don't know what—I don't speak either language. But the Vietnamese staff were frightened, and one of the doctors sedated her.

"The next day, and for the rest of her stay, she was so depressed—or drugged—she didn't talk at all."

"That's not unusual, is it? For a woman who's just lost a baby?"

"No, but one reason I remember her is that she had a huge bruise on her abdomen, right in the middle. It looked like someone with a big foot kicked her."

"Christ!"

It explained so much. Hue had been depressed and paranoid after her miscarriage. When Bobby begged Thinnes to move in with her, she hadn't protested, though it caused a scandal with the neighbors. After she got to know Thinnes better, she'd "confessed" that an American "officer" was harassing her. She wouldn't tell Thinnes who, just that he was "very powerful." She'd begged him not to tell Bobby because "he'd kill him."

At the time, Thinnes believed that she was afraid Bobby would kill the harasser, and she'd refused to tell Thinnes the man's name for the same reason. Since the "officer" didn't bother her after Thinnes moved in, he'd let the subject drop.

"Who is she?" Bea asked.

"Was. Hue An Charcot, then. Or she'd probably have been listed on your patient roster as Charcot An Hue."

"Doesn't ring any bells." She handed Thinnes Hue's picture, then studied the picture of Ragland and Jasmine.

"I remember them, but I don't know much about the girl. She had a Vietnamese name. I do recall him—a soldier, an educated black man. He brought her into the hospital after some bastard beat the b'jesus out of her. She didn't want to be there, but he insisted. Insisted we care for her 'like a round-eye'—his words. He said he was going to marry her. One of the aides told me Cọp Trắng was her pimp and he'd beat her because she wanted out."

"So what happened to her?"

"I don't know. She just came in that once. I never gave either one of them another thought."

They sat in silence for a while. Thinnes wondered what he would've done if he'd known what caused Hue's miscarriage. Probably gone on a tiger hunt and gotten himself killed. Hue probably saved his life, and Bobby's, with her silence, but it cost her life in the end. She'd no doubt been killed because she could ID Cọp Trắng. And her death was proof the bastard made it out of Saigon!

"When did you finally leave?" he asked Bea.

" 'Seventy-five. Almost didn't get out. Graham Martin—that moron—never authorized an evac plan. He kept insisting Viet-namization was working. Thank God for Homer Smith." She shook her head. "You saw the news. You felt so bad for your friends who weren't getting out because they weren't high enough on the food chain. Effin' waste."

She stared at the window with its film of condensation, masking the view of the parking lot. "You know, I can't cry anymore. I can drink like a sailor and swear like a stevedore. But I can't cry."

THIRTY-SIX

Thinnes told me I could trust you," Franchi said. "If I ever had a problem."

"Come in." Caleb offered her a seat. She selected the center of the couch as she had the first time they met.

She was nervous. Her eyes went all around the room—not seeing it, he'd have bet, looking for a way to begin. He waited, let her sort it out. She'd been a smoker, he remembered. Now she acted like a person in the grip of nicotine withdrawal.

"I used to have a crush on Thinnes, the first time in my life— I mean since I was a teenager and had crushes on movie stars." Caleb raised an eyebrow; she continued. "He's everything I ever wanted in a man—principled, intelligent, professional—but he's married. I never let him suspect, you know? He adores his wife, but with guys—sometimes love's got nothing to do with it. If they get tempted . . ."

Caleb smiled inwardly. Thinnes had told him something similar.

"Anyway, I wouldn't want to tempt him even though I don't think he'd screw around on Rhonda. It would make it harder for him to work with me, you know? Uncomfortable."

Caleb nodded. "So you've gotten over your crush?"

"I think so—don't get me wrong, if Rhonda ever left him— But she won't. She's crazy about him, hard as it must be to be married to a cop."

"So what brings you here?"

"There's someone else—a suspect in a murder."

"I see."

"I can't stand it. The first time I saw him—I don't believe in that love-at-first-sight crap. But it was lust at first sight for sure. I'm supposed to interview him and I can't look at him without fantasizing . . ."

Caleb concealed his amusement. "Can't you ask Detective Thinnes to interview him?"

"No. That's what makes the final straw. Thinnes got pulled off the case because of an anonymous tip that the guy's Thinnes's illegitimate son."

"Paternity is easy enough to establish."

"If the parties involved cooperate. Our suspect won't. And we don't have any standing to compel him."

"What choices does that leave you?"

"A rock and a hard place. They got me working it with Viernes. He's good, but we're in over our heads."

"What are you doing about it?"

"Having coffee with Thinnes every day, getting tips. Everybody knows, but they can't prove anything. Besides, Evanger wants this thing cleared."

"What would you do if you weren't attracted to this suspect?"

She shrugged. "Prove he did it and nail him. Or exonerate him and try to jump his bones."

"Well?"

"It's hard. Every time I'm near him, I just want to . . . you know!"

"You could ask Detective Viernes to do the close-in work."

This time she smiled. "You mean tell him I'm allergic or something?"

"Would that work?"

"It just might. What if we close the case?"

"Then you're on your own."

THIRTY-SEVEN

Ten A.M. Thinnes, Franchi, the sergeant, and the custodian were the only ones in the squadroom when the phone rang.

The sarge got it. "Thinnes, your kid's on the phone."

Thinnes picked up.

"Dad?"

"Rob, what's up?"

"I'm at Highland Park Hospital."

"Christ! You hurt?"

"I'm okay. But Dad—the car's totaled."

"Hang tight. I'll be there." He put down the phone and told Franchi, "I gotta go. Rob just crashed my car."

"Is he all right?"

"Yeah."

"You got wheels?"

"I'll sign out a squad."

She took out her keys. "You're not in enough trouble?" He shrugged. She tossed him the keys. "I take it you got insurance?"

He nodded. "Thanks."

Highland Park Hospital was a red brick complex located west of Green Bay Road, north of Park Avenue West. Thinnes followed the EMERGENCY signs to the ER entrance and parked as close as he could to the door. Inside, he gave his name to the receptionist and was referred to a short, middle-aged man in a white lab coat.

"How is he, Doctor?"

"He's shaken up, but he'll survive. In there." The doctor pointed to a room beyond the ER desk.

Thinnes followed his direction.

Sitting on the exam table, Rob was pale and looked younger than his age. He jumped down when he spotted Thinnes and started toward him, then stopped—obviously unsure of his reception. "Dad, I'm really sorry."

Thinnes rushed forward to hug him. "You're okay?"

"Yeah."

"What happened?"

"I was coming up Sheridan Road—just cruising, minding my own business—when this deer ran out in front. I swerved and lost it. I . . . I think I killed the deer."

"At least you didn't kill yourself. Let's go."

Out in the parking lot, Rob brightened when he spotted Franchi's Corvette. Thinnes cursed himself for not signing out a squad. He said, "Do you know what they did with the car?"

"They said they were having it towed to the Safety Center." Rob grinned. "Can I drive?"

"Don't push your luck."

When they were southbound on the Edens Expressway, Thinnes said, "You sure you're okay?"

"Yeah.

"Dad, I'm really sorry."

"Forget it."

They traveled several miles in silence. Then Thinnes said, "Did you ever wish you had a brother or sister?" He watched from the corner of his eye as Rob thought about it.

Rob looked out at the traffic, then back at Thinnes. "I guess I never really thought about it. I mean—I guess I liked having you and Mom to myself. But that's just how it's always been." He lowered the window, raised it when the heat from outside hit. He looked at Thinnes. "Are you trying to tell me you have a kid in Vietnam?"

"What makes you think that?"

"The box of Vietnam stuff you left in the kitchen. And you never asked me about being an only child before."

Smart kid. A few miles farther on, Rob said, "You didn't answer my question."

"I can't. I mean . . . I didn't fuck around over there. But I got wasted a few times. So I can't swear . . ."

"Then what's this about?"

Thinnes told him about the anonymous accusation.

"Sounds like bullshit to me. What're you gonna do?"

"Try to find out who made that call, I guess."

"That's why you got out the Vietnam stuff?"

"It had to be someone who knew me in Vietnam."

When he got back to the Area, Thinnes was grilled about the crash, then kidded about borrowing Franchi's car. Ferris, particularly, tried to make something of the fact that she'd never let anyone drive it before. Nobody bit, so Ferris asked if anyone had heard of Bambi's revenge.

"No, but I'm sure we're going to," Viernes said.

"These four hunters are coming back from Wisconsin with a deer on the luggage rack on top of their car. It's late. It's dark. Drizzling, so the road's wet. And this deer runs out in front of the car. The driver hits the brakes and loses it. Car hits a bridge support, gets crushed like a pop can. Two guys in the front seat get mashed. One of the guys in the back breaks his neck. The other wasn't wearin' a seat belt; he gets decapitated."

"Hunters one; deer four, huh, Ferris?"

"True story. I couldn't make up something that weird."

At a glance, Thinnes made the guy filling the conference room doorway for a cop. Near retirement age. Fit.

"You Thinnes?" An investigator, probably a former CPD dick. "I'm Paul McKenzie. With the State's Attorney."

"What can I do for you?"

"It's what *I* can do for you. I heard you got two open murders in Uptown that look like professional hits."

"Yeah?"

McKenzie handed him a sheet with fifteen RD numbers.

"What's this?"

"Cold cases—hits mostly—from Uptown. Some of 'em while I was at Area Three—back when it was Six, some of 'em I inherited. I think they were the work of one guy. You may want to review 'em, just in case I missed something."

"Why'd you give up on 'em?"

"I didn't. But you know, this ain't TV."

Thinnes nodded. They couldn't drop everything else unless it was a heater case. Even without the aggravated batteries and assaults, there weren't enough bodies in Violent Crimes to keep up. And the murder rate was job security. You did what you could.

"Thanks, McKenzie."

THIRTY-EIGHT

Maharis was still MIA, but Arthur reported he was improving and would probably be back soon. Arthur sat like a golden bear in his rocker, ankle resting on his knee, and rolled his ballpoint back and forth across the end of a yellow legal pad. He'd left the blinds half open and sun barred the polished oak floor with a tiger-pattern of light and shade.

"Alec," he said, "why don't you start?" Alec was sitting on a folding chair to Arthur's right. Between them, a small round table held a Tiffany lamp and a box of Kleenex. Behind Arthur, the ancient window unit at the bottom of the tall window struggled to banish the heat. Heat, Caleb reflected, not unlike that of Saigon. Stupefying.

Between Alec and Butch, Joe sat with his arms crossed over his chest and his legs splayed out in front. Caleb wasn't sure he was awake. Butch was awake, watching like a dog at dinnertime.

Arthur continued, "You've been having flashbacks?" Alec nodded. Arthur said, "Of what?"

"This . . ." Alec started. He stopped. Cleared his throat. "Guy where I work. Ah . . . worked. I don't anymore. Don't work there. Can't. It was in the paper . . ."

"Take a deep breath," Arthur said. Alec did. "Now start over."

"I used to work," Alec began, "at a commercial real estate agency. The name's not important. It was a small place—an owner/manager, fifteen agents, two secretaries, and me. They worked on commission—except me and the secretaries. It was kind of high-pressure but not too bad. I thought. Until, one day, Ambrose Penn—Penny—came to work with a gun and tried to kill us all."

Alec started sobbing. Arthur handed him the Kleenex box. Finally, Butch said, "Facts, man. What kind of gun?"

Alec stopped crying and snuffled. "I don't know." He blew his nose and added, "I didn't see it. Somebody screamed, 'He's got a gun!' and I dived under my desk. I just heard it. Loud. I was afraid to look out. He shot everybody else. Killed three of them. I'm the only one he didn't shoot. Somehow he missed me."

"Like Corazon Amurao?"

"What's that?"

"Who, not what. She was that nurse that survived when Richard Speck killed all the others. She hid under the bed and he forgot her. Or maybe he couldn't count." Butch shrugged. "Anyway, she lived; all the others died."

"I keep having these—" Alec rubbed his eyes with the heels of his hands. "They're like waking dreams where he comes back for me. I was so scared I couldn't even dial 911. I couldn't move. I couldn't make myself . . ."

"What could you have done?" Butch's tone was derisive. "Beside get your*self* killed?"

"I don't know. The point is, I just hid while he slaughtered everyone else."

"So you're feeling guilty 'cause you're not dead."

"Of course. I didn't even try."

"You bein' dead, would that bring back any of 'em?"

Alec shook his head.

"Have you had any firearms training?" Arthur asked.

"No."

"Combat experience?"

"No."

"Self-defense?"

"No."

Caleb said softly, "I've seen seasoned veterans freeze under fire."

"So?"

"It wasn't your day." Joe spoke for the first time.

"It wasn't anybody's day," Alec said.

"No, I mean, it wasn't your day to die."

Alec looked at him as if he'd lost his mind. "After the SWAT team took Penny away, they pulled me out. I'll never forget walking past the secretary's desk. She was lying in blood. Her eyes were open. It was raining when she came to work and she left her umbrella open to dry behind her chair. It was splattered with her blood."

"Bad luck to open an umbrella indoors," Butch looked at Caleb. "I bet you got a rotten-luck story, too. Don't you, Jack?"

A tiny breeze ruffled the treetops but didn't make it down to ground level. The air seemed to be half water, heavy, palpable. It muffled the chatter of unseen monkeys. Fluffy cumulus showed through the canopy beneath which Caleb lay trying to estimate the trees' height. Taller than a city bus was long. Taller than the hundred-year-old oak trees in his yard back home in Kenilworth.

He couldn't see his squad mates but he could smell them. He wondered idly why; he must have smelled, too. None of them had bathed in weeks; their clothes were moldy from repeated soakings, from sweat and humidity. Their cigarette smoke tempered the BO the way perfume covered the fish smell of the whores they patronized on their days off.

"How's your headache, Harlan?" Professional courtesy. Caleb didn't really care. It wasn't life-threatening.

Hidden to his left, Harlan said, "Better, Doc. Thanks."

Caleb had given him APCs—aspirin-phenacetin-caffein tablets, the standard medicine for every small pain. The only real remedy was a trip back to the world, a cure Caleb couldn't prescribe. He sat up. To his left, Froggy was asleep. To his right Ethan Allen—so called because he was from Vermont—was changing his socks.

"Fuck. You should at least be carrying a sidearm, Doc," Ethan Allen said. He'd been trying to arm Caleb since he was assigned to the squad to replace Hemingway. Hemingway had gone home minus a leg but still breathing.

As if he'd read Caleb's mind, Preacher called out, "Think Hemingway's back home yet?"

Caleb shifted so he could see Preacher and watch the smoke dissipate from his cigarette. Preacher took another drag. Gunner lay beyond him, fingers laced behind his head.

"Who the fuck's Hemingway?" Ethan Allen demanded.

Gunner, who was black, said, "Fuckin' dead white guy."

"A dead fuckin' writer," Harlan corrected. He was the platoon's RTO. "Don't you assholes know anything?"

"He was a guy in our squad who used to write a lot," Preacher said. "So we called him Hemingway."

Ethan Allen said, "How the fuck d'he die?"

"Fuck!" Gunner laughed. "*Our* Hemingway ain't dead. He gone back to the world."

"You assholes are fuckin' nuts," Ethan Allen said. He told Caleb, "You still need a fuckin' weapon."

"My second canteen is more likely to save my life."

Ethan Allen snorted. "You meet Charlie, you fuckin' gonna throw water on him?"

"Maybe," Caleb said. "Worked for Dorothy."

"Who the fuck's Dorothy?"

Harlan sat up and grinned. "We sure as hell *ain't* in Kansas anymore."

From the tall grass between the trees and the river the sergeant's voice croaked, "Shut the fuck up! Ethan Allen, you got watch. Rest of you bastards get some shut-eye."

It started to rain the next day, midmorning, just as the squad stumbled into a landscape of rice paddies. The hamlet attached to the fields wasn't a free-fire zone, so the lieutenant told them, "Search it. Carefully."

Like most places they'd been, it was eerie—just old people and small kids who never said a word when the legs rousted them and searched their hooches. It started raining and the villagers—perhaps a dozen people—stood out in their black pajamas and conical straw hats, staring like cattle. The grunts didn't care. They were soaking, too.

There weren't any water buffalo, though something must have been used to plow the acres of paddies. They didn't search the people. Some companies did that, but the new sergeant had enough sense to not allow it without evidence it was necessary. They didn't find anything. The RTO reported as much, and the lieutenant told them to move out.

They cut across the paddies, through the rain and water, trampling the young rice plants. They didn't walk on top of the dikes between fields because Charlie liked to booby-trap anyplace easy to walk. But they had to cross the dikes to get from one field to the next. About half the platoon had scrambled over the last of them when Ethan Allen started screaming. He swung something whiplike around his head, shaking the hand it was attached to.

"Hold still, man," Froggy screamed.

Harlan yelled, "Medic! Doc!"

There were bursts of rifle fire. The whiplike something flew away from Ethan Allen's arm. He fell into the rice paddy. Preacher hauled him out and half threw him on the dike.

Firmly attached to the fleshy part of Ethan Allen's hand was the head of a huge cobra. Ethan Allen lay staring at it, screaming. "Get it off me! Get it off!"

He might have thrashed himself to death if Preacher and Harlan hadn't held him down. Gunner took out his bayonet and was starting surgery by the time Caleb got to them. Gunner pried the head loose and threw it halfway across the rice field, where it landed with a splash among the seedlings.

Ethan Allen's hand was white. Bright blood beaded the skin in rows where the snake's teeth penetrated. Caleb applied a tourniquet above the elbow.

Meanwhile, Gunner picked up the body of the snake and whipped it against the dike, splattering blood and mud and water into the air, screaming, "Fuck! Fuck! Fuck!"

As Caleb started an IV, Ethan Allen whimpered. His arm

swelled and started turning purple. His pressure dropped. But fluids won't enter once circulation stops.

Quite suddenly, Ethan Allen was dead. Acute shock, Caleb thought, or maybe he'd just died of fright.

Staring at the corpse, Harlan gulped. He turned to Caleb. "Quick! Dorothy, click your heels together three times and say, 'There's no place like home!' "

Preacher took his helmet off, paying his respects.

The sergeant came up and slapped him on the back of the head. "What're you, some fucking FNG?"

The only dry place for a dust-off landing was the hamlet cemetery. They'd been in country long enough to recognize it for what it was. They didn't care. As the Huey set down in the middle, Preacher muttered that disrespecting the dead would bring bad luck. The rest of the guys stood smoking, watching as Ethan Allen was loaded in the chopper. All the while a steady rain was falling.

They pitched their butts among the graves as the Huey lifted. It got almost to the woods beyond the paddies when Charlie began throwing RPGs at it. One caught the chopper in the tail; it went down smoking. And blew up on impact.

Two fields away, the men in the cemetery took cover, squatting behind the dike in a foot of water. The machine gunner opened up while Harlan called in their location.

Before long, artillery rounds ringed their position with fire and brimstone. The trees beyond the fields disappeared in black smoke and red and yellow flame. The hamlet vanished under a hail of rockets. Artillery shells cratered the rice fields, flattening the seedlings with tsunamis of steam and smoke, raining mud and shrapnel on the ruins and the tiny burial ground.

When Caleb finished speaking, the group was quiet for a long time. The window air-conditioning unit throbbed.

Butch finally broke the silence. "So you goody-goodies wiped out a village?"

"Not intentionally."

"That make 'em any less dead?"

THIRTY-NINE

Caleb got the news at two in the morning and went straight to the hospital. He beat his father's personal physician there by fifteen minutes—something that wasn't supposed to happen when the patient was as famous as Arthur Caleb.

As it happened, death had beat them both by an hour. The night nurse was beside herself because she'd been prevented from starting resuscitative measures by the DNR order on Arthur Caleb's chart and by the resident. Caleb had made it very clear to him, earlier, that under no circumstances should that order be ignored.

He spent the better part of the next hour comforting the nurse. And reassuring the resident. And telling the physician that nothing more could have been done. It was an hour after that before Caleb could confront his father's remains.

The death had not been unexpected, though no one anticipated it would come so soon. Arthur Caleb died alone—pretty much as he had lived.

Caleb stood over the bed. No one had dared pull the sheet up, though the old man's eyes were closed. Caleb marveled briefly at how he'd shrunk in the last two months, the giant who'd towered over him in childhood reduced to a fragile remnant, a cinder, a shade.

Caleb took brief note, too, of how little he felt. His father had died for him long ago. Now he experienced only regret for the passing of someone who might have shared his knowledge had he lived.

He didn't touch the corpse. He pulled the sheet over his father's face and left the room, turning the light out before he closed the door.

Arthur Caleb had lived in Lake Point Towers. Caleb accompanied Rosemary there to select something for the funeral home to dress him in. Caleb was going through Arthur's cufflink drawer when he came across a familiar memento. He was staring at it when Rosemary came out of the walk-in closet with Arthur's favorite suit.

"What've you got there?"

He handed her the Silver Star he'd received for killing the sniper in Vietnam.

Their newest lieutenant stalked up to the hooch where Caleb was sharing a six-pack with Froggie and Preacher.

"Corporal Caleb," the lieutenant snapped. "You're going to be awarded a Silver Star this afternoon."

"No, thank you, sir."

"You don't have a choice, soldier. You will present yourself at the parade ground, in uniform, at sixteen hundred hours. You will fall out when told to do so, stand at attention while they pin your medal on, salute smartly, and fall back in. What you do with it after you're dismissed is your business. But if you fuck it up, you'll be serving the rest of your tour at the LBJ ranch. Is that understood?"

The LBJ ranch. Long Binh Jail.

Caleb had said, "Yes, sir!"

"Where did he get this?" Rosemary asked. "I'm sure he would've let us know if it was his."

"It was mine."

"When did you give it to him?"

"I didn't. After the ceremony, I pitched it."

"But you went back and retrieved it."

"No. I've no idea how Arthur got it. Maybe one of my buddies saved it in case I changed my mind."

"Maybe we'll never know."

"Maybe when we go through his things we'll find a diary."

She looked shocked. "Father a diarist?"

"He had the ego for it."

"Anyway, I think you should keep it." She handed him the medal, and he put it in his pocket.

He still had the Silver Star when he got to the funeral home to inspect the arrangements. Robert had selected the venue, one of the most expensive on the North Shore. Pure guilt. Caleb would've chosen a place convenient for Rosemary and the few friends the family had left. But they hadn't discussed it. Robert made the big decisions and left it to Rosemary to handle the details—like going to Arthur's condo for his clothes and taking them to the funeral director. He hadn't consulted Caleb at all.

From everything Caleb heard, Robert was a success. But though a competent surgeon, he was too cautious to approach Arthur's brilliance. Robert wasn't a raving narcissist. He was too concerned with his patients' welfare to take the chances with their lives. And he was too jealous of his older brother to appreciate his own gifts. All his adult life, he'd hated Caleb for not being the son Arthur wanted, for being a shrink instead of heir to Arthur's legacy, for being gay. Robert resented Caleb's abdication. Caleb understood. But he wondered if Robert ever would.

There was a discreet cough, and the funeral director sidled up. "Dr. Caleb? Come this way if you would."

Caleb followed him into a lavishly appointed parlor. At the far end, can lighting illuminated the bier. The usual ranks of folding chairs filled the middle ground.

Caleb approached the coffin. Surrounded by a truckload of floral arrangements, Arthur looked as real as he ever had. The ensemble Caleb and Rosemary had chosen was suitably dignified. The morticians had managed to make Arthur look like something from Madame Tussaud's wax museum.

Caleb turned to his host. "Could I have a moment alone?"

"Certainly." The man turned and vanished.

Caleb put his hands in his pockets and tried to decide what he felt. Nothing. No loss. No remorse. Arthur had paid the bills and set impossibly high standards. He'd never been a presence in Caleb's life.

Caleb found his fingers brailling the Silver Star. It was another of the many things they'd disagreed on. For Arthur, it meant supreme achievement. For Caleb, official recognition of failure to live up to his ideals.

He slipped the medal into the pocket of Arthur's suit.

FORTY

When Thinnes came into the squadroom the next morning, the place was nearly deserted—just Franchi, the sergeant, and the custodian emptying wastebaskets.

After Thinnes filled his coffee mug, Franchi handed him a letter addressed to *Det. Thins, Chicago PD.* Someone had added, *Thinnes, John, Area Three.*

He opened the envelope and read the enclosed note: *I herd you was disturbin' the dead, old buddy, so I thought I better drop you a line. Some things are best left buried.*

It was from a guy he'd met in 'Nam. It wasn't signed, but Thinnes knew who'd sent it.

The postmark was Palatine, which meant it was mailed in one of the north suburbs. He handed it to Franchi.

"When I was in Saigon, there was a guy named Mike Corso, a corporal in the infantry—I don't remember what division, but he was from the Chicago area. I'm pretty sure this is from him. Any chance you could look him up?"

Franchi nodded and gave him back the letter. "You think he's our white cat?"

"No. But whatever's going on, he's getting a cut."

An hour later, Franchi handed Thinnes a sheaf of printouts. "Fifteen Mike or Michael Corsos listed in the city, ten more in the suburbs. I leave it to you to narrow the list. But if you find him . . ."

"You'll be the first to know."

A phone rang. The sergeant answered. "Thinnes, you got a visitor." He put the receiver down and added, "On his way up."

The visitor was Tien Lee. He strolled into the squadroom like a cat in familiar territory. He took his time getting to where Thinnes and Franchi were waiting. He nodded at Franchi and said, "Detective."

Her reaction was probably too subtle for Lee to notice, but Thinnes could tell she was off balance. He wondered if she was pissed because Lee had come to see him.

"I was going through my mother's things," Lee said. "I found this." He handed Thinnes a letter in Vietnamese.

Thinnes looked it over and made an *oh, yeah?* face.

Lee grinned. "You don't read Vietnamese?"

It was gibberish to Thinnes.

"It's from a friend of my mother," Lee said. "Hoa Nhài. You were asking about a woman named Jasmine. Hoa Nhài means Jasmine."

Thinnes said, "No shit!"

Lee almost smiled. "The letter is mostly chitchat. There's no date. The relevant part says she's afraid she'll be devoured by the White Tiger."

Thinnes felt the prickle of adrenaline tugging his back hairs upright. Then he realized Lee was saying something in Vietnamese. "What was that?"

Lee repeated, *"Tat den nha ngoi cung nhu nha tranh.* Roughly, it means all cats are gray in the dark. So why a *white* tiger? Do you suppose she meant a Caucasian?"

"She may just have meant a deadly SOB."

FORTY-ONE

The funeral home had Oriental rugs, pricey wood furniture, and a highly polished staff. They'd cranked the A/C up high enough to form condensation on the windows. Thinnes was grateful. In a lot of places the temperature was eighty-eight degrees.

He went to a lot of wakes and funerals in his official capacity. This was different. This time he signed the book, even put down his home address. This time he waited in line to offer condolences to the family and stand over the casket to view the body. Not to pay respects. He hadn't known the deceased, and Caleb never mentioned him. That made it harder. He had no idea what to say beyond the standard, *Sorry for your loss.*

Out of habit more than anything, he studied the crowd. There were fifty or sixty people, lots of men in two-thousand-dollar suits, women in things that looked equally pricey. Doctors and lawyers, mostly. He knew from the obit Arthur Caleb had been a respected surgeon, so it was a good bet most of the people were medically inclined. No one looked over sixty, though. Caleb was forty-six, so his old man had to have been up in years. Odd at least a few friends his own age hadn't showed. Nobody looked particularly broken up, either. But people showed their grief in all sorts of ways.

Franchi came and took her place in line. The line moved forward. Caleb was standing next to an attractive thirty-something woman who—judging by the resemblance—was the daughter mentioned in the obit. Caleb's sister. The man with her was most likely her husband—they were holding hands. And had matching rings. Thinnes picked out the brother, too—*son Robert,* who maintained a puzzling distance.

"Detective Thinnes?"

He turned. The knockout redhead seemed familiar.

"I was a brunette last time we met."

And observant and quick. "Miss Morgan." The girl he'd met two summers ago, when her mother was murdered.

She giggled. "Call me Linny. D'you know Jack's dad?"

He shook his head.

"Me neither."

"Are you here by yourself?"

"My dad's around somewhere. Talking shop." She gave him a dazzling smile. She was only sixteen, just trying out her developing powers.

"You go to a lot of these?" she asked.

"Too many."

Her eyes widened, then she must've realized he meant professionally and she relaxed. "What do you say? I mean, *Sorry your dad croaked* seems pretty lame."

He grinned. "You don't have to say anything. Sometimes a handshake or a hug is enough."

"I'll watch you."

When Thinnes's turn came, Caleb greeted him with a handshake and introduced him to the family—Robert, Rosemary, and Victor—as a friend. No mention of his occupation. Robert accepted the introduction with an obvious effort to be gracious. Hostility from strangers came with Thinnes's job; Robert's attitude was a mystery. Some animosity toward Caleb extending to his brother's friends? Thinnes decided to hang around and learn more.

So he watched with amusement as Linny followed his example, improvising to the extent of hugging all the family enthusiastically. Even Robert seemed touched.

Franchi hugged Caleb and shook hands with Rosemary and Victor. She greeted Robert politely, but watched him the way a cat watches a bird.

• • •

As Thinnes put a hand on the men's room door, he heard a voice snarl, "Cure thyself!" Robert Caleb's voice.

Thinnes froze. He couldn't hear the response. Curiosity kept him from opening the door. Or backing away from it.

Robert persisted. "You felt *nothing* for him!"

"I never felt he was my father." Caleb's voice.

"You were his favorite!"

"I didn't ask to be."

"What did you expect? You were his firstborn."

"Once I matured enough to understand him, nothing."

"You're hopeless!"

The door jerked open. Robert Caleb blinked. His face hardened. He said, "Excuse me," and pushed past Thinnes.

Caleb had seen him when the door opened, so Thinnes went on in. If the doctor was embarrassed, he didn't show it. He said, "John," then walked out of the room. As Thinnes took care of business, it occurred to him Caleb had left abruptly to avoid making him feel uncomfortable.

When Thinnes came out of the john, Caleb was in the foyer, talking to Linny Morgan's dad.

Thinnes let the door go, and it closed with a soft thud. Caleb and Morgan increased the distance between them with a practiced casualness. Thinnes wondered why. But he didn't ask. He simply nodded as he passed.

He wasn't sure why he hung around. Curiosity, maybe. By nine-fifteen, he was the only nonfamily member left. Robert Caleb stopped on his way out to talk to the funeral director, not with his family. Victor and Rosemary hugged Caleb, shook hands with the funeral home staff, and left. The staff disappeared.

When Thinnes approached Caleb to say good night, the doctor asked, "Are you in a hurry?"

Thinnes shook his head. He wasn't now.

"Would you join me for a brandy?"

The invitation was irresistible. To his surprise, Caleb led him to the funeral director's office. As plush as the rest of the place, it

164

had the same pricey rugs and furniture, but comfortable chairs as well, and side tables with reading lamps and Kleenex boxes. Caleb offered him a seat, then opened a cabinet containing an assortment of glasses and an impressive stock of booze.

"There're other things here . . ."

"Brandy's fine."

Caleb poured it into snifters and put the bottle back. He handed a glass to Thinnes and sat down. "To peace."

"Peace."

They sat in comfortable silence. While Caleb got to the point, Thinnes played with the liquor, swirling it, watching it climb the glass's sides. He was good at waiting.

Eventually Caleb said, "When we were children, Robert considered Arthur God. I was the one he asked for help, the good example.

"I was fifteen when my mother died. And I went from straight-A student to total fuckup."

"That a technical term?"

"Absolutely.

"Anyway, Robert never bothered with psychology; he was seriously disillusioned. When I abandoned the role of good son, he dutifully stepped in and assumed what's turned out to be a thankless position. He's never forgiven me. He's become a well-regarded surgeon, but he's not happy. He adopted our father's beliefs about homosexuality as well. When I came out, he was doubly disappointed."

"But you seem happy; you've done well enough."

"He can't see that."

They were quiet for a while. Thinnes swirled the brandy. It was one of those timeless moments when life's on hold while you do what you need to do, however unrelated to what you've been doing. He waited, turning the tables on the shrink.

Caleb eventually went on. "My father tried to warn me I'd be drafted if I didn't straighten up and go to college. Naturally, I started skipping school and smoking pot. I dropped out when I turned sixteen. I wasn't a C.O. from the onset. I wasn't interested in the war. Not that I was averse to defending my country; I just

165

knew without thinking deeply that the war was about drawing a line in the sand and being too macho to back off. And I was too wrapped up in skirmishing with my father to give any thought to a place I couldn't locate on a map.

"When I filled out my draft registration, I put down conscientious objector more to be contrary than anything else—sort of along the lines of, *You can make me register but you can't make me fight.* What would be diagnosed today as oppositional defiant disorder.

"Since I wasn't a Quaker the draft board had me in to justify my request for C.O. status. I didn't back off, so they classified me as 1-AO. It counted the same for their draft quota as 1-A. I guess they figured the Army would straighten me out.

"My friends told me I was nuts. 'There's no way you're gonna get a deferment. They're gonna ship you over there to get shot at and you won't even have a gun to shoot back with.'

"Sure enough. A month after my eighteenth birthday, I got a draft notice.

"The army rightly recognized C.O.s as a contagion threatening its war machine. In basic, I was singled out and harassed. It made me determined not to give in. I perfected the art of passive-aggressive resistance."

"Passive-aggressive resistance? Is that a Freudian slip?"

"Not at all. I paid close attention to everything they taught and never missed a chance to point out inconsistencies—like being drafted to fight for freedom. I made sure I was the best in my group at every noncombat duty they assigned. I got fit. I was always pressed and polished, clean-cut and clean shaven. I read the manuals and learned the regulations. I even stayed straight and sober so I was ready for verbal combat at all times. But I never would touch a gun or a bayonet. It drove them crazy. I think they probably threw a party when my orders were cut to report to Fort Sam Houston."

After another pause, Caleb continued. "Like most, I interpret what happens to me in a way that reduces cognitive dissonance."

"Yeah?"

"We judge the grapes we can't reach to be sour; we look for silver linings."

"Ah."

"Those of us who went to Vietnam cite survival, or character development, or the close friendships we developed as good consequences of a tragic mistake."

"If life gives you lemons . . . What's your point?"

"Vietnam made me who I am today. If I hadn't gone I'd probably have drifted through life until I died of AIDS or OD'd. As it is, I've become a better man than my father. Isn't that what we all strive for?"

"Those of us who had good fathers try to measure up."

Caleb nodded. "Robert can't see any of that. He's never seen Arthur for the narcissist he was."

"He never did military service?"

"Robert? No."

They thought about that for a while. Finally, Thinnes said, "If you knew then what you know now, would you have gone?"

Caleb shrugged. "Moot question. I'm not the same man."

FORTY-TWO

The day after Arthur Caleb's funeral, Thinnes stopped by Tien Lee's dojo. It was lunchtime and the place was deserted. Lee suggested they sit on the visitors' chairs along the wall. "What's on your mind?" Lee asked.

"Did you ever hear your mother mention Theo Ragland?"

"I doubt they ever met. Is there a connection to my mother's murder?"

"I don't know. Tell me more about your parents. Anything about 'em that'd piss someone off enough to kill?"

"It's hard to know what would make anyone kill."

Thinnes waited.

"My father was a man of unbending principle. That sometimes put him in conflict with others.

"When I was very young, he would take me to work with him. I was quiet, so he'd let me hang around while he conducted business. Sometimes he'd ask me to get coffee or photocopy something—errands. He never introduced me. He never intervened when someone mistook me for an employee or servant or spoke to me disrespectfully. Occasionally he would ask what I thought of this person or that, and he would always make me justify my opinion. As first I was hurt by this. I felt that if he weren't ashamed of me he would introduce me as his son.

"One day I was so insulted by a man pursuing my father's custom that I spoke to my father about my feelings. He said that the true test of a man's character is how he treats those he believes have no power. He asked whether I would do business with the man who had insulted me. And when I told him no, he said, 'Neither would I.' "

Lee gave a little smile. "After my father died, that same man was quite anxious to acquire his business."

"Did he?"

"No."

"Revenge is sweet."

"Not at all. When he came to discuss terms, he was clearly surprised to find Étienne Lee was Asian. I could see on his face the precise moment he realized I was the child he'd treated badly years before. I could also see him decide to pretend we'd never met. He hadn't changed. He was still the sort of man with whom my father would never do business."

Franchi was in the squadroom when Thinnes got back. "You get anything on Lee's financial situation?" he asked.

"You're off the case, Thinnes."

"No, I know."

She didn't look willing to budge.

"Look, put yourself in my place."

She let her breath out slowly, so he could see her aggravation. He waited. Finally she looked around the empty squadroom and flipped open the file on her desk. She paged through it, then slammed it shut and said, "Sold his father's consulting firm two years ago for ten million. Bought Martial Artists for cash. Nothing here on what he did with the rest of the money. What he said about money not making up for his mother's death is true on the face of it—assuming he doesn't have any *Mommy Dearest* issues."

"Did he have any other offers for his father's business— besides the one he accepted?"

She shrugged. "Is it important?"

"Maybe."

"I'll take it under advisement."

Later Franchi dropped a photocopy in front of him.

"Tien Lee turned down eleven million for Lee et Fils. The losing bidder charged discrimination. He's white. Lee's Asian; the CEO's Korean. My source says the guy wanted to sue but couldn't get anyone to take the case. Lee et Fils is a veritable UN, and Tien was personally loved—going back to when he was a kid. Lee was quoted as saying the overall package offered by the competing firm was better for the company's employees.

"You knew that, didn't you?"

"I heard something about it."

"From whom? C'mon, Thinnes. Give or that's the last you hear about this case from me."

"Lee told me."

"Are you crazy? What were you doing talking to him?"

"I had to know if his mother knew Ragland. Hue's friend had the same name as Ragland's girlfriend—who was killed by the same asshole that killed Hue."

"Have you told Evanger?"

"Not yet."

"Lee tell you why he turned down the higher offer?"

"He didn't mention money. He said the bidder wasn't the kind of man his father would do business with."

Franchi gave him an *Oh, yeah?* look.

"He's either the most principled man I've run across since I met Bobby, or the best liar I've met in years."

"You trust him!"

"About as far as I can throw a bus."

"Then why are you jeopardizing our case?"

"We don't have a case. Just a dead woman with no enemies. But someone had a reason to kill her. Whatever it is, it involves me. And since she's dead, the only person who might connect the dots is her son."

"Fine. Just let me and Joe sort it out."

"How? You weren't in Saigon. What makes you think you'd recognize a motive or even the players?"

She shook her head. "I'm gonna dig deeper. If Lee as much as failed to return a library book, I'll find out."

"Then what?"

"We'll see."

"Why all of a sudden are you so anxious to nail him?"

"On paper, he looks too good to be true. Nobody's that good. And what if he *did* kill his mother? He may be stringing you along to find out what you know."

"And killed Ragland to shut him up?"

She frowned. "Possibly."

"Then we'll nail him. I need to know what kind of man he is. To do that, I gotta spend time with him. Besides, he speaks Vietnamese. He can translate for me."

"And tell you whatever he wants you to hear!"

"I'll give you names. You can go back with a translator."

"Thinnes, you're nuts! This is nuts! I'm nuts to even consider going along with it."

FORTY-THREE

Thinnes looked up from the report he was reading when the desk sergeant interrupted the conversation Franchi was having with the custodian.

"Franchi, someone downstairs to see you, a Ms. Crone."

"She say what about?" Franchi asked.

"Probably trying to serve you with papers."

"Yeah, right!" She dug in her suitcase-sized purse for her notebook and paged through it. "Here," she told Thinnes. She tapped the notebook. "Sabra Crone. Met her at Ragland's funeral; asked her to come in for an interview." She looked at the sergeant. "Have them send her up."

He nodded, then said to Thinnes, "When are you going to do something with those files you ordered?" He hooked his thumb back toward his counter.

"What files?"

"Damned if I know. You ordered 'em."

"Oh. Yeah." The cases Paul McKenzie had put him on to. More work.

"Hang on to them for me. I'll get to them as soon as I can."

To Thinnes's surprise, Sabra Crone was Asian—or at least half Asian. She was tiny, dressed in a smart navy suit that looked like one of Franchi's outfits. Franchi led her into the squadroom and offered her a seat, then gave Thinnes a look that said, *Get your notebook out.*

He brought coffee for the three of them, then parked out of the women's line of sight.

"At the funeral," Sabra began, "you said to call if we had any information about Theo . . ."

Franchi nodded encouragingly.

"He was engaged to my aunt. Long ago. In Saigon. Aunt Nhài was shunned by our family because she was a prostitute and engaged to a *người Hoa Kỳ*—an American.

"But when we came here, the rules changed. Being from a good family wasn't as important as having a sponsor in the States. And Uncle Theo treated us like family, even though he and Nhài never married. He helped us get jobs and deal with paperwork. He brought some of us home to meet his family.

"I know he would never kill himself. He was a Christian. I want to help catch whoever killed him."

Franchi nodded again. "You have some information?"

"I heard my parents arguing about Uncle Theo. I'm sure they know something, but they're afraid to go to the police. My mother would, but my father forbid it."

"Do you have any idea about what?"

"No, but it must be very important. They never fight."

"Could you persuade your mother to talk to us?"

"No. But maybe you can. Maybe if you tell her that you know she knows . . ."

Franchi had court that afternoon. And the next morning, Thinnes had an early meeting with Columbo, the assistant state's attorney. So they didn't get to look up Sabra Crone's parents until nearly lunchtime.

Crone was a veteran, his wife Vietnamese. Their restaurant was in Uptown—surprise. The place was staffed by their respective family members.

Crone told Thinnes and Franchi that he met his wife when he helped pull her from the South China Sea after the fall of Saigon. "For a while, all our profits went into buying her family free.

And we still get letters from 'relatives' no one ever heard of, begging us to sponsor them. But it's all about family, and we're doing okay."

He wasn't enthusiastic about letting them talk to his missus. "She knows nothing about Theo," he insisted. "I hired him. I supervised him."

"You speak Vietnamese?" Franchi asked. Atta girl!

"A little."

"So you can't be sure she and Ragland never spoke."

"No."

Franchi raised her eyebrows and waited.

Crone finally said, "I'll get her."

Mrs. Crone was a small, serene woman who listened politely to Franchi's questions, then looked at her husband before answering. As Crone predicted, she told them she hadn't known Ragland. She could not imagine why he was murdered. And she had no clue about who had killed him.

Thinnes didn't believe her, especially her answer to the last question—she couldn't make eye contact as she spoke. And she was *way* too relieved when Franchi said, "Thank you, Mrs. Crone."

He didn't think Franchi was any more satisfied, but it was clear they wouldn't get anything out of her with her husband around. Still, he gave it one more try. "Your daughter was at Theo Ragland's funeral, Mrs. Crone. Was he a friend of hers?" He thought she looked as frightened as when Franchi asked if she knew who'd killed him. But all she said was, "I don't know."

At the restaurant door, Thinnes said, "Long as we're here and it's lunchtime . . ."

"You trying to get me hooked?"

While they waited for their orders, a crew of efficient, interchangeable young Asians brought them tea, utensils, egg rolls, and a large bowl of rice. Thinnes doubted he could pick one out of a lineup.

The restaurant never got less crowded. As soon as a table opened up, the young men cleared it, and Mrs. Crone repopulated it from the line at the door.

The food was good and plentiful. They finished eating and were waiting for a check when a crash on the street out front sent them—along with half the other patrons—to the front window to see what was happening.

A CTA bus sat in the middle of the street, blocking both lanes of traffic. The driver's side of a shiny black BMW was wrapped around the bus's right front fender. The Beemer's air bag had deployed; the driver was unhurt. He gestured wildly as he talked into a cell phone. The bus driver, a middle-aged black female with cornrows, was leaning resignedly on her steering wheel with her radio handset to her ear. Obviously the Beemer had been nailed when it cut off the bus.

"Once in a while there's justice," Franchi said.

They went back to their places; other patrons did the same. Thinnes signaled the waitress, and she hurried over. When she glanced at the table, her eyes widened. She put a hand over her mouth.

"What's the matter?" Thinnes asked. He looked down. Everything was as they'd left it but the rice bowl. Someone had stuck a pair of chopsticks in it. Upright.

The waitress said, "Nothing. I'm sorry." But her eyes strayed back to the bowl. "You're finished?"

They had been but Thinnes said, "No. Give us a few minutes." When she was gone, he told Franchi, "I need to make a phone call. Keep an eye on our rice."

"What? What's up?"

He pointed at the bowl. "Did you notice how the waitress reacted when she saw this?"

"No, but—"

"Did you put those chopsticks there?"

"No."

"Well, somebody did. And it means something."

He went outside and used his cell.

Tien Lee answered, "Good afternoon. Martial Artists."

"Mr. Lee, just the man I need to talk to."

"How may I help you?" In the background, Thinnes heard a chorus of "Hai's." Lee must have hired another teacher.

"Any significance to chopsticks stuck upright in a rice bowl?"

"Something you've seen recently, I take it? What makes you think it might be significant?"

"I recall hearing something. And I just saw someone react strangely to a rice bowl stuck with chopsticks."

"Ah. Then you'd better take care. For the superstitious, chopsticks standing erect in a bowl of rice is a sign of impending death."

Franchi looked like she was dying for a smoke, though she'd quit nearly a year earlier. "What's up?" she demanded.

"We're gonna need a doggie bag."

"Are you nuts?"

"And let's ask Mrs. Crone to come out so we can compliment her cooking." He signaled the waitress and asked for Mrs. Crone. The waitress backed nervously away.

This time, Franchi noticed. "What's with her?"

"Watch Mrs. Crone when she comes."

"You going to tell me what you found out?"

"We're being threatened. Or the Crones are." He repeated what his "source" had told him.

"Ridiculous," Franchi said. "A coincidence."

"I don't believe in coincidences. Anyway, let's see what our hostess thinks."

Mrs. Crone tried to be cool but she couldn't keep her eyes off the bowl. And she only half listened as Thinnes praised the food. When the waitress brought a plastic box and doggie bag, Mrs. Crone watched wordlessly while Thinnes shoveled the leftover rice into the container and stuck the chopsticks in the bag as well.

She followed them to the cash register and tried to keep them from paying, but Thinnes put a ten and a twenty on the counter and handed Mrs. Crone his business card.

"The change is for our waitress," he told her, "and if you re-member anything about Theo Ragland, please give me a call."

She nodded glumly. She didn't look at him, but she couldn't seem to take her eyes off the bag.

On the street outside, a crowd had gathered around the crash site, and several people were trying to get the bus driver to open her door. She wasn't having it, or letting her captive witnesses out of the bus, either. The Beemer driver was still ranting into his cell.

Thinnes sighed and handed Franchi the leftovers and the car keys. "Better see what's holding up patrol."

He took out his notebook and walked to the group waiting to board the bus. He flashed his star.

"Anybody who actually witnessed this can give me your name. The rest of you, move along."

"Where to next?" Franchi said as Thinnes approached the car. She was in the driver's seat. She'd started the motor and—thank, God!—the A/C. He opened the driver's door and jerked his thumb at the passenger's seat. Franchi shook her head but scooted over. When he was inside with his seat belt on, he answered. "The Crime Lab. See if Cọp Trắng left anything in our rice besides chopsticks. Or any fingerprints."

"You think he was actually in there?"

"Probably not. But he always had lots of help."

FORTY-FOUR

Mike Corso," Franchi reported as they headed west on Belmont, "was honorably discharged from the Army in September of '73 and hired by Chicago PD the following spring. Says here he worked part-time for an uncle while he was waiting to get on the job. He quit the job after someone beefed him for brutality in '77." She shut her notebook.

"Must've been grounds," Thinnes said. "You'd have to be half dead to get anyone to take a complaint seriously back then."

"Whatever. Anyway, he bought this bar—paid cash—and he's been running it ever since. Apparently he's keeping his nose clean—the only complaints are nickel-dime stuff."

"Or maybe he's got a powerful Chinaman."

Time hadn't done anything to improve Corso. He was sitting behind his bar, studying a racing form. It was only eleven A.M., but he was drinking MGD from a bottle. A cigarette smoldered in an ashtray full of butts at his elbow.

"Well, well," he said when he spotted Thinnes. "If it ain't Mr. Clean. What brings you in here?"

"I think you already know, Corso."

"You heard this was the best place on the North Side for a shot an' a beer?"

"Guess again."

"Drucker was right—you're too smart for your own good."

"Getting warmer."

"Maybe you gone over to the dark side. Lookin' for a payoff?"

"You got something to pay off for?"

"I'm clean as a fifth of Smirnoff. What do you want?"

"I'm still looking for the man who killed Jasmine."

"Who?"

"The hooker who was stabbed in the House of Flowers."

"A dead dink? A dink whore who's been dead twenty-five years? You're nuts!" He looked at Franchi for the first time. "You know how nuts your old man is?"

She smiled as if he'd paid them both a compliment.

"I hadn't thought about 'Nam for a long time," Corso told Thinnes. "I was hoping to keep it that way."

Thinnes kept waiting.

"Word was the White Tiger got her."

"Was there word about why?" Thinnes asked.

"That was twenty-five years ago!"

Thinnes kept waiting.

"I heard she wanted out. And she must've known the Tiger personal. That kept her in for life."

"Did you know Theo Ragland?"

"Name's not familiar. Refresh my memory."

"Black GI. Jasmine's boyfriend."

"Doesn't ring any bells. Anyway, the Tiger's girls didn't have boyfriends—except when they were working." Thinnes followed Corso's line of sight down the bar. Two men who'd been nursing beers when he and Franchi came in were still at it. "We done?" Corso said. "I got customers."

"Just one more question. White Tiger's real name."

"Your real name's the one you make for yourself. And he had a name for not leaving anyone alive who knew him by any other."

"The next winner," Franchi said, when they were back in the car, "is your deserter, Alvin W. Smith, a.k.a. Alvin Smythe, a.k.a. Smitty Grimes. Court-martialed for desertion in '72, dishonorably discharged a year later. Arrested since then for aggravated battery, possession with intent, pandering, and receiving stolen goods. Never convicted. Which is why he's still in the gun business."

"Maybe the same Chinaman," Thinnes said.

"Humph. Well, the shop he leases belongs to a land trust. He's been there fifteen years. Guy I spoke with in Gang Crimes said they think he supplies guns to the Kings *and* the Disciples but nobody's been able to prove it."

"I'll be damned!" Smitty said. "Duddly Do-Right! *Du mama,* Duddly." He leered at Franchi. "But then I guess you got something better to do."

Franchi was inspecting the handguns in the display case. She ignored the insult.

"Time hasn't improved your manners, Smitty," Thinnes said.

"You haven't changed, either, John-Boy. Still minding other people's business."

Franchi slapped her hand on the countertop, startling both men, getting their attention. She pointed to one of the guns in the case. "I'd like to see this one."

"You got a gun card?" Smith asked.

She flipped open her purse to show him her star.

Smith looked at Thinnes. "Still playing with white mice, I see. Though this one looks like a better breed." He sounded pleased with his clever analogy.

"You sure you want to play it this way?" Thinnes asked.

Smith laughed and pulled a fat bunch of keys from his side pocket. He opened the display case and pulled out the handgun Franchi'd pointed out, a small .38 revolver with an internal hammer. "Sure you can handle this, little lady?"

She picked up the gun, broke it open, spun the cylinder, flipped it back in place, and snapped off an imaginary round, all fast enough to make Smith blink. She shook her head and put the gun down. "Doubt this would have enough firepower."

Smith shoved the gun back in the case and clicked the lock shut. He glared at Thinnes. "You didn't come here to show off your girlfriend. What do you want?"

"The same thing I wanted last time we talked—who's the White Tiger?"

Smith laughed. "Ya know, that was a long time ago. I forget. *Xin loi.*"

Back in the car, Franchi asked, "What does *'Sin-loyee'* mean?"

"It means sorry about that. And *du mama* means just what it sounds like."

Ferris put down the report Thinnes had just finished on Smith and said, "A typical vet—nuts—like Ragland and Maharis."

"None of them was typical," Thinnes said. "And Ragland wasn't nuts. Millions of guys came back and just took up where they left off."

"Yeah?" Ferris sneered. "Name two."

"Including Thinnes?" Franchi asked. "How 'bout the sergeant over there, or Evanger, or Lieutenant Holton at Wentworth, or Chief Hillard? Ten bucks says a quarter of the guys on the job served in 'Nam."

"What about you, Ferris?" Thinnes asked. "You serve?"

Ferris reddened. "Yeah."

"In 'Nam?" Thinnes asked.

"No, but I served."

"What branch?"

"The National Guard."

"Guarding what?"

"Shooting students?" Franchi asked.

"Aw, fuck off!"

FORTY-FIVE

Maharis was back. "Sorry about your dad, Jack," he said as he took his usual place. The others had expressed their condolences at the wake. Now they made a point to ask how Caleb was doing. He wasn't eager to share his feelings about his father. And Maharis didn't want to talk about Ragman's death. So the group discussed reasons for the delays that sometimes occur between the trauma and PTSD.

Joe reported that he'd had no symptoms for years. Then one afternoon he found himself on the Jackson Boulevard Red Line platform, staring at the third rail. He had no recollection of how he'd come to be there. Or why.

He'd remember when he was ready, Caleb decided. He didn't seem ready today.

Alec had already told them about his traumatic experience. The result had been immediate—flashbacks, insomnia, and fearful, exaggerated reactions to every unanticipated event. He was working it through, and they listened without much comment.

Arthur gave him suggestions for homework, then directed everyone's attention to Caleb. "Why now? The event you flashed back to happened decades ago."

"I tried to reconstruct that. After I called you, I made myself watch the late news. The murdered woman's name was Lee, which sounded Chinese. But many Vietnamese have Chinese names. I read in the *Tribune* the next day that Lee was her married name. Her husband was Robert Lee, from Virginia. The two of them met during the war."

"So what was the connection?"

"I'm still not certain. Perhaps just the mention of a Vietnamese woman."

"What comes immediately to mind?"

"In 1970, when my first tour ended, I had a month off. I could've gone home, but I know I'd've ended up deserting. So I went to Bangkok—another story. When I got back in country, they sent me to Charlie Company, to replace their medic, who was KIA. He was the second medic they'd lost in three months, so the guys told me I was either going to be the charm or the third in their string of bad luck.

"Most of the combat units in country were undermanned most of the war. There were eight men in the squad, including me. It took me a week to sort them out."

The day Caleb arrived, the sergeant, who was black and older—twenty-five at least, was sitting on an ammo crate with his sleeves rolled to his biceps. He had a pack of Kools tucked into the left side. His legs were crossed at the ankles, jungle boots untied. The cigarette dangling from his mouth bobbed when he talked. He was sailing playing cards into an upturned baseball cap.

When Caleb got near, the sergeant looked him over. "You a fucking virgin, soldier?"

"No, Sarge," Caleb said.

"Why not, boy?"

"Virgins don't fuck, Sarge!"

The sarge nodded. "Where's your weapon, kid?"

"I'm a C.O. I don't carry a weapon."

"How the fuck you expect to stay alive if you can't shoot back, C.O.?"

"With respect, Sarge. A weapon didn't do your last medic much good."

The sergeant laughed and shook his head. "You can bunk with the Frog and the Preacher."

The Frog—Froggy—was Canadian, white, twenty-four;

Preacher a black Baptist, and all of twenty-three. The two had been together since basic, in country four months.

The other five guys were FNGs—eighteen- and nineteen-year-olds—and black. They were all into black power, not interested in getting to know any "honkies." So Caleb hung with Froggy and Preacher and got to know them pretty well.

One afternoon one of the other men asked, "What you readin', Doc?" Harlan was tall and thin with a face scarred by acne. He wore wire-rimmed glasses. He was reading, too.

Caleb held up his *Merck Manual*.

"But what *is* it?" Harlan said.

"A sort of do-it-yourself doctor manual," Caleb said. "AIT didn't cover half of what I'd have to deal with here."

Harlan nodded and held his own book up for inspection—James Baldwin's *The Fire Next Time*. "You ever read this?"

"No, but I've read his novels. Great writer."

"You could borrow this when I'm done." Caleb nodded. "Then we could talk about it. Best thing about reading a good book's talking about it." He looked around; no one else was there. "None of these turkeys read much."

"How old are you?" Caleb asked him.

"Nineteen. You?"

"Nineteen."

"Huh. You seem older."

"Maybe 'cause I've been here too long. This is my second tour."

"No shit! What the hell you re-up for?"

"I'm damned if I can remember. I must've been stoned."

"Jack," Joe said. "You're spacing out again."

"Sorry. When something gets me started thinking . . .

"I had too much time to think in 'Nam. One night, trying to get comfortable in my bunker, I thought about the fairy tale 'The Princess and the Pea.' Where do people come up with ideas like that? And what about 'Jack and the Beanstalk'? Didn't Joseph Campbell say the villain is the hero of his own myth? From the

Giant's point of view, it was a case of 'RESIDENT KILLED BY HOME INVADER.' Maybe some future generation of Vietnamese will tell the tale of an ogre who collected human body parts. And the ogre-killer will be depicted as a brave young soldier or heroic youth.

"It seemed like the whole war was a case of 'We're gonna save these people if we have to kill them to do it.' And once you start using questionable means, you're on the road to hell, *the gentle slope, soft underfoot, without sudden turnings, without mile-stones, without signposts . . .*' It changed you the way drug use did. After a while, you were completely different, but you couldn't see it."

"There was this guy in my unit," Maharis said, "that was hooked on Hanoi Hanna. He used to listen to her all the time. But then he'd get mad, 'cause she was spouting shit, he'd and change the station. Then he'd wonder what he was missing and turn her back on. He swore all she needed was a man, an' he could fuckin' straighten her out."

"What's that got to do with anything?" Butch demanded.

"Fairy tales," Maharis said. "Jack's stories aren't exactly fairy tales, but they're interesting."

"So don't interrupt."

A few weeks after Caleb joined his new unit, they were on patrol along the Cambodian border when it started to rain. Most of the men hated rain. The weather was usually hot and humid as a sauna anyway. And sometimes when it rained, you could see it turn to steam as it hit the road—where there were roads. After-ward, when the sun came out, it would rise as mist from the fields.

They took shelter under a rock formation that looked like a temple. A couple of the bloods started a card game; Preacher wan-dered over to watch. The game went on as the clouds blew away and the sun came out.

Caleb noticed Froggy casually check on the whereabouts of the others, then slip through the wet curtain of vegetation ringing the clearing. His furtive behavior gave Caleb to understand he wasn't just seeking privacy to take care of business. Caleb glanced around—everyone else was absorbed by the game.

Curiosity compelled him to follow Froggy. He quickly discovered there was no sneaking up on the Canadian. Caleb froze when he felt something small and hard press against the small of his back. He turned to face an M-16, with Froggy behind it. He felt fear, then rage, then relief.

Froggy grinned. He lowered the gun and put his fingers to his lips. Beckoning Caleb to follow, he moved off parallel to a faint game trail.

About a hundred yards deeper in the jungle, the path widened and crossed a little stream. The fall of one tree and the death of a lightning-blasted giant next to it created a small hole in the forest canopy. Sunlight streamed down into the resultant clearing, gilding the grass, highlighting a huge tiger stretched out in its warmth.

"Just between us, eh?" Froggy whispered.

Caleb understood. The others would shoot it just for the hell of it.

As softly as Froggy spoke, it was too loud. The tiger sprang to its feet and vanished.

Froggy sighed. "So beautiful. Just like the wild cats on my family's farm in Quebec. They kill so joyfully. But there is no sin in them, eh? So no guilt." He turned and started back toward where they'd left the others. "I wish I was like that."

"Guilt-free?"

"Pitiless." Froggy stopped and shrugged. He took a pack of Marlboros from his pocket and offered one to Caleb. "But God gave me a conscience. Not as troublesome as Preacher's, eh? He could never kill in cold blood." He lit his cigarette and took a long drag. "Well. Maybe to save someone else. But then he couldn't live with it. Eh?"

"And you could?"

Froggy laughed. "I'm a Catholic. We believe that if you confess, your sins will be forgiven."

. . .

"Jack, you ever gonna finish telling us about your buds?" Butch was frowning.

Caleb realized he'd spaced out again. "Where was I?"

"Nineteen seventy. Your second tour."

"Back in the world, the civil rights movement heated up, and blacks, especially draftees, were mad as hell and not going to take anything anymore. Morale was low, discipline was often poor. We were fighting NVA by then, when we were fighting at all. ARVN was supposed to take over the war. The average Vietnamese was more like us than not." Caleb looked at Butch, who—for once—didn't have a sarcastic comment. "But we sometimes saw their poverty as backwardness, their simplicity as stupidity, and we didn't recognize their compromises as adaptive. They got by as best they could. They grew catfish in the ponds that formed in the bomb craters, and shingled their roofs with flattened beer and soda cans. I don't know where they got ice without electricity, but in the towns along the highway, there were always people offering to sell us some, or 'code bee-ah' or 'boom-boom-numbah one good time with *sis-tah*.'

"I discovered Preacher felt as I did about them. Maybe he identified because of the prejudice he'd experienced. At any rate, he'd always volunteer to go along as bodyguard when I went into a local village for the Health Assistance Program.

"In one of the villages, we met a small girl—maybe ten or eleven—selling tiny red origami birds. They turned out to be made from labels off cans the Army threw in the dump outside the base. I bought two. One to take apart, to see how it was made. One for my sister. When I told Preacher, he said, 'You got a younger sister, too?'

" 'She's the one who keeps me supplied with socks and Corona salve.'

" 'No shit! I practically raised my kid sister. She's thirteen. Writes me every day.' "

"What's all this got to do with the dead woman in Uptown?" Butch demanded.

"Arthur's question started a chain of associations that reminded me of another dead woman.

"We called our hooch girl Mamasan. She came in twice a week to clean our hooches and take our dirty laundry home to wash. She was making fairly good money by Vietnam standards, but to some of us it seemed like slave labor.

"One day she didn't show. Gunner was sure she'd run off with our skivvies.

" 'Naw,' Harlan said. 'She finally heard about the Emancipation Proclamation.'

"Froggy said, 'Maybe she's sick or something. Eh?'

"We were on stand-down, with nothing better to do. So Froggy, Harlan, Preacher, and I got permission to go look her up. We found out she lived in a hamlet half a klick up the road. Sarge told us to take our weapons."

"You?" Butch demanded.

"I took my kit and what supplies I could spare.

"When we got there we found her stretched out in the street, shot full of holes. Along with three others who'd just been in the wrong place at the wrong time. We found one survivor, an old man left for dead. I did the best I could to patch him up. We buried the others."

They'd taken the old man back to the base to be evacked. The commotion brought the rest of the squad, who hung around to watch the dust-off. Walking back to the hooch, Froggy asked, "Think they'll ever find out what happened?"

"Probably not," Caleb said.

"Hey, Preacher," Harlan said, "if there's a God, why's He let all this shit happen?"

"God give us free will. He stop the shit, He take away our free will. He won't do that. It's *we* let this happen. Don't blame *God*. He makes *you* responsible for you."

"Nah," Harlan said. "If I was free, I *sure* as hell wouldn't be here."

"Maybe you's *in* hell," Gunner said. "For sure, you's a devil. Maybe you *deserves* to be here."

That got laughs, and nobody argued with it.

"What about things no one can control?" Caleb said. "Like cancer. Why does God let good people get cancer?"

"We all die. Good folks go to God. Early. Late. Don't make no nevah-mind. They's with God, they's happy. Don't matter what the folks they leave behind feels."

FORTY-SIX

When Thinnes came down to breakfast the next morning, Rhonda had already left for work. But Rob was still home. He was sitting at the table, going through the box of Vietnam stuff, studying, specifically, one photo taken in front of the MP barracks in Saigon. Thinnes helped himself to coffee and cereal and sat down across from him.

Rob put the photo down. "What was it like?"

"Really different. The people were small and dark and didn't speak English. It smelled like shit. Or incense. Or a farm. It was hot all the time. Hot and humid, or hot and dusty—but hot. It probably wasn't any noisier than here, but the sounds were different—you noticed them more.

"Certain times of the day—midday and after curfew—the city seemed almost deserted. The rest of the time it was like Mardi Gras with livestock.

"One of the things it was hard to get used to was the trees. A lot of them were palms. Growing up here, I didn't pay much attention to trees, but they're usually either evergreens or have branches all the way up. The trees in Saigon were more like tall telephone poles with party hats. Bananas and coconuts and bamboo all grew right in town.

"There weren't any really tall buildings. The poor areas— the slums—were unbelievable. And outside the city, areas that hadn't been bombed into moonscapes were beautiful—miles of flat green rice fields or little mountains covered with green jungle. People wore sandals made from old tires and cone-shaped hats. And the women wore white dresses that suggested a whole lot more than they showed but made them look incredibly sexy."

"Did you ever wish you could go back?" Good question.

"No. In spite of the buildings and the shrines, it was a dirty city—more corrupt than Washington."

They sat in silence for a while, Rob idly studying the picture. Thinnes studying Rob.

He'd graduated from high school in June and was starting at DePaul in September. He still seemed like a kid. But Thinnes hadn't been much older when he was drafted, when they gave him a helmet and sidearm and sent him across the world to keep the peace.

"I never thought much about Vietnam," Rob said. "It was just an old war—sort of like World War II must've been for you. Or the Civil War."

"It was probably more like the Revolutionary War, only none of us was smart enough to see it. And we didn't want to be the Redcoats."

Rob laughed. "You oughta teach history. I'd have paid more attention if someone pointed out stuff like that." He was quiet for a while, then said, "That charge . . . I mean—you and Mom weren't married. You had to be tempted."

"Not by Hue. Don't get me wrong. It wouldn't have mattered that she was Vietnamese. And she was beautiful. But she was my best friend's girl. That put her in the category of *Don't even think about it*—like nuns."

"I can get that."

There was a long, not-uncomfortable silence during which Thinnes marveled at how much a man his son had become. He'd be moving out one of these days, maybe bringing home a wife. Having kids!

"Supposing there was something to that allegation?" he said. "What would you think about that?"

"You mean, if I had a brother or sister somewhere?"

"Yeah."

"I dunno. I guess it'd be cool. You never—I mean—with someone else?"

"No. I was superstitious. I thought if I screwed around, I'd get a Dear John letter."

FORTY-SEVEN

Mrs. Coral is Vietnamese," Tien Lee said as Thinnes drove to her apartment. "She married a former International Voluntary Services worker she met during the war."

The building was undergoing renovation. Tuck-pointers loafed on a scaffold over the entrance were watching laborers unload boards onto the parched lawn. They moved slowly in the heat.

Thinnes stopped under a parkway tree. He and Lee got out and picked their way among the workers, between piles of sand and gravel. Just outside the door Lee bummed a cigarette from one of the men using the boards to form up a new walk. It was the only hint that he was nervous.

"I thought you Bruce Lee types don't smoke."

"Part of the image," Lee said. "Anyway, everyone's got flaws." He sucked in the smoke like a hippie toking on a joint, holding it until Thinnes wanted to yell, *Breathe, dammit!*

Lee let the smoke out very slowly. Then he pinched the burning end of the cigarette to put it out. He brushed off the charred end and put the rest in his pocket.

"Ready?"

"Tien," Mrs. Coral said. "You favor your mother."

He nodded and introduced Thinnes.

"Come in," she said. "Come in and sit down."

Her living room was contemporary American, furnished from a high-end store. A bit surprising for Uptown. There were real flowers on the coffee table and real-looking Oriental rugs on the floor. Also Martha Stewart touches like a basket of dried flowers next to the phone and designer Kleenex. She offered them seats on the couch; they sat at opposite ends. Mrs. Coral took a chair across the coffee table and moved the flowers from their line of sight.

"We roomed together," she said. "Hue and Nhài and me. At school. Catholic school." She spread her fingers and emphasized what she was saying with her hands. Her slight accent was the only hint that she'd been born in Vietnam.

"After we graduated, Hue's father got her a job with a friend. In a bank. And my father arranged a marriage for me with a man who was willing to overlook that my paternal grandfather was French." She stared into space for a moment. "It didn't work out, thank God." She crossed herself.

"But you wanted to know about Hue." She smiled at Lee as if he were a favorite nephew. "She was lucky. First the job at the bank. It let her move out of her parents' house, which—you understand—wasn't done back then. But she talked them into it because she had a roommate she'd gone to school with—Nhài. They thought it would be okay. Nhài was Catholic, too, and as far as they knew, a good girl. From a good family. Hue's parents thought the two girls could chaperone each other."

She smiled wryly and shook her head. "Hue never needed a chaperone. She worked hard and saved her money and visited her parents on weekends. She never got into any trouble until she met your father." She smiled. "He used to come into the bank every day to change his money. And he'd wait until she was free before going to the counter so he'd have time to talk with her. He even tried to learn Vietnamese. His pronunciation was so bad it made her laugh. And when she laughed, he'd be very pleased and beg her to correct him. She liked that he wasn't arrogant like most Americans. And that he bothered to learn about our customs. He used to bring her little things—an individually wrapped chocolate, or an origami bird—never anything expensive or too personal. By the time he got transferred, she'd fallen for him pretty hard, though I don't think she ever let him know.

"But he came back when he had leave, and they started going together." She shrugged. "You know the rest."

"Tell us about Nhài," Lee said.

Thinnes decided to let him do the talking. Mrs. Coral obviously had good feelings for him, and he was asking the right things. He'd make a decent detective if he ever decided to try his hand.

"Nhài was a different story. She moved out of the apartment almost right after she moved in, although Hue told me she kept paying her share of the rent. She took a job at a place where men went to dance with women for money. It wasn't a whorehouse, but just a step up. Most of the women who worked there were like Nhài—not pure-blooded Vietnamese, so their options were limited.

"In the Vietnamese culture, family is all-important. Few men would marry a woman who wasn't a virgin or from a good family."

Thinnes nodded. He wondered how Lee felt hearing this. He didn't show any sign it bothered him. But then he'd had a lifetime to get used to it. If anyone ever did. Even growing up with money, he must've been called "gook" or "slope" or "slant-eyes."

Lee only said, "Go on."

"Nhài was beautiful, so she did well at the dance place. We'd go out for lunch and she'd brag about how the men lined up to dance with her. But it was hard work being sweet to all those strangers. And some of them were very crude. Some smelled bad. Most had two left feet. The manager never let anything get too far out of hand, but after a few months, Nhài seemed very tired.

"Then she met a man who promised to make her a star. She never said doing what. But she was very excited.

"The next I heard of her—someone told me—she'd become a prostitute, working in a brothel that catered to Americans and rich Vietnamese. It was sad, but it didn't surprise me. She'd always been kind of wild. I didn't expect to ever see her again.

"But one day, she came to see me. At my house. She was happy. Engaged. She had a big diamond ring to prove it. She'd met a GI who spoke Vietnamese and treated her well. I can't remember his name, but she had his picture.

"That was the last time I saw her alive."

195

"The GI," Lee said. "Was his name Theo?"

Mrs. Coral thought for a moment. "It might have been. It was a long time ago."

Thinnes handed her the copy of Theo Ragland's picture that he'd had made up from his family's portrait. Theo in uniform. "This him?"

She studied it briefly. "I only saw a picture, and it was a long time ago, but it *looks* like the picture Nhài showed me. He wasn't all dressed up like that, though. The guy in Nhài's picture was wearing a regular uniform—green.

"He was *dàn óng den*—a black man. Many Vietnamese—those descended from the Viet people—look down on blacks because they're dark like Cambodians.

"When I spoke to Nhài about this, she was angry. She told me her soldier was an old soul and loved her, and nothing else mattered. She asked me how happy I was, married to a 'suitable' man." Mrs. Coral shrugged. "That hurt, but I deserved it. And it made me think about leaving my husband. He never loved me."

She seemed to have nothing more to say.

Lee said, "Thank you, Mrs. Coral." He stood up.

Thinnes said, "Just a minute."

They both looked at him.

"You said that was the last time you saw Nhài alive. Did you see her dead?"

Lee looked surprised. He sat back down.

Mrs. Coral looked like she'd been poleaxed. "How—?"

"Tell us," Lee said.

She looked sad and frightened. "I can't."

Thinnes said, "Sure you can."

She shook her head. "I vowed I would never tell."

"You know who killed her?"

"Everyone knew. Bạch Hổ."

Lee raised his eyebrows. "Not Cọp Trắng?"

"How do you know about him?" When Lee didn't answer, she added, "He was called that, too. Sometimes."

"Who'd you make the vow to?" Thinnes asked.

She pressed her lips together and shook her head.

"He killed a man recently, Mrs. Coral," Lee said. Her eyes widened. "And he killed my mother."

She put a hand over her mouth and started sobbing quietly. "It was Hue. I promised Hue I would never tell."

"Cọp Trắng killed her," Thinnes said. "Who is he?"

She sobbed again. Lee got up and brought her the designer Kleenex box. She sniffled and pulled out a tissue. She dabbed at her eyes and blew her nose. "I don't know."

"Then tell me what you *do* know."

She glanced at Lee, then said, "I promised Hue . . ."

Tien seemed ready to explode, but he let his breath out slowly. "You've kept your promise admirably, Mrs. Coral. But my mother's dead. Tell us! Please!"

"The night Nhài died, your mother called me. We were one of the few families with a phone. She asked me to pick her up at an address on Tu Do Street." She glanced toward Thinnes, then back at Lee. "Of course, I couldn't believe my ears. Your mother in Tu Do Street. It was the red-light district then, a place where only prostitutes would go. But she was my best friend and terrified.

"My husband was away and I was afraid to go alone, so I called a friend who had an old Peugeot. Tu Do Street was crowded and dark in places but we made good time. When we stopped in front of the House of Flowers, Hue came from the shadows, out of the alley. She was . . ." Mrs. Coral looked at Lee, her reluctance to continue obvious.

"She was pregnant at the time," Thinnes said. He was beginning to put things together. Hue's miscarriage had happened around the same time as Jasmine's murder. Why hadn't he figured it out before?

His statement disrupted Lee's maddening calm, though he recovered quickly. "Go on, Mrs. Coral."

She looked at Thinnes. "She was pregnant. But she was hurt. I told her, 'Get in,' but she said, 'I'm bleeding.' My friend said—excuse me—'Fuck the car! Get in!' He drove her straight to the hospital. She was screaming for us to just take her home, but she was bleeding badly. So we paid no attention. We told her she had to think about the baby. Bobby's baby. That made her quiet. Then she went into shock or something.

"After a while, after they'd got some fluid in her, she was better. Until they said she'd lost the baby. She started cursing in French and Vietnamese, screaming, trying to get up and leave. And she kept saying, 'I'll kill him. I've got to kill him!' She wouldn't tell me who. They finally sedated her. They said come back tomorrow and take her home. That's what I did. She wasn't threatening murder anymore. She made me promise—on my ancestors' graves—not to tell anyone, especially Bobby. She said it was too dangerous. She told me about Nhài. She said Bạch Hổ had killed her and he would kill us, too, if he got word we knew about him. She said he would kill Bobby."

Lee said, "Bạch Hổ caused her to miscarry?"

Mrs. Coral nodded. "I went to the morgue the next day. I told them I was Nhài's sister. They let me claim the body and we buried her, Hue and me. We buried her with Hue's baby, who we christened Hoa Nhài.

"I stayed with her a week. Then Bobby got her letter—about the miscarriage—and sent a friend of his to stay with her. I left before he came. My husband was coming home and I didn't want trouble.

"My husband told me we were moving to Vung Tau. Someone told him I was fooling around and he wouldn't let me out of his sight. I didn't get to say goodbye to Hue. I missed her wedding. I never saw my friend again."

Lee stopped just outside the building to dig out the cigarette he'd saved. He lit up. As he drew in the smoke, he watched Thinnes. "You knew about this." He was too cool, too in control for a man who'd just heard his unborn sister had been murdered. By the same man who'd murdered his mother.

"Some of it." Thinnes was feeling a little light-headed with rage. "Some I put together just now, from Mrs. Coral's pieces."

Lee exhaled, looking briefly like a man breathing fire. "How close are you to finding this monster?"

"I'll get him."

He gave Thinnes an 'oh-yeah?' look and took another drag.

"He's hunting on my turf now. His camouflage won't hide him in my jungle."

"We'll see." Lee took three deep hits from the cigarette and dropped the stub on the dirt within the concrete form. He stepped down deliberately to stamp it out.

"Don't get in the line of fire," Thinnes said.

FORTY-EIGHT

After he dropped Tien Lee at his dojo, Thinnes went back to Belmont and Western. The squadroom was nearly deserted. At the desk, the sergeant was studying the *Sun-Times* sports section. The custodian had pushed his broom over to the coffee setup and was helping himself. When he noticed Thinnes watching, he fished out coins and dropped them in the coffee-fund can, then saluted Thinnes with his cup and pushed the broom out the door.

Thinnes dropped his jacket and paperwork and got his LONE STAR mug. It was lunchtime, but after the interview with Mrs. Coral, he was too worked up to be hungry. And coffee helped him think.

Except for Drucker, he hadn't had much luck locating guys he'd served with. But maybe one of Bobby's pals would remember something. Two of them had attended the wedding; four others showed up for the reception. Bobby had only introduced them by their first or nicknames. And—maybe because Thinnes was an MP—they hadn't gone out of their way to socialize. He didn't remember a single surname. He knew Bobby's unit and dates of service, so he could get a list of all the men in the company. But without last names, how could he pick Bobby's half dozen buddies out of the scores—including replacements—that he'd served with?

Thinnes was still thinking about it when Franchi came in with the remains of her lunch—an iced cappuccino.

"Guess what, Thinnes," she said.

"What?"

"Mr. Hung was a colonel in the Army of the Republic of Vietnam."

"Why do you suppose he didn't mention that?"

"Maybe 'cause we didn't ask."

"Let's go ask now." He stood up, then sat down again. "Hold on a sec. I got an idea." He dialed Lee's dojo. When Lee came on the line, Thinnes said, "Do you have any pictures of your parents' wedding?"

"Yes." His voice was perfectly neutral, as if someone had just asked whether he gave classes on Tuesdays.

"Could I stop by later this afternoon and see them?"

"Of course. I'll be finished for the day at four."

"Thanks. See you then."

"What was that about?" Franchi said when he'd hung up.

"Nothing."

"*Bullshit!* You just can't leave it alone. And you're digging yourself in deeper by the minute."

"Have you developed any new leads since the last time we had this conversation?"

"No."

"Then drop it."

When they were seated on the couch in Hung Duc Minh's living room, Thinnes said, "Why didn't you tell us you're a veteran, Mr. Hung?"

"I wished to be judged for who I am, not the family I was born to or the mistakes I made when young and stupid."

"What mistakes were those?"

"I prefer not to say. Nothing to do with Mrs. Lee."

Thinnes waited to see if silence would work on him.

Hung finally said, "Strange that here, where everyone's ancestors were criminals or outcasts, and whole society ignores laws, people are condemned by mistakes forever. Criminals and outcasts who come here have a chance to start over. They do okay because no one knows them. Unless really bad, they leave the past behind and become whoever they could not be in their old lands."

"Where were you stationed?"

"You know I was in the Army. You must know."

"Our information only has your rank."

"After Saigon, I transferred to the Eighteenth Infantry under General Le Minh Dao. When Xuan Loc fell, I joined boat people."

"What can you tell us about Bạch Hổ?"

Thinnes couldn't read Hung's expression. He said, "Name of corrupt unofficial security firm in Saigon. Also head of firm. Were you ever in Saigon?"

Thinnes nodded. "Tell us about it." He could see Franchi spoiling to ask what they were talking about. He gave her a look that said, *Later.*

"I had a friend with shop in Cholon," Hung said. "He told me Bach Hö wanted fifty percent of profit or accidents would happen. My friend say, 'No way!' His shop burned.

"Most paid. One who tried to fight Bach Hö died. When I discovered this I know I can't fight Bach Hö alone. So I request transfer."

"Would it surprise you to know Bach Hö killed Mrs. Lee?" Thinnes asked.

Hung shook his head. "But here corruption's not so bad. Here if Bach Hö come, I can go to police."

Thinnes nodded. "You have my card."

Hung bowed almost imperceptibly.

Thinnes stood up to go; Franchi followed suit.

Hung looked at Thinnes. "I know what you think. You still call ARVN soldiers cowards. But when Romans conscripted men, they were sent to fight in other provinces. Americans drafted to fight on other side of world, against people who look very different. When we were drafted, we were sent to fight relatives and neighbors. It is not cowardice to resist what you cannot fight."

Thinnes couldn't argue with that.

"I need some background here," Franchi said.

The car was like a broiler. Thinnes didn't answer until he'd rolled his window down and started the motor. "The French were in Vietnam long enough to develop bribery into an art form, and

Saigon was the most corrupt city on the planet. Nobody—including the police—did their job without a quid pro quo; bribes were a cost of doing business. And it was impossible to tell where official corruption ended and organized crime began."

"Kind of like Chicago? Historically."

"Yeah, but in three languages and with a war going on. And with refugees, orphans, mercenaries, and deserters thrown in. It was nuts. I guess if you had to run a business, you paid off the biggest shark and hoped he'd scare away the piranhas."

"Why didn't you ask about Cọp Trắng?"

"I did. Bạch Hổ was another alias. What else did you dig up on Hung?"

"*Nada*. Apparently he got here with enough cash for a down payment on his building. He worked for an office-cleaning company to make payments, and worked his way up to supervisor. Now he does the hiring and firing—mostly Vietnamese."

"And he still cleans his own building?"

"Maybe it's a way to keep an eye on things." She shrugged. "Apparently he was arrested once for taking a bat to a couple of vandals. I checked. The case was dropped when no one showed up to testify."

"So he's not afraid to use force."

"You think he could be our White Tiger?"

"There's a big difference between going after someone in the heat of the moment and a cold-blooded execution."

"Yeah but he was in the army, trained to kill."

"So was I."

"Thinnes, where are you going?" He'd just turned west on Lawrence, away from Lee's dojo.

"Back to the house."

"To drop me off so you can talk to Tien Lee alone? Not a chance!" Franchi folded her arms across her chest and braced her feet on the car floor.

He considered his options.

She probably wouldn't turn him in if he refused to take her, but she'd be pissed off forever. And he still wasn't sure about Lee. Maybe Franchi would shake loose his inscrutable facade.

Thinnes shrugged and made a U-turn, heading back toward Broadway.

A slight widening of his eyes was the only indication that Tien Lee was surprised to see Franchi. He looked from her to Thinnes and said, "Come in, Detectives."

"You've been here before," Franchi said as she preceded Thinnes into the apartment.

"Later," he growled, hoping she'd forget, knowing she wouldn't.

"Please make yourselves comfortable," Lee said. Comfortable, not at home. He'd changed from his work clothes and—judging by his wet hair—had showered. He was barefooted, wearing Levi's and a black silk shirt with the sleeves rolled to the elbows. He waved toward the couch.

Thinnes took one end, Franchi the other.

"May I offer you something to drink?" Lee said.

Thinnes shook his head. Trying to figure Lee out was like watching a big cat—you knew something was going on in there but you couldn't tell what.

Franchi said, "No, thank you." She yawned, covering her mouth with one hand, stretching the way people do trying to be unobtrusive.

There was no mistaking what Lee thought about that—Thinnes'd thought it himself from time to time. She *was* hot.

He felt a stab of jealousy—though he and Franchi had never been intimate—then shame. He wondered what Jack Caleb would make of it. But Caleb would probably say everyone had some kind of Oedipal issues.

Oedipal. Did that mean he'd accepted the possibility that Lee was his biological son? Was he refusing to remember what happened that night because nothing did, or because he didn't want to know?

Mindfucking!

He realized he'd been woolgathering when Lee said, "I'll get them."

And Franchi said, "Thanks." She eyed Thinnes as if she'd caught him drinking on the job. As soon as Lee left the room, she said, "Thinnes, what the hell's with you?"

He didn't answer. She got up and prowled around, studying the place as he had the first time he was there. Franchi was better educated than he, so she'd probably know the value of the art and furnishings. But then, Lee's financial situation had never been at issue.

She was back on the couch by the time their host returned with a photo album and a bulging shoe box that he put on the coffee table between them. "I hope these help." He sat across the table, curling one foot under him.

Thinnes noticed Franchi staring and he looked at Lee more closely. The top button of his shirt was undone. His expression was still unreadable, but his attention was definitely on Franchi. Great!

"What've you got here?" Thinnes asked.

Lee dragged his attention away from Franchi and waved his hand at what he'd brought. "My parents took lots of pictures when I was very young, before they got too busy building my father's firm. And they had pictures from Vietnam."

Franchi didn't move, so Thinnes set the shoe box aside and started paging through the album. Photos of places Bobby and Hue visited. Mutual friends. Jasmine. Thinnes took her photo out and turned it over. *Nhài 1970.* She'd been beautiful and happy. Thinnes handed Lee the picture. "You know who this is?"

Lee looked, then turned the photo over. "Maybe the woman who wrote the letter to my mother?" He shrugged. "No one I ever met."

"You wouldn't have," Thinnes said. "She died before you were born." Out of the corner of his eye, he could see Franchi's disapproval. Cops never volunteer information.

Lee handed the picture back. "Murdered."

Thinnes didn't comment. He set the picture to one side and kept looking through the album.

The bulk of the photos were from the Lees' wedding. Hue's boss and schoolmates. Two of Bobby's buddies. Thinnes couldn't remember their names. He took out the picture that showed them most clearly and set it next to the shot of Nhài. "I'd like to borrow these if I may."

"Certainly."

"Your folks ever talk about the wedding?"

Lee shrugged. "If they did, I've forgotten. Kids aren't too interested in that kind of thing." His gaze shifted to Franchi, who'd scooched closer to Thinnes to study the photos—way too carefully. Thinnes wondered if there was something between them he should know about.

Franchi turned the page and pictures of the reception brought the event back for Thinnes.

Royhill and Benett, a.k.a. Robbie and Benny. As in Robby, Bobby, and Benny, the three Mouseketeers. They'd all had too much to drink and were singing the Mickey Mouse song. Hue hadn't seemed to mind.

"Thinnes!" Franchi looked annoyed.

"What?"

She glanced at Lee, then at Thinnes. "Found what you were looking for?" She must've asked that already.

"Yeah." He asked if Lee minded them going through the shoe box, as well. He wondered, as he shuffled through a time-lapse of Tien's childhood, how Lee felt.

He wondered, again, what he and Hue and Bobby had done after the reception, whether there was a chance the child he saw figuratively growing up before his eyes was his. He wondered what Franchi was thinking as she looked from the photos to the grown man.

It was obvious the Lees had loved their son, however they'd come by him. It was hard to imagine him growing up to be a killer. But more horrifying things had happened.

In the car on the way back to the Area, Franchi said, "You really think he could have killed his mother?"

She seemed disconcerted when he said, "Sure."

FORTY-NINE

The squadroom was busy. Evanger was helping himself to coffee, and Ferris, three Property Crimes dicks, two tactical officers on loan to the Detective Division, and the sergeant were all going about their business.

Sitting in the conference room, Viernes faced the window. He looked up from the paperwork he had spread out on the table and waved Thinnes in.

Thinnes crossed the squadroom and leaned into the open doorway. "What's up?"

"Lab called. The gun used to kill Mrs. Lee was found after a drive-by shooting on a Lester Williams. Williams is a South Sider. He claims he found it in an alley."

"He got an alibi?"

"No," Viernes said. "But his story's so lame, you gotta figure it's the truth. And what better way to get rid of a murder weapon than by leaving it where some mope's sure to find it?"

"They know where it came from originally?"

"Stolen two years ago, in a burglary in Northbrook, used in at least one other shooting—which Williams couldn't have done. He was locked up at the time."

"So where are we?" Thinnes asked.

"The brass wants to close the Lee case by putting it on Williams, but that's too easy. You got any ideas?"

"Keep beating the bushes 'til we flush the big cat."

. . .

"Hey, Viernes!" Ferris was helping himself to coffee, yelling rather than cross the room to keep it between them. "Your witness is here with his pet shrink."

Thinnes couldn't resist butting in. "Who?"

"The nutcase." Ferris hitched his thumb toward the squad-room door. "On their way up."

"Where's Franchi?"

"Not my day to watch her."

If Thinnes didn't know better, he'd have thought Caleb brought in a ringer. Maharis didn't look much different, but he wasn't acting crazy and he didn't smell. He did insist that Caleb stay while he talked to the detectives.

They held the interview in the conference room. Maharis and Caleb faced the window across from Viernes. He asked the questions; Franchi took notes. Thinnes watched with Evanger from outside the room.

"Why did you go to Mrs. Lee's wake?" Viernes asked.

"Pay my respects, like I told you last time."

"You said you didn't know her."

"She was a friend of Ragman's."

Viernes leaned forward. "So why did *you* go?"

Maharis leaned back. " 'Cause he couldn't. He had a out-standing warrant."

"Where did he know Mrs. Lee from?"

"Saigon."

"Yes, but how did he know she was in Chicago?"

"The market. She used to come there to shop."

"By herself?"

"No. With another woman. Vietnamese. Big talker."

Mrs. Nyugen.

"Was Ragland afraid of the White Tiger?"

Maharis's eyes widened. He asked Caleb, "How do they know?"

"They're detectives. Answer the question."

Maharis looked back at Viernes. "Yes. White Tiger."

"What's his real name?"

"I don't know. Ragman never told me." Viernes waited. Maharis added, "He said, people who know die. He was right. He's dead. Mrs. Lee is dead."

"How long did Ragland know the Tiger was in the city?"

"I don't know. He never mentioned him until Mrs. Lee was killed."

"How'd he come to tell you that? He volunteer it?"

"No, but I could tell he was bummed out, so I asked why. That's when he told me about Mrs. Lee. She was a friend of Ragman's girlfriend. He didn't know what happened to her. He used to show people her picture and ask if they knew her. Then I think Mrs. Lee told him she was dead."

"Was he mad at Mrs. Lee?"

"No. But he was gonna get a gun and go hunting for the Tiger. Guess the Tiger got him first."

They typed up Maharis's statement and had Columbo look it over. Once they had his signature duly witnessed, they cut him loose. He and Caleb were going out the door when Thinnes said, "Doctor, may I have a word with you?"

"Certainly." Caleb handed Maharis his keys and asked him to wait in the car.

As soon as he was gone, Thinnes asked, "Was he telling the truth?"

"I believe so. As he sees it."

"Think he's seeing straight today?"

"When he's not off his medication, he's remarkably perceptive." Caleb waited, then asked, "Anything else?"

"Just—aren't you afraid he'll make off with your car?"

"Evanger wants to see us." Franchi put her purse on his table and dug out a pen and a pack of gum.

Thinnes took a stick. "You know what about?"

"Progress report?" Helpful.

Thinnes put the gum in his mouth and lobbed the crumpled wrapper at the trash can. Missed. He got up and put the wrapper in the can.

"Okay." He sat back down. "Let me make a call first."

"Hey," Mabley said when Thinnes identified himself. "I was just gonna call you. Got a break on that .22." Mabley was currently assigned to fire-arms identification.

"The one that killed Ragland?"

"The DB from the burned-out building. Was that Ragland?"

"Yeah. What've you got?"

"Gun was reported stolen in Mount Prospect a year ago."

"And?"

"The owner wants it back when we're done with it."

"So?" Evanger was sitting back in his chair with his elbows on the chair arms, his fingers laced. He'd watched Viernes interview Maharis, so Thinnes didn't bother to reiterate. Without getting too specific or mentioning Tien Lee, he told him what they'd found out to date about both murders. Franchi added details.

"A tiger doesn't change its stripes." Evanger said. "So why haven't we heard about this guy before?"

"Recent immigrants are usually afraid of the cops," Franchi said. "Maybe he's just preyed on Vietnamese."

"Or maybe he's got a new racket," Thinnes said. "Something that only involves willing participants." He remembered McKenzie's old case files—they might hold a clue. He'd have to make time to read through them.

"And he suddenly decides to go on a murder spree?"

"Maybe he had to. Supposing he's been clean all these years, maybe got a good job, started a family. Then someone from his past shows up, someone who can make trouble."

"Mrs. Lee? As far as we know, she could *maybe* accuse him of a murder he committed twenty-five years ago halfway around the world. How's that a threat?"

"We'll know that when we find out who he is."

FIFTY

I had nine months left because I'd re-upped," Caleb said.
"You fuckin' nuts?" Butch asked. "Re-upping?"
"No doubt."

They'd been on a recon patrol, in an area that hadn't seen too much action—that is, that hadn't yet been deforested by bombs and Agent Orange. Stripped of military jargon, the mission was to go out and find something for the artillery to blow up.

The sergeant and half the men in Caleb's squad were short, a month or two from DEROS. They weren't keen on getting in harm's way. The lieutenant, on the other hand, had only been in country two months, and he was suffering delusions of invulnerability.

The platoon was just half strength, twenty-three including the lieutenant and his radioman. The choppers dropped them in a field of elephant grass, a flat area along a little river. The grass was too thick to see through and too tall to see over. Perfect setup for an ambush, especially since any enemy in the vicinity would've heard the chopper coming a long way off.

Caleb was carrying three extra gallons of water—the lieutenant's way of getting him back for refusing to carry an M-16. Caleb wasn't complaining. He concentrated on watching the sergeant's back. The sergeant had kept him alive since he'd been in country.

When they hit the woods, the undergrowth seemed impenetrable. There was a faint trail, but they were reluctant to take it—it was almost certainly booby-trapped. They stumbled across a nearly dry streambed, one of the tributaries of the river they'd landed next to. The vegetation was naturally sparse in the channel, which was muddy in spots with sticky heavy clay. It had dried on either side as hard as concrete. So they stayed to the sides and followed the stream uphill.

The lieutenant sent Cherry, one of the two new guys, to take point. He put Gilligan, the other newcomer, at the end of the line.

After a while, animal tracks crisscrossed through the mud. Pigs—wild, maybe—and monkeys and some small creature with feet like a housecat. No human sign.

But twenty-two months in country had made the sergeant suspicious. "I 'member reading how—in the Middle Ages—they made special shoes that left tracks like cattle, so they could go through muddy spots without alerting the enemy."

"Think Charlie's smart enough to do that?"

"You won't get old underestimating Charlie."

"Knock it off!" The lieutenant was staring upriver where the streambed curved out of sight. "Close it up!"

Just then there was a screech and shots fired from the point. Everyone hit the dirt. Except for Caleb, they all started firing.

It was the sergeant who shouted, "Cease fire! Cherry, report!"

Cherry's screams were unintelligible, answered by a chorus of high pitched squeals and grunts. Caleb recognized the sound from his summers spent in Mexico. Pigs in a feeding frenzy! He dropped the water cans and charged toward the fracas.

Around the curve of the streambed, Cherry was barely visible beneath a roiling mass of hairy flanks and flying hooves. Caleb screamed and charged them, flailing with his medical kit, kicking and striking. He heard a hollow thunk whenever he connected, but he wasn't driving the pigs from their prey. He heard shouts as the rest of the squad charged around the bend, the lieutenant in the lead. He had his sidearm out and was emptying it into the largest animal. The boar didn't seem to notice. The other soldiers stopped, M-16s ready, unable to open fire without hitting Cherry. It was the sergeant who calmly waded into the boiling mess of bacon and took aim at the back of the boar's head. The sound of his rifle startled everyone.

The boar paused, took a step, and dropped. The rest of the pigs scattered upstream and up the sides of the streambed.

An explosion brought the humans to earth as one of the retreating animals set off a trip wire, and shrapnel screamed through space and tore through flesh and vegetation.

Caleb could hear dirt and debris dropping like fine rain in the silence that followed, then a chorus of profanity. He remembered his mission and crawled toward Cherry's still form. The grunt was breathing—barely—but he was pale as fish flesh, bleeding from a dozen mortal wounds. Caleb knew it was hopeless, even as he scrambled to plug all the leaks.

"Jesus!" Gilligan said, coming up behind Caleb. He hadn't seen enough death to be inured.

Cherry grasped Caleb's arm. "Doc, am I gonna die?"

Caleb wasn't willing to lie. "You're going home early."

Then Cherry was dead. Caleb closed his eyes.

The sergeant moved in with a tarp as Caleb dragged his kit away from the corpse. He looked around for other casualties, saw bloody cuts here and there, but no one who seemed in immediate need of his services.

The lieutenant, meanwhile, was peering cautiously above the streambed. He looked upstream and down, then withdrew to confer with his RTO, who was already calling in a dust-off. Ace and Leroy were attacking the dead pig with knives and bayonets.

When Leroy noticed Caleb watching, he said, "No use letting this go to waste."

Ace said, "Fuckin' gives real meaning to that old saying, *He went out to shit an' the pigs ate 'IM.*"

"Shut up, asshole," Gilligan screamed.

Ace just laughed, but the sergeant led Gilligan away from the others.

"Hey, this a fuckin' pig or an armadillo?" Ace demanded. His bayonet made a thumping sound every time he stabbed the dead animal, the sound Caleb heard when he first tried to kick the pig off Cherry.

"Fuckin' thing's got a flak jacket," Ace said.

The pig did, indeed, seem to be covered on its back and sides with an armor made up of dried resin mixed with dirt, and bits of leaf and twigs.

"Try skinnin' it from underneath," said Bob, who was from rural Alabama.

They rolled the pig on its back and Bob told them how to skin it, letting Ace and Leroy do the work. Caleb knew the impromptu butchering party was a diversion intended to keep the participants from thinking about Cherry.

The lieutenant walked up and watched for a minute. "I need some volunteers to take the Cherry back to the dust-off site. Can't land a chopper with all these trees and we can't clear enough away for it to land before dark."

"I'll go," Caleb said.

"Nah, I need you here. Somebody else."

The sergeant appeared silently behind his superior. When he said, "I'll go," the lieutenant jumped.

He recovered quickly. "Good. Pick your team."

"Bob, Rodney, Gilligan."

The lieutenant nodded. "Take him back to where we entered the trees. You got a rendezvous at eighteen hundred hours. Then . . ." He held a folded map up for the sergeant to study, pointed to a spot among the wavy lines denoting hills. "Meet us here ASAP. Meanwhile, we'll dig in for the night."

The sergeant collected his "volunteers," then walked toward Cherry's shrouded form. The rest of the platoon turned back to the diversion of the pig.

The platoon was well fed for a change. They roasted the pig's hind leg and ate their fill. After dumping the leftovers, they marched upstream and dug in on a small rise crowned with a stand of timber.

When the sun slipped below the western treetops, the lieutenant sent one of the grunts to climb the highest tree, to watch for the sergeant and his detail. He got halfway up.

A rifle cracked. The grunt dropped like a ripe fruit.

Caleb spotted a muzzle flare to the right and pointed. "There!"

Bits of foliage rained on him as the sniper pruned the trees above his head. Covering fire answered. Caleb used it to run to the fallen soldier.

Too late. The boy's throat was shredded; his blood had pumped all over his fatigues. Caleb dragged the body back to his foxhole.

The firing ceased.

Then, before they could assess the damage, gunfire erupted in the opposite direction. They could hear distant shouts and crackling of the underbrush. Ace fired at the sounds. His shots were answered by frantic voices:

"Don't shoot!" Gilligan's voice.

"It's us!" Rodney.

"The dust-off detail!" Bob.

"Hold your fire!" The lieutenant.

Three men burst from the forest, guns overhead. Scratched and bleeding. Winded. Scared white.

Caleb stood up. "Where's the sarge?"

Gilligan turned to look back. "He was behind us." He turned again and dived for Caleb's foxhole, shrieking when he landed on the dead lookout.

Caleb grabbed Gilligan's shoulder and shook him. "When did you see him last?"

"About ten minutes out."

"You run the whole way?"

" 'Bout half."

Caleb shouted, "Anybody hurt?" No response. He picked up his rucksack and climbed out of his hole.

"Doc, get down," the lieutenant yelled.

"I'm going after the sarge."

"No, you're not. It'll be too dark to see a thing in a few minutes. We'll find him first light."

"He could be dead by then."

"He's probably dead already."

Caleb reached into the foxhole and grabbed one of the extra canteens, then sprinted for the woods.

The lieutenant's voice chased him under the canopy. "Get back here, Doc. That's an order!"

. . .

Caleb didn't stop running until it was too dark to see. Then he'd listen for sounds that seemed alien to the woods and move toward them as quietly as he could. He almost broke his neck when he tumbled down a small ravine. He stopped, knee-deep in the stream at the bottom. Over the trickling of the water, he could hear labored breathing. But whose? He hesitated to call out. If the VC started shooting, he couldn't defend himself. And if it was the sergeant, he might call the enemy's attention to him.

He waded toward the unknown. Slowly. Silently.

Caleb found him by luck, tripping on his feet. "Sarge?" Simultaneously, he heard the pin pulled from a grenade. "Ron?"

"Jack?"

"Yeah."

"Shit! I lost the pin."

"Where's the grenade?"

"In my hand. Can't hold it much longer. Hurt."

Caleb felt his way up the sergeant's body, found his hand. "Give it to me."

"What are you gonna . . . ?"

Caleb closed his hand around the other's, around the grenade. He tried to remember what he'd been told about them. He wished he'd paid attention. "Safe as long as you don't let go of the lever. Right?"

"Yeah. Can't hold it all night. Can't see to—"

Caleb worked the explosive out of his hand, careful to keep the lever tight against the body. He wished he'd played more baseball as a kid. He wished there was even a quarter moon. He hoped the trees were thinner over the little stream. He listened for the loudest sounds of water, took a deep breath, and pitched the grenade. He threw himself on top of the sergeant as he counted the seconds off. One one-thousand. Two one-thousand. Three one-thousand . . .

BOOM!

In the flash of the explosion, Caleb could see the sides of the streambed, the glint of light on water, the sergeant's grimy face.

The sarge let his breath out slowly, coughed. "Damn!"

Caleb laughed.

"Gonna bring Charlie on the run."

"We'll hear him coming. How bad are you?"

"Leg's shot. Lung fillin' up."

"You're in luck. I brought my duct tape."

"How'd you get the lieutenant to let you come?"

"Who says he let me?"

"Aw."

"Listen! Ron. You have to live. You gotta testify for me at the court-martial."

The lieutenant was sitting at the table that served as a desk when Caleb came into the command tent.

"Spec Four James Caleb reporting as ordered, sir."

"What have you got to say for yourself?"

"Nothing, sir."

Showered and in a clean uniform, Caleb stood smartly at attention, though inside he was seething. Good word. Perfect description of the anger, loathing, and disgust eating like acid at his pacifist beliefs. He felt light-headed, as addle-brained from rage as he had ever been from alcohol. Simultaneously, he understood with absolute clarity why fraggings occurred.

Unused to having orders ignored, the lieutenant was outraged. "Do you know what the penalty is for disobeying a direct order?"

"No, sir."

"Didn't they teach you anything in basic?"

"Yes, sir."

"Yes, they didn't teach you anything, or yes, they did, but you were too stupid to retain it?"

"They taught me to save lives. Sir!"

That got him out of his chair and around the table, and he slapped Caleb, hard, across the face.

Beyond clenching his jaw, Caleb did nothing; the lieutenant stood rubbing his smarting hand.

"I'm writing you up for insubordination and desertion. You're going to spend the rest of your tour at the ranch." When Caleb didn't respond, he added, "Do you know what the ranch is?"

"Long Binh Jail. Sir."

"What do you think of that?" He started pacing.

Caleb kept his eyes ahead. "I think it would be a waste of the Army's resources."

"How do you figure that?"

"I'm an experienced medic. And medics are in short supply. Sir."

The lieutenant thought about that for a minute, then said, "You're right, Private. So I'm going to give you a chance to avoid a court-martial. I'm going to let you dodge the bullet if you re-up. You think you could handle another tour?"

Caleb felt like bursting with anger, but he stayed at attention. "Yes, sir."

"What do I have to do to command respect from you?"

"Not a thing, sir. You can't command respect. You have to earn it. Sir."

"Why the hell did you re-up, Jack?" Joe asked.

"I was drinking a lot back then. I must've thought I was signing a requisition order."

FIFTY-ONE

Sometimes when you were stuck on a case, you could get back on track by digging up a few more facts.

Thinnes took the two open case files and all McKenzie's old cases into the conference room and spread them out on the table. As he read through them, he jotted observations and questions on a yellow legal pad.

The guns in both the current cases had been stolen in the suburbs. Any connection?

He could see why McKenzie hadn't been able to get anywhere with the old cases. All fifteen murders had happened in Uptown, and twelve of the victims had been Vietnamese. Two others had done business with Vietnamese. Three victims had been stabbed—no weapon found. The others had all been shot, either execution style—in the head with a small caliber hand gun—or through the heart with a larger caliber weapon. In nine of the cases, the murder weapon was left at the scene. Six of those hand guns had been reported stolen in the suburbs. There were no other clues.

Did Ragland own the gun he was shot with? If so, where did he get it?

Who owns the building Smith leases for his gun store? Thinnes wondered. Who's Smith's Chinaman?

Evanger stuck his head into the room. "Thinnes, what're you doing right now?"

Thinnes put down his notepad, covering the Lee folder. "Going over the Ragland case."

"Anything new?"

"Not yet."

"Well, table it for now. Who you working with today?"

"Nobody."

"Where is everyone?"

"Viernes is at an autopsy—that stabbing he caught yesterday. Franchi's in court."

"I've got an elderly woman found dead. Probably just a death investigation, but check it out." He handed Thinnes a paper with the address. "Where's Ferris?"

Thinnes shrugged.

"Well, find him and—"

Thinnes held his hands up. "I can do it quicker on my own."

The dead body was in an apartment on North Glenwood, in Andersonville. The Major Crime Scene van was parked next to a fire hydrant in front. Bendix stood on the parkway, puffing one of his infamous stogies. He greeted Thinnes with, "Where's the dyke today?"

"Can you afford a harassment beef, Bendix?"

"Ha!"

"What are you doing here? I'm the primary, and *I* didn't call you."

"I heard the call and I was in the neighborhood. You'll love this, Thinnes. Two winos stabbed each other to death over a bottle of Vampire wine."

Thinnes must've given away his curiosity because Bendix pointed at him and said, "Gotcha!"

"Made from fermented blood?"

"The blood of some pretty fine grapes. It's good stuff, but not worth dying for."

Thinnes shook his head and went into the building.

Evanger was right, as far as Thinnes could tell. The deceased had been paranoid and in poor health.

"She was always so nasty," the building super told him, "that no one missed her for a few days." At the urging of a public service announcement, the super had done a well-being check and found the woman dead.

Thinnes looked around—no sign of a disturbance or that anyone but the old lady had been in the apartment. Just for the hell of it—and because Bendix was still hanging around—Thinnes had him dust for prints and run off a roll of film. He called the ME's office. They were up to their asses in bodies and happy to go with his assessment. Then Thinnes called for a meat wagon.

As he watched two burly coppers haul the body out, he noticed one of the bystanders seemed a little too nervous. The thin, pale white male wore a Cubs hat over his greasy gray-brown hair. His nervousness reminded Thinnes of a pet mouse Rob had once. Thinnes walked over to him and stood close enough for conversation. "You know anything about this?"

The man crossed his arms, hugging himself as if he were cold. The temperature must have been eighty-five degrees. "Not really." Thinnes waited. "The wicked witch is dead."

"You know this how?" I'm starting to sound like Evanger, he thought.

"Her super told my landlord. And he practically went door to door with the news."

"Is there something else you know something about?"

The man thought about it for a moment, then shrugged. "My neighbor's got a gun. And I don't think he's a cop."

"He showed it to you?"

"Not exactly. He was standing in his window, pointing it at streetlights and parked cars. He was drunk."

"How do you know?"

"It's what he does. I've seen him take out his trash. The landlord has a whole dumpster just for his empties. And he was stark-naked when I saw him."

"When?"

"Last night."

"Why didn't you call 911?"

"No phone."

Thinnes sighed and dug out his notebook. "What's his name?"

The mouse-colored man told him, also the apartment number. "What's your name?"

"I don't want to get involved."

"I didn't see the gun. In order to get a warrant to look for it, I need probable cause or a credible witness. That's you."

"What if you take away his gun and he gets another one? He'll come after me for ratting him out."

"Did he see you?"

"I don't think so."

"How many apartments in your building?"

"Fifteen."

"So you got a one-in-fifteen chance he won't guess it was you. What do you think your chances are he won't shoot you if he gets loaded and you're passing his window?"

After calling Rhonda to say he'd be home late, Thinnes wrote up a pick-up order for the lush with the gun. The man's landlord had told him the guy worked days and usually stopped at a local bar to drink his dinner. So Thinnes turned the matter over to Patrol Division. The beat cops would get him eventually.

Then Thinnes did the paperwork for the death investigation. He couldn't close the case until after the autopsy—tomorrow— but he'd have put money on the cause of death being natural. Before hitching a ride home, he stopped in Evanger's office. "Working late, aren't you?"

"Mayer's kid broke his arm; I'm covering.

"By the way, good catch on that gun nut. Patrol picked him up and found a small arsenal."

"Thanks. You served in Vietnam, didn't you?"

"Yeah."

"What do you remember about it?"

Evanger laced his fingers together behind his head and leaned back. "Radio Saigon. 'The beat goes on.' Rock 'n' roll twenty-four/seven. Chris Noel—'Member *A Date with Chris?*"

Thinnes nodded. She'd opened her show with, "Hi, luv," and played Top 40s and requests. "She must've gotten tons of mail."

"She toured the bases, too—almost as good as a Bob Hope show . . ."

As he walked out, Thinnes remembered listening to AFVN. The Armed Forces radio played rock 'n' roll everywhere from the Delta to the DMZ—a sound track for the war. Sometimes he and his buddies would sit in the enlisted men's club and sing along. "Sittin' on the Dock of the Bay."

And "Bad Moon Rising."

FIFTY-TWO

Thinnes called the ME's office the next morning. The autopsy confirmed that the old lady had died of natural causes—complicated by heat and dehydration. He felt guilty for not feeling bad, but the woman had lived alone by choice. In a sense, her death was her choice, too.

He was nearly finished when Viernes came in—pissed off. Tripping over the custodian's mop bucket didn't improve his temper. "Dammit!" he said as water sloshed over the red tile floor.

The custodian hurried—if you could call his pace that—to mop up the spill. He looked old enough to be near retirement—late fifties or early sixties, which meant he was probably vested and immune to threats.

"What are you doing in here?" Viernes demanded. "Aren't you supposed to do that at night?"

The man didn't bother to look up. "Somebody barfed."

Viernes stalked away, shaking his head. Thinnes waited until he'd helped himself to coffee, then asked, "What's really bothering you, Joe?"

Viernes looked ready to fight. Then he relaxed. "This damn Lee case. I spent the morning recanvassing, and several people told me they'd already talked to the Vietnamese detective. What detective's that?"

Thinnes considered how to answer without admitting that he'd disobeyed orders. "Probably Tien Lee. I gather he's not happy with our progress."

Viernes wasn't fooled. "How'd you gather that?"

The brown belt who usually answered the phone was just putting a CLOSED UNTIL 2 PM sign in the front window when Thinnes got to the dojo. The detective flashed his star to get her to let him in, then waited until Lee had dismissed his students. When they were alone, he told Lee, "Impersonating a police officer is a felony. You should ask your attorney what kind of trouble you can get in."

"I never claimed to be a cop."

"You're interfering in a police investigation."

"What investigation? You're not getting anywhere."

"We're not prepared to talk about our progress."

Lee didn't seem to be listening. "I found someone who knows about Cọp Trắng." His excitement undermined his usual cool. "She said she won't talk to me about him, but she may change her mind if you come along."

"Just give me her name and contact information."

Lee shrugged. "Okay." He walked to the counter by the phone and jotted down a name and address. As he handed Thinnes the paper, he said, "I hope you speak Vietnamese. Mrs. Tang doesn't speak English."

Mrs. Tang lived with her two daughters and a son-in-law above her fortune-teller's shop on Lawrence. Fortunately, business was slow, and she was able to fit them in between clients. Unfortunately, she wasn't willing to tell them about Cọp Trắng. Thinnes could see a completely different side of Tien Lee as he wheedled and pleaded with the old woman. But she was adamant. Thinnes didn't have to speak the language to understand her firm no.

"She's afraid for me." Lee explained. "She says I'll be swallowed whole by the Tiger."

Thinnes saw a flash of Hue in him—her intense joy—before he hid it behind the amused smile. Did he do it on purpose? Hue used to. She'd even said once, "How can you be angry with me? Life is so beautiful, so short."

He shook his head. "Tell her you're just bait. If he comes after you, I'll kill the son-of-a-bitch."

Lee laughed and translated.

The woman appeared startled, then saddened. She looked at Thinnes as she answered Lee. In spite of the language barrier, Thinnes knew it was no good.

"I told her you're a great hunter," Lee said. "But she said my mother didn't raise me to be tiger food."

When they were back on the street, he said, "Give me a day or two to work on my cousins. They'll tell me—if they can pry it out of her."

"Mrs. Tang's your aunt?"

"Ah, yes. Are you hungry?"

Thinnes gave him a *What's that got to do with anything?* look

"Because if you're hungry, we could get something at Phở Hoa. It's close and clean. I'll buy."

The restaurant was tucked away in a tiny strip mall on Broadway, just south of Argyle, a couple doors down from the Tai Nam Market. PHỞ HOÁ was lettered in turquoise on the front window, along with a stylized turquoise line drawing of a woman with a soup bowl.

Inside, rows of plastic granite-look tables stretched between brightly painted wainscoting—yellow on the east wall, blue on the west. Above it, continuous panels of mirrors reflected the room into infinity.

There were few other patrons: an Asian family at a table in the front window, and two Hispanic men deep in conversation in the rear. An Asian man and woman were drying and sorting flatware and plastic chopsticks at a table near the cash register in the back.

Thinnes sat facing the door at a table in the rear. Lee seemed comfortable with his back to the room. Like all the others, their table had a small vase of silk flowers, a tray with condiments, paper napkins, stacked plastic spoons, and a container of plastic chopsticks.

A waiter brought menus and asked whether they would like tea. It came in a metal pot accompanied by small ceramic cups without handles. Lee poured while the man took their orders. Number one for Thinnes, number two for Lee. He quickly brought two good-sized bowls of soup, and plates of do-it-yourself garnishes—slices of lime, bean sprouts, and fresh basil. Thinnes chose chopsticks. Lee watched with unconcealed interest as he used them to fish slices of beef and rice noodles from the soup.

Lee used his own chopsticks as if he'd never used any other utensil. His gestures reminded Thinnes of Bobby. But he wasn't Bobby. In the back of Thinnes's mind was the insane allegation about Lee's parentage—impossible, of course, but there was that missing night . . .

When he finished, Thinnes pushed the bowl aside and poured another cup of tea. "Tell me more about your parents."

Lee swirled the tea around in his cup. "Most Vietnamese believe in reincarnation. You know about that?"

"They keep being reborn until they get it right?"

"More or less. I think my parents were old souls. They believed they'd been together through many incarnations. Such individuals recognize one another instantly when they first meet in a new life. That's how it was for them, or so they said."

"I can't speak for your mother, but for Bobby it was love at first sight. He told me he wanted to learn Vietnamese so he could ask her to marry him."

Lee shrugged.

"Why did they settle in San Francisco?"

"I think my father had a falling out with his family over Mother and me. He refused to speak of them. When his father died, he didn't go to the funeral. I guess for him San Francisco was as good a place to live as any."

"He or your mother ever mention me?"

"Not that I recall. I do remember seeing your picture."

"Why Chicago? Why now?"

"After my father died, I tried to keep his business going. I had some aptitude, but no interest. So, as I told you, I put the company up for sale. It took a year to finish school and find the right buyer, then I began to think about what I'd like to do with the rest of my life.

"In Saigon, my mother was considered inferior because she was half French and she was ostracized because she ignored her parents' wishes and gave herself to an American. But here, being half Caucasian was an advantage, so her Vietnamese relatives are more forgiving, especially since she has the money and connections to sponsor other family members. They got in touch. Some were living in Chicago. My mother was lonely after my father's death and realized that I'd eventually leave. So when I had the opportunity to work here, she came along.

"And Chicago has the necessities of life." He smiled. "Music, theater, improving infrastructure. Why not Chicago? And as to why now? The timing just worked out that way."

Thinnes insisted on picking up the tab. Then he drove Lee back to the dojo. "No more investigating," he told him, "or I promise you'll end up in protective custody."

"Jail?"

Thinnes nodded.

"What makes you think I'd be protected in jail?"

"What makes you think I'm worried about you being protected?"

FIFTY-THREE

Finished for the day, Thinnes bummed a ride with Franchi. She'd taken a chance driving to work, parking her red Corvette in the cops' lot. As he squeezed into it, she said, "Thinnes, when are you going to get another car?"

"When I get time."

"You mean when we've nailed this bastard?"

"Yeah." He realized he missed working with her every day. Another reason to catch the goddamned Tiger soon.

"Doesn't it take more time taking the CTA to work?"

"Rob usually drives me."

"That's another thing I don't get." She looked stressed, as if she were dying for a cigarette.

"What?"

"You and Rhonda letting the kid drive the good car after he totaled your beater." She pulled over to the curb at the Belmont station under the CTA tracks.

Thinnes just smiled and got out. "Thanks. See you tomorrow."

He didn't go home. He flashed his star at the attendant and climbed to the platform. He took the next Brown Line train to the Loop.

Caleb returned to his office, after checking on a patient at North-western, to find his receptionist reading the *National Enquirer*. And John Thinnes sitting in the chair by the fish tank. A casual observer might have thought he was there on business. But Caleb could see signs of nervousness. Since there hadn't been anything in the news about an arrest for the Lee murder, he surmised Thinnes was still wrestling with the case.

"Good afternoon, Detective. Come into my office."

Mrs. Sleighton never looked up from her tabloid.

Caleb didn't offer his friend coffee. Today he wanted Thinnes to be uncomfortable so he would get to the point.

"This is inappropriate, John."

"Why? You're our consultant. I got a work-related problem I need to consult on. If I took it to Evanger, he'd send me to see you."

The slippery slope, Caleb thought. "But you haven't taken it to Evanger."

"I'm still officially off the case. I'm not supposed to contact Tien Lee."

"But you have."

"Franchi accused me of not being able to leave things alone. She's right."

"So?"

"I'm sure Tien Lee wasn't a gleam in his daddy's eye when White Tiger was operating in Saigon. So I'm sure Lee didn't kill his mother."

"Okay. And?"

"He as good as told me he's going after her killer."

"You're afraid he'll get himself killed, and you've developed feelings."

"He's my friends' kid. And I sympathize with his need to get the bastard."

"What's the real problem?"

"I had lunch with him today—after he took me to interview a witness. I'm not sure why. I told myself I wanted to observe him, but that's bullshit. I never questioned his translation of what the witness said. He could've been asking for her opinion on the best brand of nuoc mam."

"Was this lunch an invitation or a challenge?"

"I don't follow."

"Apparently he has the means to hire a private investigator if he's dissatisfied with what the police are doing. But he seems to be engaging you by interfering in your investigation. Why do you suppose that is?"

Thinnes considered the question. "Franchi asked him if he'd heard of me before his mother's death. He told her no. Today he said he'd seen my picture in his parents' album. But if he paid enough attention to remember the picture, he must've had some curiosity about it. Or me. Kids usually ask questions when they're curious. I can't believe Bobby or Hue would've lied or put him off."

"Did he volunteer that information or did you ask?"

"I asked."

Even in 'Nam, Caleb had had the habit of listening to what people talked about and thinking about what they didn't. Ace talked a lot about women, but never mentioned a girlfriend. Thinnes was talking a lot about Tien Lee.

"Have you discussed the allegation with him that you're his natural father?"

"No, of course not!"

"Why?"

Thinnes seemed at a loss, but he must have considered the question before. Caleb waited.

"I can't."

When waiting didn't get Thinnes to elaborate, Caleb asked, "Why?"

"It'd be an insult to his mother."

"Perhaps. But he might be willing to forgive it to clear this thing up."

Thinnes shook his head.

"There's more," Caleb said.

"It's impossible! I was faithful to Rhonda."

"Why?" Caleb wasn't referring to fidelity.

And Thinnes got it. "How could I not know?"

Caleb understood. For Thinnes to admit he might have fathered Tien Lee would be to accept that he wasn't who he'd thought, a question of his very identity.

"Mr. Lee might be as troubled by this subject as you."

232

Thinnes shook his head.

"But you will never know unless you bring yourself to discuss it with him."

"No!"

"Why?"

"First I have to nail his mother's killer!"

"I feel like I ought to pay you for this," Thinnes said.

"We've been over this before."

"I need it to be privileged."

Caleb stifled a sigh. "I charge six hundred dollars an hour."

Thinnes couldn't hide his shock.

And Caleb couldn't keep from laughing. "I have a special rate for friends and indigents. Give Mrs. Sleighton fifty dollars on your way out. She'll give you a receipt."

FIFTY-FOUR

The club was quiet, dark, and hazed over with smoke. Dim bulbs lit the bar and pool table. Christmas lights were strung around the walls. The audience was young, male, GIs mostly. The few women were Vietnamese, all young, all but the singer scantily clad. A single spotlight, reflecting off the singer's white *ao dai,* hurt Caleb's eyes. Chiaroscuro.

He leaned against the bar, nursing his drink as he recalled the sergeant's lecture: "Do what you want with the bar girls, children, but don't touch the mamasans or their daughters. Gooks don't like their women raped any more'n we do. As for the B-girls, it's rape if you don't pay 'em."

The singer could only be part Vietnamese. Her song was French, filled with longing and sorrow. It made him think of *Tristan und Isolde,* tragedy and unfulfilled love.

She was as lovely as a porcelain doll, but Caleb found her escort more compelling. Tall for an Asian, the young man was nearly white-skinned. He must have been the girl's brother or cousin, judging by their resemblance. He was indifferent to her song. But he was obviously with her—scowling and snapping in French or Vietnamese when anyone got too close. You didn't need to understand either language to know you'd have trouble if you messed with the chanteuse.

She finished her song and gave her companion a quick, bright smile, a complete contrast to the mood she'd woven with her vocal cords. The spot died, and she slipped away through the bead curtain behind the bar.

A long silence followed her departure. Then someone whistled, others clapped and stomped their feet. The noise level returned to normal. Someone fed the jukebox, and "You Can't Always Get What You Want" shook the walls.

A second youth joined the singer's guardian, and his indifference was explained as the two embraced. Caleb felt a stab of jealousy, though he'd never so much as spoken to the singer's champion.

At the far end of the bar, a half dozen of the B-girls cadged drinks from the rest of Caleb's squad.

"Hey, Doc," Leroy yelled. "We're gonna have a party!"

"Yeah, Doc," Ace called. "There's plenty to go around." He slid his hand up the leg of the girl next to him, stopping it on her buttocks.

Caleb held up his glass and shook his head. He pointed at the bead curtain and said, "I'm holding out."

"Bird in the hand, asshole," Ace shouted. He squeezed the girl's backside to reinforce his point.

The others tried halfheartedly to talk Caleb into coming; he just shook his head. He ordered another drink.

"Fuck this, man! The war'll be over before Doc gets near that little pussy." Ace's exasperation was understandable. The girl he was clutching wore a tight red silk dress and was rubbing his crotch with her derriere.

"Last chance, Doc. We're outta here."

Caleb held his glass up in a salute. "Have fun."

After they left, he looked long at the two young Asian men, wondering why he found them so attractive, the lovely woman so uninteresting.

He felt a hand on his back and looked sideways to find his sergeant had sidled up.

"Had enough, son?"

Aware he'd had too much to drink, Caleb focused on the NCO.

"If you really want the girl," the sergeant said. "I could probably arrange it."

"I don't think she's for sale, Sarge."

"Everybody's for sale. The ones who say they're not just set their asking price higher than most are willing to pay." He waited for that to sink in, then added, "I been watchin' you."

Caleb felt the prickling of adrenaline—pure panic. "Ah . . . no. Thanks anyway."

"You just told the guys she's the one you want."

Caleb felt heat in his face as he blushed. "Ahh . . . I only said that so they wouldn't think I was queer. I just didn't want to be with a bar girl."

The sergeant's hand kneading his neck kept him from thinking straight. What was wrong with . . . ? "They have diseases," he finally blurted out. He wished the sergeant would stop touching him, even though it felt good.

"That's why God created Trojans, son."

"Yeah, but those have holes sometimes."

The other man laughed. He stopped massaging Caleb's neck and grabbed his shoulder in a comradely hug. "Let's go for a walk."

Caleb threw a last look at the two young Asian men, then let the sergeant steer him toward the door.

The lane was dark, empty, except for the occasional body sleeping in a doorway or alley mouth. But for the background music of cricket song, the night was silent. Caleb was aware of the medley of smells he'd come to associate with Vietnam.

"This isn't the way back to the base," Caleb said when his eyes had adapted.

"Better you be straight gettin' back. We'll walk for a while. You can tell me about yourself." He actually sounded interested, so Caleb let him set their course.

"What do you want to know?"

"You got anybody back home who'll miss you if you don't come back?"

"My sister. And my younger brother."

"Your folks dead?"

"My mother is."

"Then she's past worrying herself sick about you."

236

"I hadn't thought about it like that."

"There's always more'n one way to think on things. Like how you turned it 'round that you didn't want to go whoring with your buddies."

Caleb felt himself redden until he was sure he must be glowing in the dark.

The sergeant stopped under the only light around—a single naked bulb suspended over the road in a cloud of dancing moths. He put his hand back on Caleb's neck. "You don't gotta explain yourself, son, especially when you're off duty."

The sergeant turned him until they were facing. He held Caleb's dog tag up to the dim light and squinted. "James A. Caleb. They call you Jim?"

"No, just James."

"What do your friends call you?"

"Jack."

The sergeant nodded. "My friends call me Ron."

Caleb nodded stiffly. He wasn't sure if he was supposed to call him Ron. What did it mean that the sergeant still had a hand on his neck?

"Listen, Jack. I got a hooch not far from here. You want to stop in for a drink?"

Caleb wasn't sure. It was flattering to be invited to the old man's hooch, but there was something disconcerting about it. Maybe it was the booze, or—he wasn't sure—their close proximity. Caleb had been humping through the boonies with him for months, had seen him nearly naked when they were drying their clothes after a rain or after trudging through the rice paddies, and he had never felt anything special for him.

But now he felt the shivery anticipation he'd first noticed at the bar while contemplating the singer's bodyguard. Still, it was crazy. A sergeant—

He said, "Sure," anyway, not worrying about why.

The sergeant dropped his hand. "C'mon, then."

Touching him only to steer him left or right, he led Caleb through a series of narrow lanes—not even glorified alleys—lit by lanterns or candlelight. A dog barked. The sergeant growled something that sounded Vietnamese, and it went silent. The sergeant pushed into a street so dark Caleb couldn't see. Caleb stumbled against him.

The sergeant said, "Hold on a minute."

A tiny breeze ruffled leaves invisible overhead. Caleb could hear the brush of cloth. There was the scratch and flare of a match, and the sergeant's face materialized from the blackness. He smiled. He reached overhead and lit a candle-lantern next to the door that had appeared beside them. He pushed the door open. "Come inside."

"Inside" was a small room with bamboo-lattice walls and a floor covered with fiber mats. The sergeant lit a lantern as he stepped inside. The place was clean and smelled faintly of incense. The furnishings were spartan—a bamboo chair, a table, a bed that was not much more than a frame with mattress and mosquito netting, a small sideboard with pitcher and basin, shaving kit, toothbrush, and a vase of pink gladioli. A mirror hung behind the flowers, its silvering flaked from age. There were books on the table and a cooler beneath it. A duffel bag lay under the bed, a large striped cat sat on the middle.

The sergeant said, "Scram, meó."

The cat stood and stretched, then vanished.

The sergeant hung the lantern from a chain over the table. "C'mere an' look at this." When Caleb was standing in front of him, trying to decide what he was supposed to see, the sergeant held an index finger in front of Caleb's face. "Hold your head still." He moved the finger slowly from side to side.

Caleb followed with his eyes, though it made him slightly dizzy. "I'm straight."

The sergeant laughed. "Good." He swept the room with a gesture. "Make yourself at home."

Since he was standing in front of the only chair, Caleb parked on the bed.

"Should be some beer." The sergeant nodded toward the cooler.

Caleb extracted two cold Lone Stars. "Where did you get—How?" Ice was scarcer off base than diamonds.

"Mamasan—my landlady—works on base. I pay her a little extra to bring home ice when I'm off duty." He pulled off his uniform shirt and hung it on the wall. He patted the sleeve of his T-shirt. "No stripes." He pointed to the door. "You start to feel uncomfortable at any point, it's not locked. And if you decide you gotta go—far as I'm concerned, you were never here."

Caleb nodded.

The sarge removed his boots and socks, shoving them beneath the chair. "Smoke?" Caleb nodded again. The sergeant handed him a bag of grass and a pack of rolling papers. While Caleb rolled a joint, the sergeant dug a votive candle and matches from the duffel. He lit the candle and turned out the lantern. He put the candle on the floor by the bed and stretched out next to Caleb.

Caleb lit the joint. After taking a drag, he handed it to his companion.

The sergeant said, "You scared, kid?"

He was, a little, but he said, "Nothing that isn't armed will ever scare me again."

He came awake suddenly. Where was he?

Then he remembered. He felt good. The candle had burned out. The hooch was in complete darkness, but he could hear the sarge moving beside him.

Crying!

"Sarge, what's the matter? Ron?"

"Nothin', kid. Go back to sleep."

Caleb reached under the bed for another candle. As he struck the match, the sergeant rolled on his side, turning his back. Caleb lit the candle and held it up. The sergeant's face was wet.

Caleb said, "Is crying part of sex?"

"Don't piss me off." Caleb waited. Finally the sergeant said, "I shouldn't have taken advantage of you."

"What?"

The sergeant looked angry. "Homosexual relationships . . ."

"Fuck regulations!" Caleb put the candle on the floor and

flipped onto his back, lacing his fingers behind his head. "Maybe I just wasn't any good."

"Shut up. It's not about you. You were fine." His voice seemed softer on "fine."

"What, then?"

"Shouldn't have gotten you involved."

"Why did you?"

"You seemed lonely. And you looked good. And I was horny." After a pause, he said, "How was it for you?"

"Fine. Oh, fuck, it was great! . . . Why were you crying?"

"Nothin' to do with you."

"What, then?"

"I had a friend . . . Forget it!"

Caleb stifled his *Oh*. He killed the light, then rolled on his side and began stroking the sergeant's head, the way he'd have stroked his little sister's when she woke with a bad dream. He felt the sarge relax, then start to quake from silent sobs. He felt tears leak from beneath his own eyelids as he rolled to face the sergeant's shaking back. He folded his arms around the sergeant and held him.

He was spread-eagled on his rack when the others got back to the tent they called home on base. The sun was just rising. Leroy was passed out, suspended like a sack of rice between Bob and Rodney. Bringing up the rear, Ace looked hungover.

"How'd you guys get past the MPs?" Caleb asked. *He'd* had a note from the sergeant.

"Aw," Bob said, "they know we're goin' back out today, so they didn't hassle us—you know? The condemned men ate a hearty meal and fucked their brains out."

"Hey," Rodney said, "look at you. Hey, Doc got lucky!"

Caleb just smiled.

"How was she, Doc?" Ace demanded.

Leroy sobered enough to say, "Shhhh. Gen'leman never tells."

Ace laughed. "What's that got to do with Doc?"

FIFTY-FIVE

In the family room with Toby and Skinner, Thinnes alternated between watching the news and watching Rhonda. She was perched in the far corner of the couch wearing a sexy summer dress—a thin, flowered cotton that looked like she had nothing under it. She was reading. The dog and cat were doing fur rug imitations. The humans had their bare feet propped up on the coffee table.

"Ronnie, what are we doing this weekend?"

She looked up from her book. "Getting ready for Monday. Why?"

"How 'bout we go to St. Louis for a couple days? We could take in the zoo, maybe stop at Cahokia Mounds."

He watched surprise, then suspicion cross her face. "In August?"

He shrugged. "They've got air-conditioning."

"What's in this for you?"

"I gotta interview someone who lives there. I just thought you might like to go."

"This have anything to do with you being carless?"

He shook his head. "I could rent a car."

"Can I drive?"

He hesitated, long enough that he was sure she noticed, but finally he said, "Sure."

They left at three A.M. and got to St. Louis by nine-thirty. Thinnes drove. He hadn't been there since before Rob was born—a lot of changes in twenty years. So once they were past the signature arch, he was forced to consult road signs, maps, and the Internet directions Rob had printed out for Rhonda. They didn't have to stop for directions.

They made a second honeymoon of it, taking in the zoo like teenagers, giggling over milkshakes at the historic Route 66 burger joint, dancing after dinner, making love.

The wake-up call, later in the morning, was way too early. Thinnes got it on the second ring. Rhonda rolled over, facing him, and said, "What time is your interview?"

"His daughter leaves for church at nine forty-five and gets back around eleven-thirty. He wants me in and out while she's gone."

"Can I come?"

"You might have to testify in court if you do."

She gave him an *Is that so?* smile. "What does one wear to an interview?"

The neighborhood reminded him of Glenview, the suburb he'd grown up in, with well-maintained brick ranches on carefully landscaped lots surrounded by hedges or fences. Eliott Austin's street was quiet, dead-ending half a block past his house. Austin opened the door himself and demanded to see an ID before he let them in. Thinnes flashed his star, but Austin asked for his card, too. Thinnes handed it over. Austin studied and returned it, then stood aside.

He was as tall as Thinnes. He'd been wiry and nervous, a chain smoker, but he'd put on weight since they last met. Now he was heavy and moved slowly. His face had thickened, too. He had an old man's bushy eyebrows over drooping, lidded eyes.

As Rhonda entered, Austin asked, "This your partner?"

"Yes."

Thankfully, he didn't ask for an introduction. Thinnes didn't make one.

Once they were inside, Austin relocked the door, then shuffled down a central hall, past arched entryways to the living and dining rooms, past several closed doors. Thinnes and Rhonda followed. Austin was breathing hard when he stopped at the last door on the right. He unlocked it and went in, flicking the light switch as he did. A reflex, Thinnes decided. Over his shoulder, Thinnes could see the room was already well lit by a bank of windows set at shoulder height. Light with privacy.

The odor of stale cigarette smoke hit him, and he spotted three ashtrays full of butts. Rhonda gagged.

There was scarcely space to turn around. A wheeled office chair could only be pulled back two feet from the cluttered desk. Beyond a narrow corridor of stacked cartons, a worn couch faced an old TV with rabbit ears. The rest of the space was crammed with filing cabinets topped by piles of typing-paper boxes labeled with black Magic Marker—years, places, events.

"Take a load off," Austin said, pointing to the couch. He tried to drag the wheeled chair toward it, but was prevented by the clutter narrowing the path.

"Let me." Thinnes lifted the chair past the bottleneck.

Austin took an ashtray from his desk and shuffled to the repositioned chair. He lowered himself into it and put the ashtray on the TV set behind him. The effort seemed to tire him and he sat breathing heavily for a minute. Finally he said, "I don't remember you."

Thinnes said. "No reason you should. I was an MP in Saigon in '72. You tried to interview me once. I was under orders not to talk."

Austin fumbled a cigarette pack out of a shirt pocket. Vietnamese cigarettes. He shook one from the pack and looked at it, then at Thinnes. "You were pretty cryptic on the phone. What's this about?"

"What can you tell me about the White Tiger?"

"Ah." Austin smiled wryly. "Cọp Trắng." He thought for a moment. "He was like the shark in *Jaws*. He never surfaced, but the bodies came ashore. What specifically?" He fumbled a book of matches from another pocket and lit up, then reached for his ashtray. The way he savored the smoke reminded Thinnes of Tien Lee. But unlike Lee, Austin broke into a fit of coughing.

"Can I get you something?" Rhonda asked.

Austin pointed to his desk and gasped, "Bottom right-hand drawer."

Rhonda got up and brought out a bottle of Johnny Walker Red. Half full. "There's only this."

Austin nodded and gestured impatiently for her to hand it to him. When she did, he took a long pull. He let his breath out forcefully and coughed again. A small cough.

He held up the bottle. "My doctor says I'll live another year or two if I give this up. This and cigarettes." He laughed. "For what?"

There didn't seem to be anything to say to that.

"Where were we?" Austin said.

"You were telling us about Cọp Trắng," Thinnes said.

"Yeah. You want a drink?"

"No, thanks."

Austin nodded. "Why?" Thinnes raised his eyebrows. "Why this interest after all these years?"

"He's turned up in Chicago." Austin waited. "We've had two murders, both people who were in Saigon in the early seventies. Both victims had connections to a woman murdered in Saigon in '72. As far as I know, they had nothing else in common."

"How did they die?"

"Shot, one was made to look like a suicide."

"Not his style. He always left a signature."

Thinnes shook his head. "I think he's been trying to stay below our radar. Apparently one of the victims could've ID'd him. Maybe both could. So they were executed." Nothing personal.

But in his mind's eye, Thinnes could see Hue Lee slumped on her apartment floor, her blood shocking red on the white shirt. It was very personal.

He glanced at Austin and was sure, from his expression, that the reporter had read just how much so.

"What makes you think you can nail him, even with my help?"

"He's hunting on my turf."

Austin nodded. "I was there five years—'70 to '75." He shook his head. "That was a long time ago." He took another drag and coughed again. "He was an assassin, a black marketeer, ran an unofficial insurance company—Bạch Hổ, they called it. He didn't always prevent trouble for his clients, but anyone who messed with one of 'em ended up gutted, floating in the Saigon River."

Glancing sideways, Thinnes could see Rhonda's eyes widen.

Austin went on. "I don't remember details of all the stories, but I've got 'em in my notes." He looked along the walls of cabinets and cartons. "I was going to write the definitive book, lay all the shades . . ." He looked back at Thinnes. "Too late. You read shorthand?"

Thinnes shook his head, but Rhonda said yes.

"Then I'll let *you* go through 'em. Maybe you can find something to nail the bastard. Take 'em with you. You can give me a receipt, FedEx 'em back when you're done."

Thinnes nodded. "Thanks."

"Maybe I'll live long enough to testify . . ."

He proved there was order in the chaos of the room by shuffling directly to the boxes containing his Saigon notebooks. He also had a carton of newspaper clippings.

Standing in the front doorway to see them off, he added, "I thought the guy was SOG, but I never could prove it, couldn't even find someone who'd admit knowing the name. One thing I do remember was a rumor he killed a prostitute because she wanted to marry some GI. And he set the boyfriend up for a murder or something, to get him shipped home."

"Why not just kill him?" Thinnes asked.

"Bad PR. He wouldn't want to attract attention by killing an American. And why bother, when you could discredit the guy and have Uncle Sam take him away?"

Rhonda was quiet on the way home. They stopped to take in the Cahokia Mounds—something she'd wanted to see since hearing of them on a PBS special—but she seemed to have lost interest. That was fine with Thinnes. He'd had enough ancient history lately.

They were on I-55, approaching the Midway Airport exit, when she observed, "They say nothing could be as bad as what you imagine, but . . ."

"The worst of it was I was only eighteen, figuratively a virgin."

"How did you stand it?"

"I had your letters."

FIFTY-SIX

Vietnam's got two seasons," Butch told the group, "hot and wet, an' hot and dry. It's never cool 'cept in the highlands. We saw so much death, after a while it didn't get to you."

"Speak for yourself," Caleb said.

"Bet you don't remember the first guy you saw killed."

"I do," Caleb said.

"They sent our squad to set up in a hard spot maybe half a klick outside the base perimeter. We knew we were being used as bait when the lieutenant said, 'C'mon, you worms. Time to go wrap yourselves around the hook.' "

As he spoke, he remembered details. He'd only been in country a month; he hadn't yet seen combat. It was the beginning of the dry season. Most of the tall grass they were humping through was desiccated and it rustled thunderously as they pushed along. May as well set off air-raid sirens. The sharp edges of the grass razored through bare skin and dragged at clothing like hacksaw blades. Nature seemed to be saying don't go there, though nothing was supposed to go down until after dark.

A half hour before sundown, gunfire erupted. The kid walking point turned with a surprised expression. A red flower blossomed on his olive-drab chest. His mouth opened but no sound emerged. Or maybe it was drowned out by the ear-slamming staccato of the squad's M-16s and the boom of RPGs exploding around them. The bright flower on the boy's shirt grew. Stoplight red. Red that stopped thought.

For an eternity Caleb couldn't remember what to do. Then, in the nanoseconds between incoming rounds and returning volleys, inspiration struck. The cry, "Medic!"

Training and a sudden fear of failure goaded him to reach the kid. He put a hand on his chest and pushed him to the dubious safety of the space behind a termite mound. Bits of mound and termites rained on them as Caleb cracked his med kit. The world shrank. Time slowed. Sound ceased.

What now?

A pink froth dribbled from the kid's mouth. Crimson streamers oozed from the red spot on his shirt. He coughed.

Sucking chest wound! You had to plug the hole. Restore the vacuum that pulled in air when the chest expanded.

He tore the kid's shirt open. Dragged tape from his kit; fumbled it from the wrapping. The process absorbed him; he watched himself perform, his actions automatic: Cover the hole while the kid dragged air into his lungs; uncover it as he forced the air out; cover it again on intake. The kid's breathing became less labored. Caleb held two fingers on the hole while he scrubbed the flesh dry around it, then slapped the gauze on. Tape over the gauze. Bandages to hold the tape in place when sweat loosened the adhesive.

The kid coughed again, breathed a little easier, managed to wheeze, "Am I gonna make it?"

Caleb took a deep breath. "If you don't try to talk."

The sergeant's voice startled him. "Cease fire!"

Caleb's ears pounded from the concussion, then hummed in the sudden quiet. He was saved from thinking about what he'd just done by another cry for help. He stumbled toward the voice. Ace was kneeling next to Rabbit, who had a small black hole above his left eye. Caleb stared. What was the procedure for serious head wounds?

A dark hand clamped his shoulder. The sergeant muttered, "Nothin' you can do for *him,* son. Go help McG."

Caleb moved like a robot.

Ace screamed, "You can't leave! You gotta help!"

Sarge's soft voice answered Ace. "He ain't God, boy."

Red flowers sprouted on McG's green shirt and grew like the time lapse of a blooming field of poppies, flowers overlapped until the shirt was blood-red, McG's face white.

Caleb looked at Butch. "Your first, you always remember."

FIFTY-SEVEN

There was no way Thinnes was going to let Rhonda read Austin's notebooks, even if it wouldn't be against regulations. He dropped them off at the Area on their way home.

He was in early the next morning to sort through them, but apart from the dates and locations on the covers, they were gibberish. He was waiting with fresh coffee for the boss when Evanger came in.

Evanger looked suspicious. "What do you want?"

"We got anybody who reads shorthand?"

"Azul."

"Can I borrow him for the day?"

"Why?" When he explained, Evanger sighed and said, "I suppose so."

When Azul came in, Thinnes had the notebooks and his files spread out on the conference room table.

"What do you need, Detective?"

"Read through these." Thinnes pointed. "Translate anything you find that refers to Cọp Trắng, Bạch Hổ, or White Tiger."

Azul picked up one of the notebooks and flipped through it. "I can do that."

An hour later, Thinnes asked him, "How's it going?"

"Beats reading traffic reports," Azul said. "Is this stuff for real?" Thinnes shrugged. "This White Tiger the guy you're looking at for the Ragland hit?"

"Yeah."

"I'll keep reading."

By three P.M., Azul had finished the last notebook and was typing a summary of his findings. He gave Thinnes the condensed version: Austin had kept track of crimes attributed to White Tiger, a.k.a. Cọp Trắng, and guessed that Cọp Trắng and Bạch Hổ were the same individual. He'd also speculated that the CIA and at least a couple of SOG guys knew the identity of the killer and let him stay in business for reasons known only to themselves.

"What's SOG?" Azul asked. "He never goes into that."

"Studies and Observation Group. A black ops outfit that operated in 'Nam, Laos, and Cambodia during the war. Special Forces, Commandos, SEALs, and Green Berets, mostly. There were rumors about assassination, kidnapping, and stuff we'd call terrorism if the other side did it."

Azul nodded. "He's got a lot of dates, places, and details here. I'll put 'em in my report."

"Thanks. He name any of the SOGers or CIA agents?"

Azul sorted through the papers and handed one to Thinnes. "I'm not done with this."

"I'll copy it and bring it right back."

Austin had been good enough to include ranks, units, and military ID numbers for some of the names on the list. Thinnes gave it to Franchi, who tracked down most of them overnight via the Internet. Nearly all were dead.

Thinnes had the coffee ready when Evanger came in. "Boss, I got a lead, but I have to go to Indiana to follow up."

"Their phone lines down?"

"Guy I need to talk to doesn't have a phone."

"You know this how?"

"Talked to the local sheriff, trying to get some background. I quote: 'He won't talk to you. He never leaves home.' "

"How'd you find out about this guy?"

"Franchi tracked him down. You might as well let us do this together. Our cases are joined at the hip."

"Is this going to be like last weekend? If I say no, you gonna take your wife?"

"Probably have to."

"It's a wild goose chase."

"What else have we got to chase right now?"

Evanger shook his head. "You and Franchi and Viernes got one day to track down this Indiana guy and the rest of the week to close your cases. After that you put them on hold 'til the Slow Season." The Slow Season. The mythical time when nothing much happened and Violent Crimes dicks could catch up on backlogs.

Spring brought people out of their houses, into contact with neighbors and aggravating strangers. Summer meant heat and short tempers and crowds at events where liquor freely flowed. In the fall idiots argued, lethally, over baseball playoffs and football games. And in winter there were holidays where families gathered to pour alcohol on smoldering resentments. Winter, spring, summer, and fall, men beat their wives, parents killed their children, drunks settled arguments with fists and knives and bottles, road-raged motorists, with cars and guns. The Slow Season was as likely as the Cubs winning the Series.

Viernes had court the next day, so Thinnes and Franchi went without him. They got there midafternoon. Neither of them knew enough about farming to time the visit right. They ended up watching the farm until four-thirty, when the guy running the tractor took a break and went to the house.

The door was answered by a Vietnamese woman. She seemed afraid of them, but when they flashed their stars and asked to see her husband, she invited them inside. "Please wait." She indicated the couch, and they sat.

There were pictures in the room—children at various ages. Teenagers. College kids. Amerasians.

The woman disappeared and came back with the tractor driver. He didn't introduce himself. "What do you want?"

"Information about Saigon," Thinnes said.

"I haven't talked about the war with anyone. Don't see any reason to start now."

"Tell us about SOG."

"Mindfucking. You can get what's been declassified on the Internet. Can't give you anything more than that."

"White Tiger," Thinnes said.

Behind him, Thinnes was aware of a change in the woman, a listening quiet. Fear. He turned to her and said, "Maybe *you* could tell us?"

She shook her head.

Thinnes turned to her husband. "White Tiger."

"Why should I get involved?"

"He's killed two people recently."

The man shook his head. "Nothing to do with me."

Thinnes was aware of Franchi staring at the woman. She'd gone even quieter than before. "One of the victims was the wife of a good friend of mine," he said. "She was Vietnamese."

The man looked at his wife. Thinnes couldn't see any sign from her that would sway his decision, but he could see him giving in.

After a long pause, he said, "Winning the hearts and minds of the people, more often than not, translated to trying to make the Vietnamese fear us more than Charlie. Not possible. We never got to know them well enough to really scare 'em. We didn't know their history, or their myths, or even what bogeymen they used to scare their kids. They didn't look like much, but they were tough little bastards.

"The key thing was deniability. We didn't know too much so we could credibly deny anything we were asked about. So I can't tell you much about Bạch Hổ. Just that he was American. We let him be, in exchange for certain jobs . . . dirty stuff."

"Can you tell us his name?" Franchi asked.

"Sorry. I can tell you he got his name because he was just like a tiger. Deadly. And merciless."

Thinnes got the message first thing next morning: "Boss wants to see you."

He wandered over to Evanger's office and tapped on the door-jamb. Evanger waved him in. "Close the door." When he did, Evanger pointed to the chair opposite his desk.

"I'm getting heat about you poking into the Lee case."

"From who?"

"Keller told me *he*'s getting heat." The deputy chief.

"Did he say from who?"

Evanger's look said, *You know how the game's played.*

"Know if he served in 'Nam?"

Evanger shook his head. "Why?"

" 'Nam is all I had in common with the Lees and, presumably, Hue's killer. And somebody—probably someone who also served in 'Nam—wants me off the case."

"Says you."

"Could you look into Keller's service record?"

FIFTY-EIGHT

Arthur's air conditioner had finally given up; the window it had occupied stood open. A new box fan pulled in what passed for fresh air. The blinds sliced afternoon sunlight into golden strips. The group seemed on the verge of sleep.

Joe was more than usually depressed.

"What is it?" Arthur asked.

"I can't sleep. When I close my eyes they're waiting."

"Who?"

"Dead Iraqis."

"If they're dead, what's the problem?"

Everyone but Joe glared at Butch. Joe looked as if he were seeing dead Iraqis. With his eyes open.

"What are they doing, Joe?" Arthur asked.

"Nothing." Arthur waited. They all did. "Just lying there. Dead. It wasn't a fight—nothing left alive. It was like those pictures of Hiroshima, only instead of dust and shadow silhouettes, the Iraqis turned to cinders."

The Highway of Death. February 27, 1991. The Iraqi retreat from Kuwait. Caleb recalled an article in *Time* magazine. All he remembered was that he couldn't bear to read it. His consciousness was already raised too high.

"Where were the TV camera crews?" Joe demanded. "And the fucking reporters? They were Johnny on the spot when some asshole general wanted to make a speech . . .

"I was on burial detail. We collected bodies and laid them out in rows, then buried them in mass graves. I tried to count, but I lost track around two hundred. There didn't seem much point in starting over. There were too many. Thousands. Tens of thousands. I kept thinking we make such a big deal about one American MIA, but there were thousands of Iraqis missing. No way their families are ever gonna find them. Most of 'em looked young, the ones that weren't so charred you couldn't tell that they were human. Civilians, too. Cars and buses of civilians. They must've thought that they'd be safe with the convoy. But we found little cinder people. And cinder mothers holding little lumps of charred—"

"We *got* it," Butch interrupted.

"I thought you liked war stories, Butch." Tears streaked Alec's cheeks.

Sitting on the floor next to him, Maharis tucked his hands into his armpits. He was rocking forward and back. "Black and white and red," he said. "No. No red this time. Only black and white."

"Here's a story for you, Butch," Joe said. "Sometimes when we picked a body up it would crumble to dust. And the dust would mix with the dust from the desert, and we'd breathe it. I'm sick to my soul from all the dust I breathed."

Caleb had a flash of recollection. Corpse powder. What Navajo witches were said to use to make their enemies sick. Some cultures made it seem so simple: Do wrong, be ill. How many of the Gulf War Syndrome victims were really just soul-sick? Perhaps there was a sort of symmetry here.

Not!

"I guess I'm lucky," Joe said. "One of the guys I served with shot himself. And one tried to shoot his CO. And I know for a fact one's locked away in a psych ward."

And the real perpetrators of the massacre wouldn't lose a night's sleep. Politicians banging the tin drum, generals out to destroy the Iraqi army, pilots playing life-and-death-sized video games, dropping real bombs on game-piece people. Remorse was left to the Joes of the war.

But what if they held a war and Joe didn't go? And Maharis stayed home, or Ragman? What if the generals had to *lead* the brigade? He shook his head. Silly speculation.

Maharis rocked faster, shaking his head. "No justice. No justice for Iraqis. No justice for Ragman."

Caleb wished he were wrong. He didn't see anyone dragging George Bush or Stormin' Norman into the Hague anytime soon. But he would see what he could do for Ragman.

FIFTY-NINE

Thinnes had talked to Jay Helms, Ragland's parole agent, before and after they'd located Ragland. Now he called him again.

"You get queries about Ragland from anyone besides me?"

"That's a pretty broad question," Helms said.

"Maybe because I haven't got enough of a handle on this to narrow it down. Did anybody ask for his address or contact information just before or after he disappeared?"

"Not that I recall, but let me check the file."

The phone went silent. Thinnes watched the action in the squadroom while he waited. The desk sergeant read his *Sun-Times*. Two of the Property Crimes dicks kibitzed over the coffee setup. Franchi typed furiously on her laptop. Viernes ripped a sheet of paper from one of the old manual typewriters, crumpled it, and lobbed it at a wastepaper basket. When he missed, the custodian retrieved it, giving him a dirty look. Evanger wandered out of his office with his BIG DOG mug.

"Detective." Helms's voice brought Thinnes back to business. "I had two queries about Ragland before you called. Someone from the Eighteenth asking if I had a current address. When I asked if I could call him back, he said he'd get back to me and hung up. Then a day later, a plainclothes cop stopped by and asked the same thing."

"Who?"

"Don't think he gave his name. Or I forgot to write it down. Anyway, he flashed his star and said it was urgent and he'd be pissed if he had to get a subpoena."

"So you told him?" Thinnes said.

"Why not?"

"No reason." Though it may have led to Ragland's death. "You think you could pick him out of a photo array?"

"I don't know," Helms said.

"Could you try?"

"Yeah, sure."

"I'll get back to you." Thinnes hung up and followed Evanger back into his office.

"One more thing, boss—think you could find out if Keller made detective?"

SIXTY

Another stifling afternoon, Arthur's new A/C unit worked overtime.

"What are you doing here, Butch?" Caleb asked.

Arthur seemed content to let Caleb play the shrink.

"Can't get enough of the war stories."

Caleb just looked and waited.

Butch capitulated. "My wife says I got anger management issues. She's gonna leave if I don't work 'em out."

"What do *you* say?"

Butch grinned. "She may have a point."

"What's your story?" Maharis demanded.

"Like I'd tell you."

On that rock the conversation foundered. Arthur seemed content to let silence work on their various neuroses. Caleb studied the others. Alec traced the seams of his slacks. Maharis rocked forward and back. Slowly. Absentmindedly. Joe took out his pocketknife and cleaned his nails. Butch stared at something only he could see.

Carl, Arthur's cat, broke the logjam. He strolled into the room, tail in the air, and made a circuit of the group, sniffing each man. When he got to Butch, the man patted the cat's head. Carl rubbed against Butch's legs.

"Butch keeps coming in, day after day," Arthur told Caleb, "listening to your stories because he has one of his own he needs to tell. When he's ready."

"Is that right, Butch?" Joe asked.

Butch kept petting the cat, but he nodded. So they all waited.

"There were lots of animals in country," Butch said finally. "Flies and rats and snakes. We had a entertaining form of rodent control. We'd douse the rats with kerosene, then set 'em on fire and bet on who could hit 'em. Even with an M-16 on full auto, it was hard." He shook his head. "Anything some sick bastard could imagine, someone did over there." He glanced around, judging their reactions. Caleb did the same, finding only interest. Butch's reaction to the cat vouched for his character.

Butch went on. "Did you ever have to do something that you knew was wrong, that you didn't want to do, that you knew was going to hurt someone but you had to do it or someone was gonna hurt you worse?"

"Yeah," Joe said.

" 'Member how it felt to be there?"

"Like shit."

"Well, multiply that by a thousand. That's how it felt to be in country. They ordered you to harass people you had no quarrel with, smash their property, bust up their families, and flatten their towns. If you did it, you were a baby-killing motherfucker. If you didn't, you'd end up at the ranch or in Leavenworth, fucked up for life with a dishonorable. If you deserted, you could be shot. But where was there to desert to anyway?

"Sometimes we'd be sent to pick up the Zippo squads. We called 'em that 'cause they used Zippos to torch the villages. Burn 'em down and put all the people in trucks and move 'em to these concentration camps they called 'fortified villages.'

"These guys'd come in from the bush and their eyes'd be dead. They'd stink to high heaven, too, but you wouldn't say nothin'. You fuck with those guys . . . I see 'em in my sleep.

"And other things:

"You know those pictures of forests after a tornado, where there's trees lying every which way—just snapped off and dropped? It was like that after a battle. Only it was bodies lying around. When they were ours, we'd swoop in and pick up the pieces— literally! There's no way we could've got all the right parts together. The dead gooks, they'd search and dump into piles and torch."

He shuddered. "Sometimes we'd drop napalm. There'd be

these mini-mushroom clouds of black smoke rising over the fires. It'd even float on water for a while—with little flames rising over it like rows of sharp teeth or, if there was enough, like a field of grass from hell. Burning everything—plants, hooches, people . . . If you were high enough, you'd just see the black smoke with little patches of fire glowing through and you could make yourself forget that there were people down there. One time the smoke was white. Or maybe it was fog and all you'd see was the tops of some of the biggest trees. And some of *them* were burning . . ."

The silence went on too long, until it was clear Butch wasn't going to finish.

"Butch," Caleb said, softly so he'd have to listen carefully. "Back then we had a choice between bad and worse, kill or be killed."

"Or be court-martialed," Joe put in unexpectedly.

"Yeah," Butch said. "Now we got a choice between guilt or anger."

"Only if those are the only options you can see."

"Oh, yeah. Right!"

"You could choose to put the blame on the system. Or on the military for sending kids into a hell they weren't prepared for. Or on incompetent, ill-prepared officers. Or on the silent majority that backed a senseless war because it was easier than thinking."

"Bullshit!" Butch said. "That's a fuckin' cop-out!"

Arthur held his hands up in a *Hold everything* gesture. "It is if you see it that way, Butch. But you *do* have an alternative you apparently haven't considered."

"What's that?"

"You can forgive yourself and get on with your life."

"Forgive myself for what?"

"You tell me."

"The worst—we had to fly these ARVN rangers upcountry—three of them. We didn't think much of 'em. They were all smaller than us and a little older—I was nineteen at the time. Only one of 'em spoke English. We picked 'em up in a hamlet they'd 'pacified'—a couple hooches and some paddies.

"They had a prisoner—a skinny kid in black pajamas—no more than sixteen. They had his hands tied behind his back, and they'd wrapped a long piece of cloth over his eyes and mouth.

"I remember the wind from the chopper blades fanning the water, blowing the rice stalks as we took off. When we got over the treetops, the dinks took the cloth off the kid's head and started hanging him out the door, laughing when he screamed. The translator said they were trying to scare him into talking.

"Then they just pushed him out. We must've been two hundred feet up. There wasn't anything I could do. He was there one second, then gone. The bastards who dropped him were laughing like fools and passing a joint back and forth.

"I lost it! I turned my M-16 on 'em—blew all three to hell.

"The pilot freaked; he almost lost it. And he was screaming so much, you couldn't understand a word he said.

"Lucky for me, I talked him into setting down and cutting the radio. After I told him what happened, he said we had to cover our butts. We cooked up a story that the fuckin' kid they'd offed had tricked ARVN into setting down in an ambush, then grabbed a gun and blew them all away.

"We dumped the bodies. Just to make it look good, we fired a couple rounds at the side of the chopper. Nobody questioned it."

"Didn't the pilot talk?"

Butch shook his head. "He got blown away a week later. He'd only been in country two fuckin' months."

SIXTY-ONE

Thinnes." The sergeant handed him a case folder. "Reports back on the guns they took off that nutcase in Twenty-four." District Twenty-four. "Lots of 'em stolen. Nice work!"

Thinnes took coffee into the conference room. He spread the files out and read through each report. It only took three-quarters of a cup of coffee to see a pattern.

Half the fifty-six firearms confiscated had been stolen. No surprise there. Only one still had a serial number. The others had their ID numbers filed or drilled off. On a hunch, Thinnes called the Northbrook police, who'd originally reported the gun missing. When he explained what he needed, the operator transferred him.

"Detectives. Irene Pederson."

"John Thinnes, Chicago PD. We just recovered a Sig Sauer you reported taken in a burglary six months ago."

"Do you have someone in custody?" Pederson asked.

"Just for illegal possession and possession of stolen property. He's not talking, but he doesn't look like your burglar."

"How can I help?" She sounded way too cheerful.

Thinnes wondered if it was part of a good cop/bad cop routine. If so, where was the bad cop? "There a chance you could fax me a copy of the report?"

"Certainly. If I recall, six or seven handguns were stolen. You only found the Sig Sauer?"

"The guy we arrested had fifty-six weapons in his possession, but that's the only one that had a serial number. I can ask our weapons officer to send you a copy of the report, if you like."

"I'd appreciate it. We have a decent clearance rate, but we're always trying to improve."

"Is there a chance I could get the reports on your other open cases involving weapons thefts?"

When he got the faxes from Pederson, Thinnes called the victim who'd lost the Sig Sauer. He got the man's wife, who gave him her husband's work number. Thinnes dialed it.

"Who is this?"

Thinnes identified himself and explained that the man's Sig Sauer had been recovered.

"When can I get it back?"

"You'll have to talk to the state's attorney about that. Probably not until after the trial. It's evidence."

"What about my other guns?"

"That's the only one that still has a serial number. If you can prove the others are yours, they'll be returned."

"Christ! One of them's an antique—one of a kind."

"Can you identify it?"

"I have pictures of all of them."

"There a chance I can get copies?"

"If it'll help me get 'em back, sure."

"It may. Where'd you get them originally?"

"I inherited two and bought three at the Lake County Gun Show. The others came from the Smithy."

On a hunch, and because he didn't believe in coincidence, Thinnes called the other Northbrook burglary victims. Five of the seven, bought guns at the Smithy. Two thought they could positively identify their weapons. He was on a roll; he started calling other suburban police departments. Oak Park, Evanston, Wilmette, Winnetka, and Morton Grove told him they banned possession of handguns, but an Evanston officer confided—off the record—that a resident burglarized a year earlier had reported a stolen gun, then amended his report when told possession was illegal. Cops in fourteen other suburbs, from Lake Forest to Brookfield, all agreed to fax the burglary reports.

At quitting time, Thinnes reported his preliminary findings to Evanger and got permission to work overtime. Then he called Rhonda to say he'd be home late.

SIXTY-TWO

When he left Arthur's, Caleb felt he was on the verge of remembering something important, but the harder he tried to recall what, the more elusive it became. Let it go, he thought. Don't push the river.

Instead of going home, he got his car and headed north on the Drive. Rush-hour traffic occupied his conscious mind for the next half hour. By the time he'd cut over to the Edens, it was coming back . . .

The view from twenty thousand feet was like a postcard, soft, spring-green rice paddies, brown rivers, silver pools and blue ponds mirroring the sky.

Stepping out of the plane was like entering a sauna. Until the smell registered. Mildew and decaying vegetation, open sewers, rotting meat. Caleb and his buddies were loaded into buuuu that had windows covered over with chicken wire—to keep grenades from flying in.

The road to Bien Hoa was a frenzy of activity—motor vehicle traffic, cyclos, bicycles and motorbikes, animals and pedestrians, all churning up the dust. Dust that turned to mud on the sweat-soaked skin and clothing.

Roadsides and riverbank were awash with it; mud paved the alleys and entryways of huts roofed with corrugated steel sheets or shingled with flattened beer and soda cans. The poverty made the poorest village Caleb had visited in Mexico seem like a resort town. The pace of traffic made the busiest Italian rush hour seem to fly.

The sergeant who ordered the FNGs to fall in when they arrived was tall and good-looking, a muscular, medium-complected black man. Old, Caleb thought, thirty at least. Caleb was nineteen.

The sergeant regarded the new arrivals with a stern expression. "Which one of you's the medic?"

Caleb felt a profound reluctance to respond.

The sarge looked at his clipboard. "Caleb, James!"

Caleb stepped forward and saluted.

"Well, Doc. I guess if you made it this far, you got guts or brains or a hell of a lot of luck. Which?"

"I don't know, Sarge."

"Do what I say, you may live long enough to find out."

A few days later, they'd followed the sergeant like a litter of pups after an old hound. Just outside the base perimeter it was like a bizarro version of the market in Mexico City. Vendors hawking every conceivable thing—but in French or Vietnamese, not Spanish.

It was nearly noon. An old woman dressed in black pajamas and a conical straw hat was stirring a pot of thick soup over a fire that looked like burning cow dung. Caleb didn't point it out to the others, who were fixated on the soup, which smelled very good.

One of the grunts offered the woman a quarter. She grinned, showing gaps where teeth had been. She nodded vigorously and ladled soup into a small chipped ceramic bowl. He gave her the coin. She offered him a flat-bottomed spoon, which he declined. He sipped the soup directly from the bowl. "Man, this is good. What is this, Sarge?"

"Soup."

"What kind?"

The sergeant asked the woman something in Vietnamese. She said, "*Pho cho.*" The sergeant grinned. "Dog soup."

The grunt lowered the bowl. "Sarge, don't do that!"

The sergeant grinned. "You didn't know they eat dogs?"

"This isn't funny!"

"Not meant to be. These people are poor. They don't waste nothing. One of our trucks kills a dog, they don't get sentimental. They don't let it go to waste, either."

"Shit!" The grunt spat on the ground and drew the bowl back as if to heave it away.

But the sergeant caught his hand and pried the bowl from it. He studied the handful of Vietnamese watching the show. A small boy at the edge of the group seemed to catch his attention. The child was barefoot, dressed in a torn shirt way too large for him. He had a deep scar on his forehead that pointed to a clouded eye.

The sergeant offered the soup to the boy as a maître d' might serve a recommended entrée. Everyone watched the child suck down the contents, the Vietnamese with obvious appreciation, the GIs with a horrified fascination.

"Sarge!" The grunt looked ready to puke. "How *can* you?"

With a grave expression, the sergeant said, "You live long enough, son, you'll learn not to waste food, too."

When Caleb first arrived at base camp, the sergeant introduced him to his platoon mates. One of them had scribbled ACE over the name on his uniform shirt. He sat down immediately and pulled off his boot, cheerfully presenting his smelly foot—with the first real case of foot rot Caleb had ever seen. "Hey, Doc, take a look at this."

Caleb's first "mission" lasted a week. He was appalled by the way they smelled when they came in from the bush. He and his buddies stripped down and hit the showers, abandoning their clothes in piles. He nearly puked when he came out of the shower and passed the filthy heaps.

At first he'd kept track of their missions, asking why they were searching this village, torching that. The sergeant would always tell him, "None of your business, Doc. You're just a grunt—lower than a grunt, a fucking C.O. pacifist." But then—if the mission wasn't classified—he'd tell him what they were doing, or at least what he thought was the purpose of the exercise.

Caleb dispensed salt tablets and malaria pills, aspirin, antifungal cream, and remedies for diarrhea. He discovered early on the therapeutic value of touch. His position as medic seemed to exempt him from the prohibition against touching men. And sometimes all he could do for a guy was put an arm around him.

At Lake Cook Road, Caleb turned his Jaguar east for a half mile, then into the Chicago Botanic Garden. The gate attendant spotted his member decal and waved him through. He parked in lot two, which was all but deserted.

His favorite place was the square fountain beyond the exhibition hall. Surrounded by pines, yews, and silver maple trees, its stone perimeter was a cloister. The fountain itself was simple, a circular mosaic of small granite cubes with forty-nine vertical jets spurting upward. The water splashing on the stone made a white sound like a waterfall.

There were no seats or benches. Caleb perched on the back of a golf cart parked on the walk. He sat cross-legged, cupping one hand in the other, palms up. He closed his eyes and breathed in deeply. The air smelled of water and damp earth. No decomposing bodies. No shit. But it brought back Vietnam.

The company's base camp was situated just outside a small town on the Vam Co Dong River. One afternoon, when he'd been in country a month, the sergeant took him aside.

"Let's go get a drink, kid."

Caleb had been flattered, nervous, curious. To his surprise, the sarge led him out the base main gate instead of toward the hooches. It was near sundown. The heat hadn't abated, but long shadows cut into the golden light.

The sergeant strolled along as if he had all day, smiling and nodding at the mamasans hawking their goods along the roadway, giving way to trucks and farm carts and farmers with animals aboard or in tow. A crowd of street kids surrounded them demanding handouts. Sarge told Caleb to beware his watch. He put a hand over the pocket holding his own wallet and growled at the kids in Vietnamese. They scattered. The sergeant laughed and picked up his pace, plunging down streets narrower than alleys in Chicago, streets menacingly deep in shadow. Caleb realized he had no weapon, just a pocketknife, but the sergeant seemed at home, so he swallowed his objection and followed.

It was obvious the sergeant had been that way before, probably many times. Old men smoking in doorways and women gossiping as they chopped vegetables or tended small children—people they passed smiled or waved.

They went down streets flanked by traditional peasant hooches made of bamboo and thatched with straw, and turned onto one presenting houses of stone and stucco, two-story affairs with tile roofs and wrought-iron balconies. After the fifth or sixth turn, Caleb was hopelessly lost.

A small boy approached them with a bicycle basket lined with palm leaves and filled with ice. He had a church key on a lanyard around his neck.

"Hey, Joe," he said. "You wan code be-ah?"

The boy's eyes widened when the sergeant asked in Vietnamese for three Cokes. The boy put down his basket and dug three red and white cans from under the ice, opening each before handing it to the older man.

The sergeant handed one to Caleb and gave the kid a Vietnamese bill. The boy's eyes widened even more when the sergeant waved away the proffered change. *"Didi mau,"* he told the kid with a grin.

"You numbah one, Joe." The boy stashed the bill and took off.

They continued down a street that passed between shacks thrown together from packing crates and sheets of rusty corrugated. Eventually the sergeant stopped in front of a bamboo gate set into a hedge of twelve-foot-high bamboo. He rang the wooden gong on the gatepost. The gate opened, and a young Buddhist monk stuck out his head. The sergeant spoke to him in Vietnamese; the monk bowed and swung the gate wide. As soon as they were inside, he closed it and sat next to it on a flat stone.

The sarge dropped a coin in his begging bowl, then slipped his shoes off. He gestured for Caleb to do the same.

The stone path down which the sergeant led them was still warm from the sun, though shadows had long since claimed it. The path led through a tiny formal garden to a small shrine with a bronze statue of the Buddha. The sergeant put one of the two Cokes he was carrying at the Buddha's feet and sat on his own feet in front of it.

Caleb tried to do the same, though the best that he could manage was to sit cross-legged. He gladly accepted a cigarette and smoked it as he waited.

"You believe in God, kid?"

Caleb thought about it. God hadn't saved his mother, had let his hated father live. "No."

" 'S all right. Don't matter. What matters is you understand others do."

Caleb nodded.

"Three things you gotta remember." The sergeant seemed to be waiting for his absolute attention.

"Do your job the best you can," Sarge said. "You can't save anyone. You're not God. 'Member that they'll live or die, that's not up to you. What *is,* is that you do your best to give 'em a chance." He finished his Coke in a long pull and dropped his cigarette butt in the can. "You do that and you'll make my job easier."

Caleb nodded again.

"Second thing—part of your job—is to comfort the dying. That makes you feel bad, tough shit. You do what you got to do to make 'em comfortable."

"Okay."

After a long silence, Caleb said, "What's the third?"

"Don't give nothin' to beggars; you'll turn 'em into bums. Make 'em work for what they get."

Caleb opened his eyes. The sun was down, the fountain nearly invisible in the twilight. He realized who had killed Ears. *Froggy.*

And why. Froggy had saved Preacher from doing something he'd never forgive himself for doing. But he hadn't done it without guilt.

And what Froggy, and Joe, and Butch, and Alec, and he himself had all been seeking was forgiveness—for surviving, for failing to save their friends. For not being God.

They were all wounded. And the comfort the sarge spoke of so long ago was absolution. Caleb hadn't known it. He had offered Froggy forgiveness because it was all he had to give.

SIXTY-THREE

The next morning, Thinnes rousted his chauffeur at six o'clock. He made coffee while Rob got dressed.

As he was driving Thinnes to work, Rob asked, "Dad, when are you gonna get another car? I could chip in."

"You need every penny you've got for school."

"I made plenty this summer."

"It always costs more. And it always takes longer."

"What does?"

"Everything."

He took up where he'd left off. Around noon, a messenger delivered photographs of the Northbrook man's missing weapons collection. After lunch Thinnes finished calling police departments and burglary victims in the surrounding suburbs. Then he took the photos and the police department faxes to the CAGE unit working out of Narcotics and Gang Investigations at 3440 W. Filmore.

The sergeant in charge of identifying recovered weapons glanced at Thinnes's new folder and groaned.

"I got something that I think might actually help," Thinnes told him.

"Oh, yeah? Like those fifty-six guns we just got?"

Thinnes handed him the envelope of photographs. "Any of these look like your Andersonville guns?"

"Oh, now they're *mine*."

"Possession, you know."

The sergeant shuffled through the pictures. "Hey!" He fanned the air with one of them. "We've got this!"

Back at the Area, Thinnes sorted his paperwork into piles by suburb, date, and where the stolen guns originated. Then he called Franchi. "What's wrong with this picture?"

She studied his careful arrangement and said, "Wow! Why hasn't anybody seen this before?"

"Nobody was looking. You've gotta have more than one or two to make a pattern."

"I guess I better start researching Mr. Smith."

"I'm putting in that turkey who fingered the Andersonville gun nut for a good citizen's award."

Nobody bothered to announce Jack Caleb's arrival. The doctor had been to the Area Three squadroom so many times he was almost part of the furniture. But this time he'd remembered to ask for a visitor's badge.

Thinnes was ready for a break, so he ushered Caleb over to the coffee setup and poured them both a cup of four-hour-old sludge. "What can I do for you, Doctor?"

"I take it you haven't yet arrested Theo Ragland's killer?"

"Nope. Sorry. We're still working on it, though."

"You don't sound optimistic."

"I'm not. But I'll keep plugging."

"I want to help."

"How?"

Caleb shrugged. "Any way I can."

Thinnes tried to think of a diplomatic way of saying, *Just keep out of my hair,* when it struck him that Caleb could offer the evidence a new pair of eyes. He was, after all, a consultant. "What the hell?" Thinnes said. "You feel like reading over the case file?"

"Certainly."

Thinnes took the doctor and the file into the conference room and closed the window blinds. Then he went to find Franchi.

. . .

"Your turn to get coffee." Franchi made a skeptical face but got up to collect their empty mugs. Caleb kept reading.

Franchi stopped just outside the conference room door, staring into the squadroom. "What's he doing here?"

Thinnes came out to see who. Tien Lee stood just inside the squadroom door.

"Trying to help us find his mother's killer," Thinnes said. He caught Lee's eye, and the younger man started toward them. "As long as he's working with us," Thinnes told Franchi, "we can keep an eye on him."

"Or we could just have him arrested for interfering . . ."

She trailed off when she looked in at Caleb, who was following their disagreement with apparent interest. She shook her head and stalked away.

Thinnes ushered Lee into the conference room. "Dr. Caleb, may I present Tien Lee?"

Caleb nodded. "Mr. Lee."

"Tien, please." He offered his hand; Caleb took it.

"Dr. Caleb is our profiler," Thinnes said. Not entirely a lie. "Have a seat."

Lee settled himself as Franchi returned with four full mugs, a handful of sugar packets, and a Coffeemate can. She'd been quick—probably didn't want to miss anything. She put the additives down and distributed the mugs.

Caleb looked around the group. "What do we know?"

Thinnes said, "White Tiger moved here after the war."

"Why here?"

"Could be any number of reasons." Thinnes ran his fingers through his hair. "He may be from here. Or maybe because this is an international shipping crossroads. Or because Chicago has a large Vietnamese population with no organized crime—nothing like the Tongs on the coasts."

"He knows *you*," Lee said.

Thinnes nodded. "And he knew your mother in Saigon."

"Chances are she was murdered shortly after he discovered

she was in the area. So we need to find out where she might have met him."

"Since we moved here, she went to church, the Lyric, museums, plays, restaurants, visiting relatives, shopping. Not much shopping."

"Piece of cake," Franchi said. "We just get the names of everyone at all those places, and see who had a connection."

"You always eat at the same places?" Thinnes asked.

"No. We were sampling the city's variety."

"I'll need a list. What about shopping? Same thing?"

"No. She liked the Asian markets. And we sometimes went to Dominick's. She didn't drag me along when she shopped for clothes but sometimes she went with Mrs. Nyugen. You have her credit card statements." He paused, seemed to recall something, then said, "This White Tiger must have been in San Diego for a while."

"Why do you say that?"

"My parents left there abruptly, cut off all ties with old friends, left no forwarding address. The logical explanation is that they were afraid of something. And it wasn't the government or they'd have changed their names and gotten new Social Security numbers. My father certainly had the expertise to do that if he felt it necessary. Back then it was relatively easy."

Something pissed Franchi off—maybe Lee's casual mention of identity forgery. She scowled at him. "What are you doing here, anyway?"

"I was just wondering what progress you've made."

"You could've called."

"It's much harder for people to stonewall face to face." He turned to Caleb. "A pleasure to meet you, Doctor." He nodded at Thinnes and walked out.

As soon as the squadroom door closed behind Tien Lee, Caleb changed seats so he had a clear view of both detectives. He watched their reactions as he said, "An interesting man."

Thinnes seemed resigned.

Franchi was stiff with anger. Ignoring Caleb's bait, she turned to Thinnes. "Who'd have had the clout to make your Jasmine file disappear? Back in Saigon."

"Someone with the CIA or SOG. Someone high enough in the MPs to make it look like the order came from someone even higher. Someone in the South Vietnamese government."

"He must've gotten out with the money to set up here," Franchi said. "What about Mr. Hung?"

"Why wait three months to kill her?" Thinnes said. "And whoever he is, he's got an in with the department."

"Why?" Caleb asked.

"He knew from the start that I'd been assigned to the case, and what to do to get me off it."

Caleb said, "That suggests this White Tiger is someone who knew you well enough in Saigon to know you'd eventually have solved Jasmine's murder if you kept at it."

"Who therefore knows you won't quit until you get Lee's killer," Franchi said. "Which means he's probably a cop." She sounded ready to spit.

Thinnes was still discussing the Lee case with Caleb when Amy Nyugen came. She asked for Detective Franchi or Detective Viernes. Viernes was out. Franchi invited the visitor to have a seat. She didn't ask Thinnes to sit in on the interview, but she didn't tell him to leave. In a reversal of their usual roles, he stayed off to the side with pen and notebook while Franchi asked the questions.

Amy introduced herself as Mrs. Nyugen's oldest daughter. She was twenty-two, a recent graduate, who'd worked her way through college interning for the marketing company where she was still employed. She'd been vacationing in Italy when Mrs. Lee was killed. She was grief-stricken when she found out. "Mrs. Lee was always kind. My mother thought there might be something I could tell you that would help you solve the case. I don't see what, but here I am."

"What can you tell us about her son?" Franchi still seemed teed off about something.

"Isn't he gorgeous?"

Franchi snorted. "He and his mother get along?"

"Oh, yeah. He used to take her out all the time."

"They ever argue?"

"I never heard them. My mom said they fought about marriage. She wanted him to; he didn't."

"He have a girlfriend?"

"Not that I know of. Come to think of it—maybe he's gay." She glanced at Thinnes, then looked back at Franchi. "I mean, there's lots of cute girls in our building, but I never even saw him look at one. And he's got great fashion sense." As if that were conclusive evidence.

"How did Mrs. Lee spend her time?"

"Oh, shopping and church and an occasional movie. And, she went to one neighborhood police meeting with my mother. She told me it was very interesting but didn't explain."

"When?"

"Three weeks before she died."

"Why didn't your mother tell us this?"

"Mom said you only asked her what Mrs. Lee did in the two weeks before her death."

Luckily, the Nineteenth District Neighborhood Relations officer was in. Susan Evans perched on one of her visitor's chairs. She shoved another toward Franchi with her foot and pointed Thinnes toward a third. "What do you need, Detectives?"

Franchi swung the chair around and straddled it. Thinnes parked next to her. "We need to find out who was at last month's CAPS meeting," he told Evans.

"Deputy Superintendent Keller?" Franchi asked.

"I doubt it," Evans said. "He'd have been talked about. The commander was there."

The district commander. A guy with a reputation for being squeaky clean. Not likely he was the Tiger. The beat coppers would be there—part of their job. Community activists. Residents. Maybe cub reporters. "We'll need a list," Thinnes said.

SIXTY-FOUR

Franchi held up what looked like a fax. "The owner of record of the building housing Smith's gun store is a trust at the First Personal Savings Bank."

"That sounds familiar."

"It should. Same company holds the mortgage on the building where we found Theo Ragland."

"I just remembered something else. Corso and Smith said hello in almost identical words—almost as if someone told them to expect a visit and what to say. Let's find out who really owns Smith's building."

"I'll go talk to Columbo," Franchi said. "See what we need to do to get a subpoena."

It took Franchi a day to pry the property owner's name and Social Security number from First Personal's Trust Department.

Mabel Hannigan.

"That's her maiden name," Franchi said. "Married name, Keller.

"Oh, and I called my dad." Franchi's father was a retired cop. "He asked around for me. Smith served under Keller when he was a patrol sergeant in the Third." The Third District. "Dad didn't like either of them. Smith was an abusive bully and Keller looked the other way."

"So now we know the name of Smith's Chinaman."

. . .

"Thinnes!" Evanger was standing in his doorway, holding the door. As Thinnes approached, the lieutenant backed into the room. Thinnes followed; Evanger closed the door.

Trouble!

"Have a seat." He didn't sound pissed off, so Thinnes relaxed a little. Evanger said, "I thought you were kidding about Keller."

"No-o." Thinnes dragged the word out, letting his boss know he was wondering why Evanger would think he'd kid about something like that.

"He was in Special Forces," Evanger said. "He served three tours—'65 to '68—then resigned his commission to work for a private company. In Saigon. He was there 'til '75."

"That was SOP for SOG," Thinnes said. "It gave the government plausible deniability when one of them was caught."

"That's all I could find out without raising flags. It's certainly not enough to accuse a deputy chief—"

"Well, Franchi dug up a few things."

Thinnes told him the rumors about Keller covering for Smith. "His wife is beneficiary of the trust that owns the building where Smith has his gun store. That's where a number of stolen guns came from originally."

"You know who stole them?"

"No, but I got enough to get ATF interested. What's to stop guys like Smith from selling their customer lists? Or even arranging burglaries so they have untraceable weapons to sell to 'special' customers?"

"Interesting point. What are you doing to follow up?"

"We're trying to match up what we've recovered with what was taken in suburban burglaries."

"Meanwhile?"

"Mrs. Keller's bank also holds the paper on the building where we found Theo Ragland. The key to *his* murder is what happened in Saigon. I can ask Keller if he knew Ragland or if he knows anything about Saigon."

"You can't bring him in."

"I'll go to his place. It's not ideal, but just knocking on his door ought to spook him a little."

"Take Franchi and Viernes. If it comes down to he said/she said, I want you to have witnesses. And while you're yanking Keller's tail, I'll give Internal Affairs a heads-up."

"Oh, thank God you're here!" The woman who opened the door for them was middle-aged and motherly—but a cop's wife. She'd recognized detectives even before Thinnes flashed his star. "He's in the basement."

"Who?" Thinnes said. For a fraction of a second he imagined a home invader or a burglar. It'd be just their luck to have their case blown by some idiotic coincidence.

"My husband," the woman said, as if he were stupid. She looked at Franchi, then Viernes. "He's gone crazy! He's burning trash in the furnace!"

"Christ!" Thinnes said. "Show us!" he told Mrs. Keller; to the others, he said, "Exigent circumstances."

Mrs. Keller led them to the top of the basement stairs and pointed downward. "There."

Viernes said, "Where's his gun, Mrs. Keller?"

"In the living room."

"Show me."

She turned back to Thinnes. "Please don't hurt him!"

As soon as she turned her back, they pulled their weapons. Most cops had backup guns, and they weren't taking any chances with one who'd gone "crazy."

Thinnes took point.

The steps were carpeted, but halfway down, one creaked.

"Mabel?" Keller's voice.

So much for the element of surprise. "No, Keller," Thinnes said. "John Thinnes." He kept moving down.

"What do you want?"

"I need to ask you some questions." As Thinnes got to the bottom of the steps, Keller came through a doorway at the far side of the room.

Keller reddened with rage. "You dare point a gun—" Nevertheless, he put his hands out to his sides.

"SOP," Thinnes said. "Your wife called 911."

"Get out!"

Thinnes turned sideways, giving Franchi a clear view and shot.

"Both of you, get out!" Whatever was going on, Keller was angry enough to do something nuts.

Thinnes held his ground.

"I'm not armed," Keller said.

"Turn around. Put your hands on the wall so I can confirm that."

The muscles of Keller's jaw tightened, the skin paled, but he complied. Thinnes did a quick pat-down, then holstered his gun. "You can turn around."

Keller did. "What the hell are you two doing here?"

"We three," Viernes interrupted, downing the stairs two steps at a time. He was holding a .38 Police Special by the cylinder. Obviously Keller's gun. "Your wife called us."

"That's ridiculous!"

Franchi slipped her gun into her purse as Viernes continued, "You scared her."

Thinnes, meanwhile, was inspecting the room. There was nothing incriminating in plain view, no other weapons. He stepped away from Keller to get a better look at the room Keller had just come out of. While his attention was occupied, Keller stepped to his right, putting Franchi between him and Thinnes, reaching behind him.

Suddenly he was pointing a semiautomatic. He grabbed Franchi and shoved the gun against her rib cage. "Stop!"

She froze.

Keller glanced at Viernes, then caught Thinnes's eye. "Either of you move, she's dead!"

As if she wasn't anyway.

Keller poked Franchi harder with the gun and looked at Viernes. "Drop that."

Viernes bent forward and carefully put the .38 on the floor. Thinnes didn't move.

"Give me your purse," Keller told Franchi. He put his free hand out to the side. "Now!"

Smart. If he didn't reach, she wouldn't have a chance to grab him.

She slipped the strap off her shoulder and held it out where Keller would have to reach to take it.

"Here," he said, snapping his fingers.

She started to move the purse toward him, then let it drop. As it fell, she whirled. She grabbed the muzzle of the gun and swung it across her body, turning sideways to present a smaller target. With her free hand, she caught his wrist, pushing in the opposite direction she was pulling the gun. Keller let go.

Franchi kept the weapon moving in an arc aimed at his head. When he leaned back to save his face, she lunged forward and body-slammed him to the floor. She tossed the gun aside. Before he could regain his balance, she had his right hand in a lock she used to force him into a prone position. She twisted the arm so far up behind his back it was painful to watch. *"Stop resisting!"* she said, then lowered her voice so only Keller and Thinnes could hear her add, "Or I'll break your fucking arm!"

Then she dropped a knee onto the small of his back and told him, "Put your other arm out to the side. Palm up." She had to ratchet the twisted arm a little tighter before he did as he was told. Thinnes stepped up at that point and snapped the cuffs on. Viernes stood back, grinning.

Franchi got up and backed away. "All yours, guys."

SIXTY-FIVE

It took the better part of a day to follow up on Keller's arrest. The papers he hadn't managed to burn before they arrived would probably get him kicked off the force, but not indicted for anything. A preliminary look at his bank records turned up nothing that couldn't be accounted for—more or less—by legitimate income. If he *was* Cọp Trắng he'd be rich, but unless he had an offshore bank account they hadn't found, he was relatively clean. Most of his acquaintances were pretty straight-up people, too, horrified that he'd been arrested. So the question was, why?

In the Area Three interview room, Thinnes asked him. "How did you get into this, Keller?"

"He who rides the tiger never can dismount."

"Cọp Trắng had something on you?" Keller just shrugged. "Who killed Hue Lee?" Thinnes asked.

"I'd say not me, but you wouldn't believe it."

"Try me."

"Not me."

"Who, then?"

"You figured that out already."

Thinnes didn't miss the fact that Keller hadn't answered the question. He said, "Why?"

"She could ID him."

"So what?"

"No statute of limitations on murder."

"Yeah, but there's the matter of jurisdiction. What she could finger him for was a murder in a country that no longer exists. And it wasn't a war crime, so why worry?"

"Men have been ruined by lesser allegations."

"You're not convincing me. Just tell me why."

"You. You swore you'd get the guy who killed the whore in Saigon, and you and Hue Lee were an item. It figures she'd tell you what she knew, and you'd act on it."

Thinnes shook his head.

"Why else'd she move here right after her husband died?"

"Maybe to be near relatives. Especially her son."

"Your kid."

Thinnes had decided Lee was a straight-up guy, so the allegation no longer bothered him. "What gave you that idea?"

"Her old man couldn't have spawned him. And the kid was born just about nine months after you shipped out. It doesn't take Einstein to do the math."

"Circumstantial, at best," Thinnes said.

"Men have been hung on less."

"Maybe *you're* really Cọp Trắng."

"No."

"Who is he?"

"You're not gettin' that from me."

"Why not? You as good as confessed to being an accessory with that crack about riding the tiger. At the very least you're an accessory after the fact."

"And with a good lawyer, I can get off with twenty-five to life—maybe serve twelve. I give you *him*, I'm dead." Keller paused and gave a nervous laugh. "You heard about the Chinese businessman who bragged he could finger the White Tiger? The cat got his tongue. Literally."

Late as it was by the time they'd finished the paperwork and turned Keller over to the lockup, Evanger was still at work. Fielding phone calls from higher-ups, probably. Poor bastard. His office door was open, so Thinnes tapped on the jamb.

Evanger put his palm over the mouthpiece. "Come in."

"Calling it a night, boss."

Evanger nodded. "Where are we?"

"Keller lawyered up, so we sent him over to County."

Viernes and Franchi were huddled with Evanger just outside his office when Thinnes came in from an interview the next afternoon. Thinnes asked, "What's up?

Franchi scowled. "Keller got shanked last night."

"How does that happen?"

Evanger shrugged. "Some cop-hater got lucky."

Thinnes felt his adrenaline level rising. "Luck had nothing to do with it. We gotta—"

"No!" Evanger's look froze them. "You gotta stay out of it Let the sheriff's people deal with it, and the state's attorney, or IAD." He glared at Thinnes. "You stay away!"

When Evanger had closed his door behind him, Viernes said, "That takes care of that."

"Yeah." Thinnes took out his cell phone and punched in the number of a sheriff's deputy who worked nights.

"Ritts," a sleepy voice said.

"Ritts, John Thinnes."

"D'you know what time it is?"

"Two A.M., your time."

"It better be good."

"That shanking you had last night."

"Can't talk about it."

"Okay, you had any similar situations recently?"

There was a pause, then, "Funny you should ask."

"Why's that?"

"One of our detectives is looking at whether this case fits a pattern he's been developing."

"Well, ask him to call me if it does. I've worked out a pattern of my own. We might be able to help each other."

"You're at Area Three, aren't you?"

"Yeah. But our walls have ears. Have him call me on my cell phone." Thinnes gave the number and hung up.

"Evanger just told you to lay off," Viernes said.

"Just Keller's murder." He looked at Franchi. "Don't you need a cigarette?"

She'd quit smoking nearly a year earlier. The question was a code they'd established to say, *Let's go someplace private to talk.* Thinnes caught Viernes's eye and pointed at him, then jerked his thumb toward the door. Viernes looked surprised, but a minute later, he joined them in the parking lot.

"What's all this?"

"White Tiger," Thinnes said.

"It wasn't Keller?" Franchi asked.

"No," Thinnes said. "Looks like he was being blackmailed into keeping quiet. And maybe giving Cọp Trắng information and putting pressure on me. I don't see him executing two people."

"What are we doing out here?"

"Our walls seem to have ears. If we have the place swept for bugs, we'll alert him," Thinnes said. "We need to meet someplace where we won't be overheard. And let's see if Dr. Caleb's got any ideas, now that he's read the files."

SIXTY-SIX

When Thinnes called Caleb to arrange a get-together, the doctor suggested they meet at Leona's. Thinnes and Franchi rode together in the unmarked Crown Vic they'd signed out earlier. Viernes, who was off duty, took his own car.

Leona's was on the west side of Franklin, a street that ran under the El tracks just north of the Loop. Caleb was waiting at the bar, a half level up from the street. The hostess seated them in a quiet corner of the nonsmoking section; the waitress came with spiral-bound menus. Illustrated. She rattled off an impressive selection of drinks—nearly a full page. Thinnes read along.

They held off talking shop until they were finished eating. Viernes's cell phone rang and he went outside to answer.

When he returned, Thinnes asked him, "What was that about?"

"You'll never guess who set up the Keller hit," Viernes said. They waited. "Keller."

"What?"

"My source says he dissed Arcángel. He had to know that was suicide. It makes sense," Viernes continued. "He gets convicted, he loses his pension and his life's over anyway. He kills himself, his life insurance company won't pay off."

Thinnes nodded.

"But if he's murdered in jail, his family collects on his insurance and has a nice suit against the county. And chances are the wife benefits some other way because Keller was never convicted."

"Can you prove it?" Franchi asked.

"Nope. And from what I gather, Mrs. K's a decent woman who didn't have a clue about what her husband was up to until he went nutso and started burning his papers." Viernes shrugged and said, "Who cares?"

"Great theory," Franchi said. "But Keller's last words were, 'I did nothing.' He was saying he was innocent."

Viernes grinned. "That's your proof?"

"A dying declaration?"

"Not unless he said, 'I'm dying. I didn't do it.' "

"If a man's dying he's not gonna be too formal."

"And anyway," Viernes said, "a dying declaration would have to be against his interest to mean anything."

Thinnes said, "I got a hunch he knew exactly what he was saying. And it wasn't 'I didn't do it.' "

"Thinntuition?"

Thinnes shook his head.

"It's a quote," Caleb said. "*All that's required for evil to triumph is for good men to do nothing.*"

"So he didn't do the murders," Viernes said. "But he didn't do anything to prevent them."

Franchi looked glum. "Which leaves us back where we started with our two unsolved homicides and McKenzie's fifteen cold cases."

Thinnes said, "What insight can you give us, Doctor?"

"Not much, I'm afraid. We're dealing with a classic sociopath—no conscience, no empathy, no remorse. He's intelligent, apparently. And, like a tiger, he'll be extremely dangerous if cornered. Be very careful."

Franchi made a face. "I hate to say it, but it's obvious he's a cop."

"Not necessarily. You may be looking for an ant lion."

"What?"

"A creature that lives in the side of anthills to prey on the ants. Because it lives among them, it smells like an ant, so they don't recognize it as an enemy."

Franchi got her cell phone from her purse.

"Who're you calling?" Thinnes asked.

"The desk. The sarge probably knows the guy's name."

As she dialed, Thinnes drew his index finger across his throat. She covered the mouthpiece. "What?"

"He may be there listening. Or he may have the phones bugged."

She looked annoyed. To the phone, she said, "Sarge? This is Franchi. Is the custodian still there—what's his name? Leo?" She waited. "Yeah, listen. I lost an earring. I wonder if you could ask him to keep an eye out for it. It's got sentimental value. Yeah, thanks."

She ended the call. She was putting her purse under the table when Thinnes's phone rang. He said, "Excuse me," and pushed his chair back from the table. "Thinnes."

"Detective Thinnes, this is Tien Lee. I've put the word out I'm hunting the White Tiger."

"Dammit! That makes you his next meal."

"Exactly. I thought you'd like to bring your guns and set up a blind."

"Where are you?"

"I'm home. Safe for the moment."

"Stay there."

"Ciao."

The line went dead. Thinnes disconnected. The others waited for the flip side of his conversation.

When he told them, Viernes said, "The fuckhead! I'm on it." He stood up and took out his wallet.

"I'll get that," Thinnes told him. "Get going. We'll take Dr. Caleb home, then arrange to relieve you."

Viernes nodded and walked out.

In the car, Franchi said, "Thinnes, did you give Lee your phone number?"

His business cards had been printed before he got his cell phone. He'd never bothered to get them reprinted with the number, but he sometimes wrote it on the cards. "No."

"How'd he get it?"

"Caller ID?"

They were approaching Michigan Avenue, a few blocks from Caleb's condo, when Lee called again.

"Detective Thinnes, Cọp Trắng has just invited me to meet him." Lee gave Thinnes the address: 1111 N. Elston.

"You still at home?"

"I'm two blocks away."

"Wait where you are," Thinnes said.

"I'm sorry. He said to come alone and to be punctual."

The line went dead. Thinnes hit call-back; Lee didn't answer. Thinnes slammed the steering wheel. "Goddammit!"

"What?"

Thinnes put on the headlight flashers and made a sudden U-turn. "Call Viernes. Tell him to meet us. And tell him to put on his vest."

SIXTY-SEVEN

Eleven-eleven N. Elston was a four-story brick structure, a former city records storage facility. Undergoing renovation, it was surrounded by CAUTION tape and temporary fencing, and lit by security and exit-sign lights. Lee's red Mustang sat empty halfway down the block. There was no sign of Lee, or the security guard who should have been on duty.

Thinnes parked in front of the entrance and got out, telling Franchi and Caleb to stay put. One of the glass double doors was slightly open, propped with a crushed Coke can. He left it and came back.

"How're we gonna surround this place?" Franchi asked. "It's huge."

"Call for backup."

"Done."

A few moments later her cell phone rang; she activated it, "Franchi." She listened, said, "Joe's here. In the alley."

"Tell him to cover the back 'til backup gets here."

"If we go in now, who's gonna cover *our* backs?"

Thinnes caught Caleb's eye in the rearview. "Jack?"

"Yes."

"Just stay in the car and out of sight, in the front seat so you can get patrol on the radio if you need to."

They went in with vests on and guns drawn. Beyond the glass doors was a small lobby. Overhead, fluorescent fixtures glowed but alternating panels were off, making the light dim and harsh.

To the left, a granite counter formed a partition between the terrazzo-floored lobby and a receptionist's cubicle with a door in its back wall.

Franchi covered Thinnes while he vaulted the counter and checked out the tiny room—desk, chair, phone, standard electric wall clock, a bowl of water on the floor. *Sports Illustrated* was open on the desk, along with a clipboard for signing in, another for logging door checks and call-in times. According to the log, the absent guard's name was Webber, his last check-in forty-five minutes earlier. The phone jack had been jerked from the wall. Thinnes plugged it in and tried the phone—dead. He opened the door and swung it wide. An unlit passage stretched ahead into the darkness. He held his breath to listen. No sound.

He took the Mini-Maglite from his pocket and flashed it into the darkness. Polyethylene sheets hung from the ceiling, closing the corridor off ahead. The floor was thick with white construction dust. Footprints led from where he stood to a side passage on the right. He held a finger up to tell Franchi, *One minute.* Entering the main passage, he kept to the right-hand wall and looked into the side hallway. Doors flanked it on either side; it ended at another door, as did the trail of footprints. He retraced his steps.

On the far side of the lobby, signs flanked ornate elevator doors: NO ENTRY WITHOUT A HARD HAT and USE SERVICE ELEVATOR IN REAR. The doors were blocked with yellow CAUTION tape. Halls stretched into darkness to the right and left, their terrazzo floors protected by sheets of oriented-strand board.

They went right. The hall T'd into another hall, which dead-ended, to the right, at a door marked STAIRS and EXIT. They turned the other way. The flashlight beam showed a long passage with doors on either side. Ten yards down, a pool of liquid gleamed black in the dim light. Thinnes flashed the beam around as they approached it—ceiling, walls, dust-covered floor. And footprints.

The liquid was blood! Drag marks trailed blood beyond a closed door. Franchi covered him as he kicked it open.

A uniformed security guard lay just inside the room. Webber, no doubt. Unconscious, white from shock or blood loss. His feet were propped up on a collapsed folding chair. A bloodied rag formed a tourniquet around a mangled upper arm. Another rag, tucked beneath his neck, elevated his head. Someone's attempt at first aid?

Franchi turned suddenly and yelled, "Stop!"

Thinnes swung his light and weapon. Frozen in the flashlight beam, Tien Lee stood—shirtless—on a chair by the door, a second chair raised overhead.

"Putting this down," he said as he leaned over and set it carefully on the floor. He stepped down slowly.

"Up against the wall!" Franchi demanded. "Face it!"

Rage showed in the rough way she cuffed him.

Thinnes wondered why she was so pissed. He took his phone and rang up Caleb's cell, heard, "Hello," then, "Don't move!"

Thinnes yelled, "Hey!"

A strange voice came back. "Police! Who *is* this?"

"Detective Thinnes." He gave his star number. "Call for backup and an ambulance. We have a person down here, and a killer loose in the building!"

"Yes, sir," the cop said.

"There's a detective in the alley who needs backup."

"Ten-four."

"And bring Dr. Caleb in. Maybe he can help."

"Okay."

Thinnes disconnected. He frisked Lee, finding keys and a set of handcuffs. He put the keys back in Lee's pocket, the handcuffs in his own.

Franchi took Lee by the shoulders and sat him on the chair. Thinnes shone the flashlight on his face.

"What happened?" Thinnes said.

"When I got here," Lee said, "the building was open. So I came in. I told him my story . . ." He nodded at Webber "He didn't believe me. He took Cop Trắng's note and put those hand-cuffs on me." Lee shifted in the chair, nodding toward Thinnes's pocket. "Then his dog took off. He told me to hang tight and ran after it. I waited. He didn't come back, so I got out of the cuffs and went looking for him."

"How'd you get out of the cuffs?" Franchi asked.

Lee grinned. "I've been studying Houdini."

"Then what?" Thinnes asked.

"I went to the office to call 911. The phone was out."

"Where's *your* phone?" Thinnes asked.

Lee nodded at Webber. "He took it."

"It's not on him."

"Whoever stabbed him must have it." Lee shrugged. "Anyway, I went looking for the guard and found him in the hall. I dragged him in here and locked the door in case his attacker returned. I did what I could for him." Which explained Lee's missing shirt. He looked at Thinnes. "I figured you'd be coming. But when I heard you out there, I thought you might be the guy who did this coming back."

Caleb's arrival with the beat cops ended the discussion. He hurried to Webber's side.

Thinnes went into the hall with the coppers to bring them up to speed. "We need more bodies," he said. "We gotta search this whole place." He went back in the room.

"What about him?" The cop who'd followed Thinnes pointed at Lee.

"Detective." Caleb held a square of paper up by its only unbloody edge. "This was in his pocket."

Thinnes took it carefully. The note, asking Tien to meet here, was signed, "John T."

Thinnes looked at Lee. "Where did you get this?"

"Someone slipped it under my door."

"You got any idea who?"

"One of my students has gone over to the dark side?"

"How'd you know it wasn't from Thinnes?" Franchi said.

Lee looked at her insolently, it seemed to Thinnes. "Detective Thinnes has never addressed me by my given name."

Another cop stuck his head in the room. "The paramedics are here."

・・・

They left Caleb and the medics working on Webber. They took Lee and the bloody note outside, where half a dozen patrol cars blocked the street, blue lights flashing. Cops waited for orders. Thinnes pushed Lee into the back seat of one of the squads and belted him in.

"What *is* this?" Lee demanded.

"Protective custody," Thinnes said. "I warned you not to interfere. Keep an eye on him," he told the driver. He stashed the note in the trunk of his own car.

Viernes walked up with the patrol sergeant. "How you wanna do this?" the sergeant asked.

"Can we get a K9 unit here?"

"Probably not for an hour."

"Our offender could be long gone by then. Who knows how many ways out there are?" Thinnes looked to see if he had everyone's attention. "Okay. We think the guy we're looking for is Leo Eccles. He may have worked as a custodian, probably has keys. And the security guard's gun and radio are missing. I think we can assume Eccles has them. So keep it off the air and be careful."

The sergeant nodded.

"We'll start in the basement and work up."

"How're we gonna get in the locked rooms?" Viernes said.

"Webber must have had a set of keys. See if he's still got 'em. If not, we'll just have to kick down doors."

SIXTY-EIGHT

Webber still had keys. In a drawer in the office, he told them, before the medics took him away. Thinnes told Caleb to stay out with the car.

They pried the lobby elevator doors open and made sure the cars really were out of service. The sergeant assigned a two-man team to guard each of the stairwells. Thinnes, Franchi, Viernes, and two tac cops started at the bottom.

Except near the stairs, where EXIT signs glowed above the doorways, the basement was black. There was no ventilation. The air was hot and dusty. Their flashlights pulled fantastic figures from the darkness and animated each shape they examined: piles of concrete forms and scaffolding, sawhorses, a compressor, and a forklift.

Gradually, they worked out the geography. The huge open room was interrupted by the pillars supporting the building. Rubble covered the concrete floor—remnants of walls that had once partitioned the space. Inside a padlocked cage, two of three electrical panels were disconnected, a third padlocked. Above them the ceiling crawled with pipes and conduits, and was strung with cables and unlit work flights. The floor of the garbage chute next to the service elevator had been jackhammered apart and left there, a jumble of sharp-edged boulders bristling with rebar spikes.

They found a body at the bottom of the lobby elevator shaft. Thinnes had a sinking feeling as their flashlights conjured the indistinct mound on the concrete floor. They moved closer.

And found Webber's dog. Someone had opened a door on an

upper floor and chased or lured the animal to its death. One more charge to White Tiger's account.

When they'd cleared the basement, the patrol radioed that reinforcements were staging in the lobby. They had the manpower to search all the floors at once, but not enough keys.

The ground floor set the pattern for the levels above. The building was a square ring with a central light well. A central hall ran through each floor, with offices opening on it from either side. Without electricity the rooms were dark, though the orange glow from streetlights lit the outside windows. The windows of the inner rooms opened on a central light well—now in total darkness.

Starting on the ground floor, the hunters opened doors on one side of the hall, then the other, "clearing" each room, checking for open or unlocked windows. It took a long time. Some rooms were empty, others piled with furniture that had to be examined carefully. Dust covered everything; the floor was tracked by passing feet. But it was impossible to tell when the feet had passed.

On the street, Caleb declined the patrolman's offer to wait in the air-conditioned car. The temperature was still in the eighties, but he felt chilled, as he had in the heat of 'Nam. He was on patrol again, a noncombatant detailed to watch a prisoner while his squad hunted the enemy. He glanced at the car where Tien Lee was captive. Handcuffed and belted in the seat, he rocked and squirmed.

Caleb studied the patrolman. He paced a three-yard beat, glancing often at the prisoner, more often at the building. His body language said it all: He longed to be in on it. His radio muttered with the business of the streets, not with the present action. The cop took out a cigarette and held out the pack. "Smoke?"

Caleb felt the craving, but said, "No, thank you."

"This is nerve-racking."

Caleb agreed. He glanced at the patrol car; Tien Lee had disappeared. Curious, he walked over and looked in.

"Officer, your prisoner has escaped."

299

. . .

The freight elevator car was parked on the third floor. It seemed as dead as the lobby elevator, but Thinnes pulled the emergency stop anyway. He left a tac cop guarding it and broke radio silence to tell the cops on the lower floors to move up. Then he and Viernes and Franchi cleared the third-floor rooms.

The fourth-floor hallway had ten-foot ceilings and more light than the levels below—from streetlights glowing through the skylights.

They had their quarry cornered. If he was still in the building. But if he could get to the roof or to a fire escape, he might still get away. The roof-access hatch near the elevator was padlocked. Thinnes told Viernes to guard the metal ladder leading up to it anyway.

They deviated from the procedure they'd followed on floors one through three by checking rooms with fire-escape access first. No Eccles. It was hard to be patient. They had the tiger cornered, but where? How to flush him?

Then Thinnes had an idea. "Franchi," he whispered.

"Yeah?"

"Get out your phone." He gave her Lee's cell number and listened as she tapped it out. Somewhere down the hallway, a phone rang. Thinnes started toward the sound. A door burst open. A figure flew out.

BLAM!

The shot sent them diving for cover. Thinnes radioed Eccles's position to the backup teams and peered carefully around the corner.

Eccles was nearly to the end of the hall. Thinnes caught him with the flashlight beam and aimed his .38. "Eccles! Freeze!"

Eccles stumbled, caught his balance, ran faster. Thinnes couldn't shoot him in the back. Franchi had no such qualms. She took a shooter's stance and fired. The report echoed as her bullet struck sparks and ricocheted. Eccles disappeared.

"Viernes, he's coming your way!" Thinnes yelled into the radio. "North side, heading east!"

"Ten-four."

They raced to the corner where Eccles had disappeared. Thinnes dropped to peer around at knee level. Eccles was a gray silhouette near the middle of the hall. He slowed to look back at Thinnes. Stopped when a dark figure dropped from a skylight into his path.

Thinnes fixed Eccles in his flashlight beam. Behind him, the light caught what had landed in his path. Tien Lee. Light gleamed off the gun Eccles aimed at Thinnes.

Lee sprang. Eccles whirled to face the closer threat. Too slow. Lee struck his arm. The gun flew toward Thinnes, bounced, and skittered away. Eccles moved six inches toward it, hesitated, tried to dodge past Lee.

But Lee was on him like Jackie Chan in the movies. Faster than Thinnes could follow, Eccles was spread-eagled on the floor. Still, Lee stepped beside his head and drew his foot back for a coup de grace.

"Tien!"

Lee stopped. Turned.

For a heartbeat, Thinnes was staring at a panther startled from its prey. "Don't!"

Another heartbeat. Then Lee smiled. He stepped back and bowed. Formally. Like a student to his sensei.

The spell shattered. Thinnes let his breath out. Eccles whimpered like an injured beast.

Franchi rushed up to cover him while Thinnes rolled him face down and snapped the cuffs on. A search yielded keys, cell phones, Webber's radio, and a bloody switchblade. Thinnes rolled him on his back and shone the light on his face. Eccles blinked and squinted, showing no emotion.

Another body tumbled from the skylight with a thud and a yelp and Jack Caleb sprawled across the floor.

Thinnes said, "Doctor, are you okay?"

"I'll live."

"Better give Evanger a heads-up," Thinnes told Franchi. To Lee he said, "See if you can help the doctor."

Lee bowed again. Something had changed between them. Thinnes had passed some kind of test.

Thinnes radioed the sergeant. Then he and Franchi got Eccles to his feet and started toward the service elevator, with Lee and Caleb bringing up the rear.

Waiting by the elevator, Viernes said, "Nice work." He flashed his light on Eccles.

Distracting Thinnes.

Eccles lunged sideways, shouldering Franchi against the wall. Thinnes grabbed for him, but Eccles head-butted him, throwing him off balance. Eccles kicked. Thinnes dodged. Eccles broke and ran.

But his hands were cuffed. And he had nowhere to go. The elevator doors were closed. Viernes blocked one end of the hall, Thinnes and Franchi the other. Eccles rotated three hundred and sixty degrees, then dived for the trash chute by the elevator. The waist-level door was three feet square and hinged at the top. It opened inward. Eccles hit it head-on and kept going until he'd disappeared to his waist.

"Goddammit!" Thinnes dropped his light and grabbed Eccles's legs. Eccles kicked. He put a toe against the wall and wedged himself farther in the chute. Thinnes yelled, "Help!" but Eccles's foot caught him on the mouth. He lost his grip. Eccles squirmed frantically.

And vanished.

The chute door clattered shut. Viernes and Franchi tore up from opposite directions.

The others circled the chute as Thinnes grabbed his light. He pushed the door open and stuck his head and shoulder through, aiming the beam down.

Eccles lay broken on the concrete below, impaled on bloody spikes of rebar.

Thinnes withdrew.

"Where'd he go?" Lee asked. "What's down there?"

Thinnes told him.

"A tiger trap."

SIXTY-NINE

On Labor Day Thinnes had a barbecue. Just close friends.
Rhonda asked Franchi before Thinnes had the chance. When he
invited Caleb, the doctor said, "I have a houseguest."

"Bring 'im along."

"Her. I'll ask."

Caleb brought a six-pack of Dos Equis and a case of Cherry Coke.
The girl hanging on his arm when Thinnes opened the door was
jailbait. He was shocked until he remembered Caleb was gay and
realized the girl was Linny Morgan. She came in all eyes and ears,
almost shyly. She wasn't shy. When she spotted Thinnes, recognition lit her face, then amusement. Shades of her mother. Or her
mother's shade.

In the backyard, Thinnes introduced Linny to Rhonda and
Franchi. Caleb greeted them and asked, "Where's Rob?"

"I sent him for ice," Thinnes said. "Linny, there's pop in the
cooler and stuff." He gestured toward the picnic table laden with
the usual picnic things.

At that point, Rhonda went inside; Toby trotted out, wrig-
gling with pleasure at having visitors.

Linny seemed equally delighted. "What's his name?"

"Toby."

"John," Rhonda called from the kitchen window, "there's a
man here to see you." Not someone they'd invited, or she'd just
have sent him out.

· · ·

Tien Lee was in the family room. He apologized for interrupting the holiday. Thinnes told him to sit down and waited for him to get to the point.

"I need to know—who was Cọp Trắng and why'd he kill my mother?"

"His wife told us—now that he's dead, she's willing to talk. He was a supply clerk stationed in Saigon during the war. Probably where he learned the value of camouflage. He served three hitches, then mustered out and went back as a private contractor supplying cleaning personnel for American facilities. None of his employees stole from his clients or planted any bombs. He had other businesses, too—drugs, black market goods, prostitution, gambling . . .

"He was on one of the last choppers out in '75, eventually arranged to bring some of his 'employees' here."

"Why here?"

"He was *from* here. But in '75, the Chicago outfit and our local gangs were controlling the kind of action he'd been into in Saigon, so he took a job with the city as a custodian. He preyed on the Vietnamese, did murders and arsons for hire. He got a cut from a crooked dealer who sold guns to criminals. But he kept a low profile. By the time the city privatized its custodial work, he'd worked in most of the city's buildings and clawed his way to the top of the food chain. As supervisor, he handed out assignments. After he killed your mother, he assigned himself to work at Area Three to keep track of the investigation."

"And derail it?"

"He tried."

"Why'd he kill her?"

"She knew who he was. He probably went to CAPS meetings to keep up on things. He saw her at one and didn't want her calling attention to him. He probably killed Theo Ragland for the same reason."

"There's something else," Lee said. "It's personal, or I'd have come to your office to ask about Cọp Trắng."

304

"What do you mean, personal?" Thinnes felt as uneasy as when the paternity allegation first surfaced.

Lee handed him a sealed envelope. Pink. Expensive personal stationery. "My mother left instructions to give this to you after her death."

"What is it?"

Lee shrugged. "It was addressed to you."

Thinnes opened the envelope and read:

Dear John,

If you are reading this letter it is because I have gone to join my ancestors. You once offered to do anything for us, for Bob and me, and we took you at your word though we did not ask. Tien is the child of our love and your biology. He was conceived on our wedding night, after the three of us returned to our apartment, and you passed out from too much liquid Joy. We were also very drunk. The absinthe made you dream I was your beloved Rhonda. That is what made us think we could have a child, one who was doubly beloved because he would be a reminder of our dearest friend. Perhaps you would have done this for us willingly. In the moment, there was no way to ask.

I have no wish to make trouble for you or your family. When Tien came to the age that he understood Bob could not have been his father, I told him his life was a gift of love from our best friend. I have never told him more than that, never said your name.

The letter was signed Hue. Thinnes read it twice, then looked at Lee. "Why wait till now to give me this?"

"I didn't trust you before."

"Just a minute." Thinnes called Rhonda from the kitchen. He handed her the letter.

There were tears in her eyes when she finished reading. She smiled at Lee and handed him the letter, then left them alone.

Lee's expression didn't change as he read. He looked at Thinnes. "You've asked me—twice—why I moved here, why now. I confess I wasn't entirely truthful. I knew of this." He fanned the air with the letter. "Though my parents never told me. When I was old enough to know my father couldn't possibly have sired me, I began to search my parents' papers and albums for clues to who did. Yours was the only name, the only picture that seemed to matter to them." He shrugged. "I thought—I tried to imagine how I came to be, how my mother could . . .

"I didn't imagine this. I wanted to know what sort of man you were. I had an agency locate you. I found a business I could buy here and convinced my mother she would be better off near relatives.

"I suppose that makes me responsible for her death . . ."

Thinnes shook his head. "She should have told me about Cọp Trắng in Saigon. Or asked for help when she was threatened in San Diego."

He stopped when Rob burst in, arms full of groceries. He kicked the front door shut behind him and came in the room. "Dad, that red Mustang's parked out front!"

Thinnes grinned. "It belongs to Tien. Tien, Rob."

Lee said, "How do you do?"

"Awesome car!"

"Thanks. Would you like to drive it?"

Rob lit up like a five-year-old at Christmas.

"If it's okay with your dad." Lee looked at Thinnes.

He shrugged. "It's your car."

Lee held out the key. Rob handed Thinnes the groceries and took off before Lee could change his mind.

When Caleb found himself alone with Franchi, he said, "At least one of your difficulties seems to have resolved itself."

"Tien Lee?" She smiled wryly. "Yeah."

"And I'd wager he finds *you* attractive."

"But he's seven years younger than me."

Caleb smiled. "I got my BS at UIC, where, among other things, I studied anthropology. The professor was a Dr. Charles Reed, an excellent instructor even though he was older than *Australopithecus*. He told us—this is a direct quote—'Women, on average, live seven years longer than men. So my advice to you ladies is to find a man seven years your junior and take care of him.' "

Franchi laughed. "He was very wise. As are you."

"Hel-lo," Linny said. "Who's *that*?"

Caleb followed her line of sight to where Tien Lee listened intently to something Franchi was saying.

"I believe *he*'s spoken for."

"How do you know? He's not wearing a ring."

"He's wearing a moonstruck expression."

She gave him an *Are you serious?* look.

At that moment, Rob burst into the yard, keys dangling from one hand, highly excited. He stopped dead when he spotted Linny. His eyes widened and his body language told the story. Then he recognized Caleb. "Hi, Dr. C." But his eyes stayed on Linny—who was watching him with all the confidence of a cat meeting a strange dog.

Caleb said, "Rob, may I present Linny Morgan? Linny, this is Rob."

Rob said, "How do you do?"

Linny just nodded.

Rob was undeterred. "Can I get you something?" He dragged his attention back to Caleb. "Or you, Dr. Caleb?"

"A beer would be nice," Caleb said. "Dos Equis. Linny?"

"For me, too."

Rob gave her the look adults reserve for outrageous suggestions. "See some ID?"

She burst out laughing. "Cherry Coke, I guess."

He nodded and departed.

When he came back with the drinks, he asked Linny if she'd like to go for a ride.

She brightened. "Jack?"

Caleb turned to Rob. "If you'll comport yourself as if she were *my* sixteen-year-old daughter."

He saw Rob stifle a smile. "Yes, sir!"

"Did Rob leave with Linny?"

Caleb jumped. He hadn't heard Thinnes approach. "Yes."

Thinnes offered him another beer. "God help us," Thinnes said.

"My money's on Rob."

Thinnes relaxed. "You think?" He looked across the yard to where Lee and Franchi were taking the first steps in the age-old dance. "Strange how things work out."

GLOSSARY

AFVN Armed Forces Vietnam radio call letters.

AIT Advanced infantry training.

AK-47 Russian-made rifle carried by the NVA and Viet Cong.

ao dai (pronounced OW ZAI) Traditional dress of Vietnamese women, long-sleeved tunic worn over loose-fitting trousers.

APC Armored personnel carrier; also Aspirin-Phenacetin-Caffeine tablets, a painkiller used in the late sixties and early seventies.

AO Area of operation.

ARVN Army of the Republic of (South) Vietnam.

ASA Assistant state's attorney.

AWOL Absent without leave.

Battalion Unit of approximately 900 men divided into five companies: One headquarters company, one service company, and three rifle companies—Alpha, Bravo, and Charlie.

beaucoup dinky dau Really crazy.

black ops Illegal, covert operations.

boocoo (from French *beaucoup*) Lots of, many.

brassard Badge worn on the arm; MP designator.

bunker Shelter, command, or guard post—typically made of sandbags and steel sheeting.

bush Boondocks, boonies.

butterbean lieutenant Pejorative nickname for a second lieutenant.

C4 Explosive used in claymore mines. C4 requires a detonator to explode. When ignited, it burns like Sterno and was often used to heat C-rations in the bush.

Charlie Short for Victor Charlie, the enemy.

cherry A new arrival in country, an untested soldier; also a virgin, virginity.

Children of the Dust Children fathered by American GIs.

Chinaman Chicago equivalent of a New York rabbi; a powerful patron.

claymore An antipersonnel mine used in country.

CO Commanding officer.

C.O. Conscientious objector.

Cobra Attack helicopter.

DEROS Date eligible to return overseas, date of departure for the world.

deuce-and-a-half Two-and-a-half-ton truck used, among other things, to transport troops.

didi mau Go away quick.

dink Derisive term used by Americans for Asians.

dust-off Medical evacuation by helicopter.

fatigues Regular Army uniform—green in Vietnam.

Five O'Clock Follies Press name for MACV at the U.S. Information Service.

FNG Fucking new guy; a cherry.

fragging Murder of an NCO or officer by enlisted men.

Free Strike Zone Area deemed enemy territory where anyone was a legitimate target.

FTO Field training officer.

FUBAR Fucked up beyond all recognition.

gook Derisive term used by Americans for Asians.

graduation picture Photo taken of a prisoner, prior to release, for future ID.

grunt Infantryman, also referred to in the plural as "legs."

GSW Gunshot wound.

Gulf War Syndrome Collection of symptoms displayed by Gulf War veterans.

hard spot Dangerous position in the bush.

heater (also heater case) In Chicago, a case that attracts heavy media attention.

H&I harassment and interdiction.

housecat See REMF.

310

HUEY Type of helicopter used to transport troops or supplies.
in country Vietnam.
KIA Killed In Action.
ladyfinger A type of small firecracker.
M-16 Standard-issue rifle carried by U.S. forces in Vietnam after
   1966.
MACV Military Assistance Command, Vietnam.
mamasan A mature Vietnamese woman employed to do laundry
   and other menial tasks.
MIA Missing In Action.
MO Method of operation.
MOS Military occupational specialty, or military job description.
NCO Noncommissioned officer, e.g. sergeant or squad leader.
NFA No forwarding address.
nuoc mam (pronounced NOO-ahk MAHM) Fermented fish
   sauce, very salty and smelly.
NVA North Vietnamese Army.
OCS Officer Candidate School.
papasan An older Vietnamese man.
peckerwood Derisive term used by some blacks; an asshole.
pho (pronounced FUH) Soup of thick rice noodles and meat.
platoon Division of a company, typically forty-five men, including
   a CO and NCO.
PTSD Post-traumatic stress disorder.
RD # (or no.) Case number.
REMF Rear echelon motherfucker, serviceman assigned a noncombat position, also called a housecat.
six-by A large flat-bed truck.
SOG Studies and Observations Group. A clandestine group that
   operated without IDs and outside the law performing psy-ops
   and black ops missions.
SOL Stricken on leave to reinstate, charges dropped.
SOP Standard operating procedure.
strac By the book, obsessive.
white mice Pejorative name for the Vietnamese National Police.
WIA Wounded In Action.
the world Anywhere outside Vietnam, specifically the U.S.